Praise for

A MILLION THINGS

"An original and impressively assured debut. A gem of a novel."

—Graeme Simsion, *New York Times* bestselling author of *The Rosie Project*

"Swept me into its thrall so immediately that I didn't realize I'd been holding my breath until I reached the end. . . . Fresh and slim, this novel pierces like a bullet and soothes like a psalm."

—Amy Jo Burns, author of *Shiner*

"Poignant, uplifting, and beautifully written."

—Catherine Jinks

"Direct, assured writing, hard-hitting emotion, and a wonderful sense of optimism. *A Million Things* is a debut to treasure, with characters whose dignity shines through their struggles."

—Jock Serong

A MILLION THINGS

Emily Spurr

BERKLEY
NEW YORK

BERKLEY
An imprint of Penguin Random House LLC
penguinrandomhouse.com

Originally published in 2021 in Australia by the Text Publishing Company.

Library of Congress Cataloging-in-Publication Data

Names: Spurr, Emily, author.
Title: A million things / Emily Spurr.
Description: First edition. | New York: Berkley, 2021.
Identifiers: LCCN 2020052781 (print) | LCCN 2020052782 (ebook) |
ISBN 9780593332733 (trade paperback) | ISBN 9780593332740 (ebook)
Classification: LCC PR9619.4.S68 M55 2021 (print) | LCC PR9619.4.S68 (ebook) |
DDC 823/.92—dc23
LC record available at https://lccn.loc.gov/2020052781
LC ebook record available at https://lccn.loc.gov/2020052782

Berkley trade paperback edition / August 2021

Printed in the United States of America
1st Printing

Book design by Alison Cnockaert

For Kevyn, whose quiet belief kept me going through the periods when mine faltered.

Twenty-five percent (which is still outrageous).

THE FIRST DAYS

SILENCE ISN'T REALLY silent.

It's not loud, exactly. But it sits under things, making the little sounds stand out: my heartbeat in my ears, the sharp echo of the kitchen clock, the fridge humming. I move, and the rustle of me fills my head. Splinter laps water from his bowl. His eyes tell me when it's time to eat. Alarms go off when it's time to wake.

Sleep, wake, eat, school, home, homework, dinner, TV, sleep. Wake.

Time goes weird. It keeps tripping over itself and dropping things. I stand in one room and then I'm sitting in another, but how I got there is gone.

And something grows. Pushing into my head. Something else.

DAY 14

SATURDAY

THE SMELL EVENTUALLY drifts into all the corners of the house. It's got to the point I can smell it from the lounge room. A heavy stink, seeping weighty and liquid, bad enough to drag me up from sleep.

At first, before I moved to the couch, I tried sleeping in your bed, wrapped in your duvet, one of your T-shirts pressed to my nose. Each breath in taking a little more of you, till all your scents were gone. Till only the warm, swampy smell of dog and the nothing smell of me were left and your pillow held only the shape of my head. Then this new smell started to invade.

It's time to clean out the fridge. Your meal, the last one you didn't eat. I heated it for you, had it sitting on the bench, and it was still there when I went to bed. So I covered it in plastic and put it away.

I know I should chuck it out. It's going moldy, growing life of its own. Releasing spores, probably, that are landing on every other thing in the fridge. But I don't.

I imagine you bursting through the door and asking, *What the hell is that smell?* And then, looking at me: *You're nearly eleven! Why didn't you throw it out, for Christ's sake, why didn't you give it to Splinter?*

He follows like a shadow. My Splinter, my pup, my scruffy gray stretch of mutt. I trip over him, wake to his breath on my face. He sits with his big dog head resting on my knee. I look at his brown eyes, lean my face into his and inhale the familiar humid breath, the scent of dog biscuits and bones.

I woke to Splinter's nose in my face that day too. That first day. The room was cold, colder than usual cold. I looked into your bedroom: the bed was made. Into the kitchen, and the back door was open. The air stung my cheeks; I puffed experimentally and I could see my breath. There were leaves on the floor. I couldn't see you in the backyard but I knew you were there. You'd have shut the back door if you'd gone out somewhere. I remember looking at the clock: seven. On a Sunday morning. It was still gray light outside and there was no smell of coffee. I went out, saw the big-shed door ajar. I pushed it open.

And in that second our house vanished. I stood, feet in the grass and nothing but blackness behind me.

There was a breeze. It's funny how air's just there. You don't notice it. Looking at you, I could feel it touching my face, the pressure of it on my skin, the tickle as it lifted a hair off my cheek, as it shifted ever so slightly, making the rope creak.

The back door slammed and the sound sent a familiar shock up my spine. Or it would have if I'd been standing in my body rather than slightly to the left. The alarm *chik chik chik* of a blackbird exploded in my ears, too loud and too sharp. I could hear the grass growing.

My ears have always been sensitive to you leaving. Each time you'd go, noises muffled and sharpened and silence got loud. I'd stand still, trying not to breathe, waiting for the door to open and for you to come back through it. The silence you left after you grabbed the keys from the bowl on the table and slammed out the door would stand like a person beside me. The bang made me jump every time. Even though I knew it was coming. Knew from the second your eyes lost focus and tightened and you stopped seeing me and saw only this thing *ruining* your *life*. You'd shout, grab those keys and stalk to the door, and bang. And I would jump.

I cried, when I was little. But you'd come back. My nose would squish into your shoulder, your arms around me and the warm smell of you in my whole head. The knot in my tummy would loosen and melt with the tingle that ran up my neck into my skull as you stroked my hair and made my eyes close. It almost made the before worth it.

You just got *angry*. It just was—like the weekends you'd get sad and stay in bed—and I stopped hiding under the duvet, stopped crying about it. The shock of the door would go through my spine but I'd stay where I was. I'd be still and Splints would sit on my feet and we'd wait. My heart racing. Sometimes you'd be back before we moved, my toes warm under his bum even as my legs went numb from the standing. Other times you wouldn't, and Splinter would move. Or I would. I'd do my homework, or clean up, or fix whatever it was that made you snatch up the keys this time.

Sometimes I'd flip through the fat blue dictionary, looking for the right word for it, the feeling inside. *Agitated* was almost right, but it didn't quite fit. It matched the chill of the tiny bubbles popping in my chest but not the stillness. *Aimless* felt close: floaty. I floated, but I always had something to do. When it was summer we'd go outside and I'd cut the grass. Or weed the veggie patch you liked *in theory*. And sometimes we'd just lie in the sun, Splinter's big head on my lap, and I'd watch the swirling red behind my eyelids. I guess I was *ambivalent*. But that wasn't right either because it hurt, you being gone. I never did find the right word.

Then you'd come back. You'd pull me into your chest and squash my nose into your shoulder and everything would be okay. I was used to that. Used to the nipping worry of not having you here. Used to the little voice that said maybe this time was different but knowing it wasn't. *Knowing* you'd always come back.

Now I don't know what to do.

But I suppose you're not really gone, not properly. Not if I know where you are.

That morning I closed the door to the shed and opened the back door and went inside. I walked through rooms that were all surface, my knees bending at the wrong time, each step ending in my hips as the floor happened too soon.

I climbed under my duvet.

My breath was warm under there and slow, like the ocean.

After a while the room was close to dark and Splints's big head rested on my leg, the weight of him making my toes tingle. Sometimes he'd lick his nose and sigh. I stayed where I was. When it was very dark a paw thumped through the duvet onto my arm. He whined.

I got up, shut the back door and fed him.

The next day I went to school.

So, here I am. Here. Not here.

Everything's here and not here.
You.
The house.
Me.
I don't know what anything is anymore.

DAY 15

SUNDAY

WHEN THE FRIDGE is clean there's nothing to distract from outside.

I've left the washing on the line and it's gone stiff and crusty and no longer flutters in the wind. I think it'd snap if I folded it. I use the clotheshorse in the kitchen instead. There's not much washing anyway.

I take your debit card and buy things. Bread, milk, cheese, eucalyptus spray, incense sticks, lavender spray, mosquito coils, three sonic oil vaporizers, ten bottles of essential oils, a large bottle of bleach, gaffer tape, some fruit, dog food, pot noodles and toilet paper.

THE OLD LADY next door sits on her porch and watches me lugging stuff home. Watching, pretending she's not, looking over her teacup. I walk past like she's not there. Like everything's normal.

I hold my breath and stuff rolled towels under the shed door. *You're a smart kid, use your brain.* I tip the bleach on the towels.

The incense sticks I place around the back door, on the outside. The smokiness works its way inside anyway, making Splinter sneeze and leaving me with a stuffy feeling and a dull ache to either side of my nose.

I gaffer the window and door cracks of the old shed. I don't look in.

I'm glad of the cold.

I set up the oil vaporizers inside. One next to the front door, one next to the back door and one in the kitchen. The oils have names: *Energy*, *Sleep*, *Breathe Easy*, *Stress Relief*... The instructions say to add five to seven drops at a time. I add twenty. They go for *up to ten hours*. I'll fill them every morning, when I get home from school and before bed. They'll just keep going.

The house isn't too bad now, if you don't mind rose geranium, peppermint and lavender. And that other smell, heavy underneath.

I watch a show about sharks, one with scary music. I stare at the giant mean-eyed, sharp-toothed fish as a diver opens packets of something yellow and oily-looking. The sharks jerk away and disappear into the camouflage of sea so quickly I have to look at the diver to check it's not in fast-forward. The biggest predator in the oceans and the smell of one of them dead makes them flee.

Their disappearing act almost makes me laugh. It's not really that funny, though.

DAY 21

SATURDAY

IT'S JUST GETTING worse. Now I can't go in the kitchen without gagging. I light more incense sticks and keep the vaporizers topped up. I hold my breath, and I go out and tip more bleach onto the towels at the door. I don't think about what I'm doing.

I tape the kitchen windows shut.

We leave the TV on and go out for a long walk.

DAY 22

SUNDAY

SPLINTER'S NOT COPING too well with being locked inside so much. I've started to let him out the back for longer sessions—more than just a quick wee or poo. At first I tried keeping him on the lead to do his business, but he'd look at me with his brown eyes, and I got the point. I always found it hard to go when you were standing in the bathroom doorway telling me to hurry up. I don't bother with the lead now. If he's not on the lead I don't have to stand with him, and it's cold out there. Colder than the rest of outside.

I ignore the hole he's dug near your shed door. I ignore the small dark shapes he chases. I know what they are. That first night, one of them came crawling through the back, wiggled its way under the house and clawed up through the wall, between posts and plaster. It popped out an air vent and scrabbled down into the lounge. I didn't see it, but I know it happened because while I was sleeping it crawled up on the bed and climbed inside me. I woke with it in there, nipping and shifting, scratching and clawing. Eating away.

I stand at the window and watch for Splints. I don't like him chasing sharp-toothed shadows. What if he catches one? What if he eats it? Everything eating everything. I don't think about that. I stand not looking, just watching so I'll know when he's ready to come in.

The grass is getting long. I've watched it grow, not looking out the window waiting for Splinter, and it's nearly halfway up your shed door now. I can't see the towels stuffed at the bottom anymore. It's all long and straggly, lanky, like it's working to make your shed disappear. The thistles are getting higher too; spiky, like the creepers in my head when you used to read Briar Rose.

I like that things are growing out there. It means it's different every time I open the door.

Splints doesn't seem to mind the jungle. He's made himself a nest near the back door. He chases imaginary things, small furry bodies that barrel away from him as he jumps over the top of the grass. He's like a wildcat, or a gazelle if gazelles were gray and goofy-looking. I watch him bounce around. There's a tiny bit of sun. A little dribble of bright in the middle of the yard. It draws insects out. I thought they'd all be sleeping, or dead, but give them a little bit of sun and here they are. Especially the flies.

Splinter's licking my foot. I look down at his furry eyebrows twitching at me. He collapses on the floor with a huff. I check the clock. I've been watching the insects for over an hour.

How long would it take for them to start running the world if we all just disappeared?

Not very, I reckon.

DAY 23

MONDAY

I WAKE AS usual to the cold pinching my face. The TV is muted but the screen lights the room, chasing away the shadows from my sleep, with their pointy teeth that rip and bite, and eyes that shine in the dark. Now it's TV light and the sound of my tight, frosted breaths.

My heart settles. The house is cold and all the quiet things are loud. The fridge, the clock, my breathing, Splinter's. He sleeps on the couch with me. I don't put him out at night.

I swing my feet onto the floorboards. Every morning for the first week your digital alarm cube came on at seven, spilling voices into your room. I'd fumble, my fingers searching over the smooth surfaces for the spot to touch that would turn it off, slipping over its pretend-wood surface. It's actually glass and hard plastic, which is why I was surprised it didn't smash when I threw it against the wall. Your room's not that big, so it didn't go far; didn't even unplug. But it doesn't go off at seven anymore. It says 11:11 and blinks madly, like it thinks it's still keeping time; 11:11: blinking, like it hasn't been destroyed. Some mornings I go in just to watch it blink. I bend down and run my fingers over the display, the hairline cracks barely registering on my skin. The quiet it left is louder than I thought it'd be.

Like all the other days, I fill the oil burners, then shower in silence. Breakfast to the crunch of my cereal and Splinter's dry food. There's no smell of toast or citrus body cream and shampoo, no one to kiss the top of my head and tell me to buy milk or bread or juice on the way home. To get annoyed at my dawdling. It's the missing sounds that make my ears hurt. I pick up my bag and leave for school.

DAY 28

SATURDAY

THAT FIRST WEEKEND is just a head-echo: snippets of the house, Splinter and closed curtains. My brain was working so hard to stay upright I reckon it didn't have room to lay down memories as well.

I have flashes of the Sunday night: packing my schoolbag, setting my alarm for the morning, standing in the shower till there was no hot water. I remember waking up on the couch, the cold of wet hair making my brain ache, the rest of me sweating under the heat of my duvet, your duvet and Splinter. Then I went to school. I slipped Schoolkid on like a jumper, without thinking. Slipped into it and didn't need to think. Home's different, though.

The second weekend I didn't know what I was supposed to do. I stayed inside with the door locked, sitting in a sickly fug of clove and pine that was meant to *relieve winter nervous tension*. Splinter paced and I watched TV. TV's rubbish, isn't it? You always said that. Especially in the daytime, though I watched it at night too. All the stuff you hate most. Soapies, cop shows, adult stuff. The ads were too loud and too bright and they woke me when I'd fallen asleep, the sound pushing through my eyeballs and squeezing my brain. I mostly leave the volume off now, except for ABC News 24. That's all finance, indexes and random babble, or it's about kids whose lives are falling apart. Bombs. Gas. Fires. Sometimes I cry. Mostly it makes me feel a bit better.

I didn't go far at first. There was an invisible elastic pulling at my middle: I didn't want to be near, but I couldn't go far. So I stayed inside, walked Splinter round the corner for a wee and a sniff and went to the gas station for bread, sliced cheese and quick noodles. Eventually the elastic loosened. My range slipped beyond school and shops. The further I went the looser the elastic became until, somewhere around Stony Creek Backwash, it fell away.

WE WALK A lot. Weekends are all about walking now. We leave after breakfast and wander home after dark, Splinter my shadow, walking with the city crouched over our shoulders like Barad-dûr. I watched *Lord of the Rings* the second Saturday you were gone, and you were right. They were really long and a bit frightening. No worse than the news, though, or the house. I downloaded all three and watched them in one go. The sun was coming up when I finished so I slept late that Sunday. That was the first afternoon we really walked. Splinter was mad to get out, and once I got down to the river the idea of going back to the empty house and slept-in couch kept my legs walking away.

The next weekend I was more organized. We were up early. I packed snacks and a bottle of water for Splinter. We crisscrossed neighborhoods. When we came to a street or alley, we walked it. Moving further and further out—or in, depending on the direction we'd started in. We've been to the CBD: Splinter wasn't a fan; Kensington: I liked the little houses; up and down the Maribyrnong with its riverside parks and crowds of people for maximum anonymity; West Footscray, Seddon and Yarraville are good places to blend in too, there are lots of kids. We're learning all the streets. We quite like the river trail around Footscray but that's best on rainy days, otherwise there's too many cyclists on the bike path, and rainy days haven't been that common.

So today we're doing neighborhoods, up and down the streets. I like to look at the houses. Maybe *like* isn't the right word. I wonder about them: how it would be to live in them. I like the imagining but not how it feels when I stop. I still look, though. I remind me of you when Splinter was still so puppy he tripped over his own paws and we'd pull-walk him through the hot streets after dinner. You'd point out all the things you liked. *This door. Those flowers.* And we'd imagine what we'd do to each house if it was ours. We'd do this every night, even though by the end of the walk you'd have frowned and gone quiet. By the time Splinter grew into his paws and could walk properly on the lead, you stayed home, mostly, and Splints and I were only allowed to go as far as the parks.

We go where we want now. I like the houses with front porches the best. Around Seddon they have tables and chairs and hanging pots with lush green leaves or flowers tumbling down the sides. I never see anyone sitting on the seats out the front, but a lot of them have cushions. They look comfortable. And pretty. Often the tables have the chairs arranged like someone was just sitting there but stepped away. Sometimes people come out, usually to get in their car or walk off. Never to sit on those chairs with the nice cushions or put their feet under the tables with the pots on top. All that lovely greenery hanging down and no one sits under it. Sometimes

I stand at a gate and stare at it all. I stand with my hand on the latch. Maybe I live there. Maybe those are my cushions.

The backpack's pretty empty by the end of the day—we've eaten the snacks and I carry the water bottle in my free hand. The gates don't squeak when you open them. The first time I just sat on the seat and looked back down the street. Nobody saw me. Nobody came out. I pick the houses that feel the most loved. The ones that actually do look like people sit there, not the ones like Christmas church Jesus displays that you know are just for show. I stop at a house with a pink front door and a heavy black knocker shaped like an acorn. The table's dusty when I touch it but the cushions are large and soft, like cushions you'd have inside. Splints doesn't sit. He stands, claws tapping on the deck as he steps from foot to foot, watching. Making me nervous. I motion for him to sit but he steps back and knocks over a pot. It cracks loudly and rolls in a semi-circle, soil spilling over the boards as the plant falls out.

I've caught my breath a bit when we find the next house. Its cushions are yellow and pink. Perfectly matched to the pansies growing in the hanging baskets on either side of the porch step. They're not those oversized ones, these cushions. They're the size you could fit easily into your bag. Some of the houses have smaller-than-backpack-sized hanging potted plants, others have little garden ornaments. Wire twisted into animals or delicate little birds sitting on the ends of pots. The sorts of things I imagine a family might go and buy at a garden center on the weekend, or maybe they get them as gifts. Some of them are really quite small. The kind of small that easily fits into a side pocket of a backpack.

It's really cold now, lip-numbing cold. We move on. The sun's dipped out of sight, leaving that not-quite-dark light that drains color away. I'm glad of your jacket, the army-green one you bought online from the States. It nearly touches the ground on me, with lining so thick I can't bend my arms properly, but it's warm and waterproof. And it has lots of pockets. A car door slams on another street. The smell of woodsmoke takes the edge off the cold in my nostrils. This house has a lantern hanging with a new-looking candle in it. I open the gate and it squeaks ever so slightly, more like a sigh. I step in. There are plants with big soft gray leaves like the ears of a baby animal, and a tiny little snail made from rusting metal. The shell part of its back is actual shell. I crouch down and reach out, the arm of your jacket crumpling softly in the quiet. I close my fingers around it and it sits heavy in my hand.

"Hey!"

I jump up. A woman in Lycra pulls her bike up to the gate. I step back, my foot sinking into the soft soil of the garden bed.

"What are you doing?"

She gestures at the snail in my fingers. I look over my shoulder and shoot a quick glance at Splints. His face pops up out of some bushes.

The woman swings her leg off her bike and click-hobbles closer, her bike shoes making her walk funny on the footpath.

"What are you doing with my snail?"

I drop it back into the garden, and it rolls under some of the lamb's ear leaves. I point at Splinter. "I'm walking my dog."

She's standing in front of me now, blocking the way with her bike. She leans down into my face.

"So, what were you doing with my snail, then?"

"I was just looking."

"Someone's been pinching things from front gardens around here."

"It's not me." I meet her gaze.

She raises an eyebrow.

"I was just looking! It's really unusual. That's all."

She straightens up and unclips her helmet, still looking at me. "What's your name?"

I look back. "Mum says not to give my name to strangers."

"Did she tell you not to steal as well?"

"I wasn't! I was just looking. You can't just accuse someone of stealing stuff. It's not nice." I glare at her.

She steps back, hands up. "Okay, okay. Fair enough. You don't want to give me your name. But it's getting dark and you must be, what, nine?"

I'm not stupid; I can tell when someone's trying to trick me into telling them stuff. I shrug.

"What are you doing out here on your own?"

Splinter snakes round to my back. He leans his weight into my thigh, and my fingers find the soft warm spot behind his ear. The woman straightens slightly at the size of him. I clear my throat. "I'm walking my dog."

"Should you be out on your own? Where are your parents? Are you lost? Where do you live?" The way she fires the questions at me, I reckon she's a teacher. No sense that she's not going to get an answer.

"I'm fine. I'm just walking my dog. We're going home now." I wave the lead at her.

She frowns. "It's getting dark. You shouldn't be out here alone in the dark. How old are you anyway?"

"I'm fine. I've got my dog." I clip the lead to his collar.

"Look"—she pats her bike seat—"let me put this away and I'll give you a lift home." She glances at Splinter. "Your dog can jump in the back. It's too cold and dark to be out here by yourself." She says it like it's the most sensible thing, for me to get into her car. I step away, pulling Splinter with me.

"I'm fine. Thank you." You'd be proud of my manners. I wonder if please-and-thank-you is going to get me out of this. I force my feet to keep moving me through the gate, my breath loud in my ears.

"Hey, I'm only trying to help." She lifts her bike up onto her porch, leans it next to the little table and the chairs with the cushions.

"I don't need help. I'm fine." I step back closer to the footpath.

"Okay, fair enough. You don't want to get into a stranger's car." *No, duh.* "That's probably very sensible. But I'll feel better knowing you get home safely, so I'm just going to follow you home, okay?" She lifts the bike down again and swings it around to face the street, snaps a shoe onto the pedal. "Make sure your mum knows where you are." She glances down at where the snail's lying hidden in the leaves.

My breath doesn't reach the bottom of my lungs. Splinter licks the jacket at my hip. I touch his collar, burying my fingers in the warm fur of his back. I reach my other arm out toward her bike—she's only got one leg on the ground—and I give her a shove to the left. Then I run.

"Hey!" I hear her crash into the garden behind me. I don't stop to look. Splinter's bouncing along beside me, trying to lick my hand, grabbing the lead. I ignore his game, yank him along and keep running. His paws get between my feet. "Splinter!" I yell at him, just keeping my balance. I look behind us. No one's following. We keep running.

I CAN'T SLEEP. Splints is restless too. The TV is annoying with the sound on and too bright with it off. With no TV it's too everything. My head's full of what-ifs. What if she'd come after me? What if she did follow me home, despite the half-hour detour we took, and I just didn't notice? What if she sees me again and recognizes me? My throat tightens. I push the heels of my hands into my eyes and focus on breathing. *Fear hates action.* It's your voice in my head, stopping my breath. *Stare it in the face.* Splints shifts his head onto my lap. I think of that lady's face, as she stood in her nice garden with her expensive-looking bike, expecting I'd answer her questions. Splints huffs a breath onto my fingers and twitches his eyebrows at me.

I tip more Winter Warmer into the vaporizers and pull on my boots. Splinter doesn't have to be asked twice.

We go back in the dark. The snail fits snugly in my pocket. We take one of her chairs too. I leave the cushion, though, sitting on her front mat.

DAY 29

SUNDAY

WE'RE UP EARLY. Out on the front porch, I take a small hanging pot from my backpack and carefully repack the soil in around the plant. It has long tendrils with leaves like pale beads. The old lady from next door is already on her porch. She's sitting on a chair with her back to us, pretending she's not watching me reflected in her window. As soon as we go in, she'll be peering over the fence to have a look. *Funny old goat*, you called her. *A whole life we know nothing about.* Nosy old goat, more like.

I ignore her inquisitive back and stand on my stolen chair to hang my new pot from the iron lacework. The spilled soil brushes off the little cushion easily as I pull it from the bottom of the bag. I give it a shake and place it on the chair. That's two odd chairs and two mismatched cushions now. And a few pots. And a wire bird on a stake. And an iron snail with a real shell. I step back and look at it all.

It looks . . . deliberate, rather than randomly collected from all over the place. Like one of those cafés where none of the chairs are the same. It looks like a lived-in house now. I arrange the chairs to give them that *we've just stepped away* look. A loved house. I think about that show I watched late at night in the first week you were gone, *Funeral Directors of Ohio*. How they painted the faces of dead people to make them look alive.

DAY 30

MONDAY

AWAKE AGAIN. TV news in my ears again. Bombs and death. I lift my head and press mute.

Now it's just the hum of the fridge and Splinter's warm breath. I roll my face back into the pillow and pretend not to notice his tongue on my hair. Monday. School. I slide off the couch and go do all those things that mean Monday morning.

Vaporizers topped up, dog fed, me washed and dressed and eating breakfast to music. My finger's hovered over your morning playlist for days and always pulled back. Today it pressed play. I push the toast out of my mouth. It sticks to my tongue for a moment before falling heavily to the plate. I can't swallow. My chest hurts, but I sit and listen. Was this you? The music fills the kitchen, spiky piano with gaps where there should be sound. I never really got it. Jazz. It sounds broken to me. But I'm trying. I force myself to hum along, filling in the missing bits. I tip the toast in the bin, rinse off my plate, put my jumper on. I listen as long as I can till my finger gets away from me and jabs pause. The silence is a relief, like letting go of a too-hot plate. I'm no closer—you're the music and the silence.

I push the thoughts away. I have school. I double-check the time. Doesn't pay to get there too early. And definitely not late. I aim for time to get my bag put away before the bell. No more, no less.

I HAVE FRIENDS at school. People seem to like me. Did you know that? Did you wonder who I was when you weren't there? I have my place in the class: solid, dependable. I make other people feel good by laughing at their jokes. I ask questions and listen to the answers, so people like having me around. No one asks much about me, I'm not that interesting. I'm friendly with most of them, not close to anyone. I float deliberately from one group to another. Welcome, but not missed when I'm not there. When you're pleasant, no one gets curious.

I'm okay with that, mostly.

I smile and chat a lot. It keeps me occupied and, between focusing on that and the schoolwork, time spins away and then it's almost the last bell.

Ms. Pham waves some forms at us. "A reminder, Student Learning Conferences with your parents are next week. This has the instructions for the online booking. Your parents will need to book a time with me. First in, best dressed." She starts passing the notices out, one to each of us. "I want you to return these marked yes or no with a parent's signature at the bottom so I know everyone got the notice. Everyone's to bring it back signed, even if your parents can't attend. So don't forget."

Student Learning Conferences. A three-word bomb. And there it is—the tight feeling I get when I think of you. It's invading this place too. I try to ignore the flutter at the base of my throat as my heart races and trips, to push it all back and focus on the desk, the whiteboard, the voice of the teacher, what I need to do, but my breath's too loud in my ears and the classroom's fading and here comes the rat, forcing its way down my throat, gnawing away from the inside as I sit frozen. It squirms its little chest inside mine. Forces our hearts to beat next to each other, one too fast, the other too slow. I sit with my eyes closed, feeling it. My feet in the grass again, the cold spikes wet on my bare ankle. I don't know how long I've been here. Forever. Never.

I press my fingers down, pushing into something solid. I look at my hands. My eyes start to make sense of it, my fingers pressing on the desk. Other sounds come back. Voices. The scrape of chairs on the floor.

I remember where I am. My feet are on the floor, in my school shoes. The tightening in my chest eases, my ribs loosen. I look up.

"All right, Rae?" Ms. Pham's watching me.

I nod. The other kids are in the hall, talking loudly and laughing. The day's over and they can't wait to get home. But I have attracted *unwanted attention*. Her concerned face sets off an alarm in my head.

I give a smile, deliberately pushing it into my eyes. "Just daydreaming."

She nods. Her gaze lingers on me a second too long.

I grin and grab the form from her hand. "See you tomorrow, Ms. Pham."

"Sure, Rae. See you then."

I bite the inside of my lip till my mouth's warm and salty and my eyes sting, your voice in my head. *Careless.*

I DON'T LOOK at the other parents waiting for their kids, all smiles. Or not even looking up from their phones, really, but there. A hand on the back, a touch on the head. I pull my cap down over my eyes and make my way through the gate.

I don't think about the last time you picked me up from school, unexpected, waiting under the tree like a shadow. The way you held my hand as we walked home, loosely, with your finger and thumb pinching and releasing the skin on the back of my hand. You got irritated with my dawdling. *Come on* and you drew my name out the way you do when you're getting frustrated, into two long syllables. You started cooking when we got home. Chopping carrots and onion, with the big heavy pot heating on the stove. But nothing went into it. When I came out from my room the butter had burned to the bottom, the carrots and onions sat in tiny cubes on the board, and you sat at the bench staring out at the shed. The look on your face made my stomach hurt.

So I don't think about that.

I walk past the other parents and out the gate. It's about 342 footsteps till home, depending on which way I cross the road. I didn't used to be a counter, not like Quentin at school, but I've found it helps when I've got a head full of bees. I look at my feet and count the steps, and the bees get less loud. Or maybe they like numbers. Some days I think of all the words for things instead, like all the words that mean walking. The best I got was ten: strolling, sauntering, plodding, hiking, marching, wandering, trekking, meandering, traipsing, shuffling. I made a few up too: streeting, avoidulating, stepolating. I wonder how you get words into the dictionary. Do you just e-mail someone? Sometimes if counting and words don't work I'll figure out how many heartbeats it takes to get home. If my heart's racing I'll have 2 heartbeats per step. That's 342 times 2 heartbeats to get to the front door, which is 600 plus 80 plus 4, which equals 684 heartbeats to get home. Though I'm not sure if that's right. Is a heartbeat the lub-dub I can feel in my chest or the single pulse I can feel in my wrist? If it's the one in the chest, that would make it 4 heartbeats per step, which would be 1,200 plus 160 plus 8, which is 1,368 heartbeats home. But that seems a lot. I heard somewhere that you should have 60 heartbeats a minute. Which means that it must be the lub and the dub together, otherwise my heart would be beating way too fast. Sometimes it feels like that, though. Other times it feels like it's stopped.

SPLINTER BANGS THE front door with his paw, making the windows rattle and the numbers fall out of my head. I stand at the letter box and watch the snuffle-snort of his giant nose squishing under the wood. I check the letter box. Splinter whines. I snap at him to shush. There's nothing but the usual scatter of pizza leaflets and a gas bill. I lean against the letter box. The sun pushes through the last of the leaves and warms my face a little. I close my eyes.

My hair follicles prickle with the tingle of *almost touched*. I snap my eyes open: a kid about my age, arm stretched out, about to tap me on the shoulder. He jumps.

"Oh." He shoves his hands in his pockets and clears his throat. I've seen him around; he moved in up the street a couple of months ago. We go to different schools.

I narrow my eyes. "What do you want?"

"I, ah—" His ears are turning red. I feel a bit sorry for him. But only a bit.

"You, ah, what?" I widen my eyes, mimicking him. Then I twist my lips into a smile. "You like invading other people's personal space and creeping up on them like a stalker?"

He steps back, glancing over his shoulder. "No, I, ah. You dropped this." He thrusts something toward me. I look at it. It's the parent-teacher notice.

"Oh." I slip my bag off my shoulder. The zip's undone. I wonder what else might have fallen out.

"It fell out on the corner."

I stare at him.

"I was coming back from the playground?" He points back up the street, the red from his ears creeping down his neck. "I saw it fall out of your bag when you changed shoulders?" I frown. "When you swapped your bag to the other shoulder, I mean. I mean that's when it fell out. On the corner. It was just that. I didn't see anything else fall out, if that's what you were wondering. When you looked at your bag, I mean."

I take the paper from his fingers. "Thanks." I turn away, so he'll know we're done.

"I'm Oscar," he blurts.

I glance back. He's got his hand stuck out again. I think he expects me to shake it.

"Right." I nod and move to walk away.

"Like the writer?" This kid does not shut up.

"My name." He's still going. "It's after the writer."

This is the point when you'd say, *Is he on drugs?* and then snort at your own joke. Splinter starts barking behind the front door. I stand on the footpath, my feet pointing toward our house, my fingers making the parent-teacher notice damp. Will talking to him make him go away faster? Or is it like feeding the seagulls? Before I can decide, he starts talking again.

"Oscar Wilde?"

My head's starting to hurt.

"Spelt with an *e*," he says.

"O-s-c-*e*-r?"

"No. W-i-l-d-*e*."

"Is your last name Wilde, then?"

"No. It's Geddes."

Perhaps I'm asleep. This is the sort of rubbish you get when people tell you their dreams. I bite my lip—it hurts. Not asleep, then.

"The writer's Oscar Wilde. I was named Oscar after him."

"Oh. What did he write?" It's out of my mouth before I realize, and I can tell from the gleam in his eye that I've fed the seagull. But I wait. I like books.

"Oh, heaps of stuff. He's really famous."

"Like what?"

"Oh, ah . . . all kinds of stuff. Classics. And stuff." His neck's going red again. His fingers scratch hard at the inside of his elbow.

I swallow a smile. "Like . . . ?"

"Books, and plays, and short stories and stuff."

"Kids' stuff?"

He nods, his eyes not focused on me. "Some of it."

I watch him squirm. "Like what?"

And snap. His eyes are back on my face and he grins. "'The Selfish Giant,' 'The Remarkable Rocket,' 'The Happy Prince.' Heaps of others."

"Cool. I'll give them a read sometime." I turn back to the house.

"You can borrow mine if you like? It's Mae, right?"

"Rae." I correct him automatically. This kid's verbal diarrhea's making me careless.

I shut the gate, ignoring his wince as it stubs his toe. He's come quite close enough.

"Who are you named after, then?"

"No one." I step onto the porch.

"What's it mean?"

I shove the key into the lock. "Nothing."

I shut the door.

SPLINTER JUMPS ON me and I dump the gas bill on the bench to worry about later. The oil burners are running low again. The orange and clove, peppermint and lavender are fading, letting that other smell win. I stand in the kitchen and breathe wisps of you in. You creep into my sinuses, my lungs; I imagine you moving from the little sacs in my chest into my blood, into my heart. Then I focus on holding my finger down on the air freshener from under the sink, counting the seconds as I point it up at the ceiling so the tiny droplets spray all the way up and then drift back down, pulling tiny little particles of you down too, to smother you on the floor in oversweet flowers. I light some incense sticks and think about where I should walk Splinter. I stuff the other questions deep into my bones, squashed down hard where I can't see them.

I have homework to do and I'm hungry. Noodles and fried egg again. I don't mind. It's tasty. I wait till after dinner to take Splints out. When I know that kid'll definitely be gone.

The scruff ball gets so excited when I clip on the lead he nearly slips over on the kitchen tiles. We often walk at night now. Who's gonna care, right? You?

It's nice. Quiet. There's not really anyone around at our end of the street. Everyone's tucked up inside, the warehouses closed and the truck yards still.

We walk up the car park end of the street and across the oval to the dog park. Not many dogs around at this time. Some. But in the dark the owners tend to stick to themselves. The dogs bounce over to say hi, though, and Splints enjoys a run with a couple of them. I jump up and down near the fence line, trying to keep warm.

"Are you out here alone?"

I jerk away from the voice. I *thought* I was alone. There's a man standing next to me, leaning on the other side of the wire. His face a little too close. I can smell cigarettes on his breath. Cigarettes and something that makes me snap my head away, something warm and rotten.

Don't talk to strangers stages a quick tussle with *don't be rude to adults*, and polite wins. Just. "No."

"Where's your mum, then?"

The question. I'm standing outside the shed again, the breeze lifting a hair off my cheek.

"She over there?" He shifts closer and leans in to point, his arm almost brushing my cheek. I can hear him rubbing up against the chain-link fence behind me. The gap between my heartbeats stretches, as loud as his breathing, and he puts his hand on my shoulder, heavy. I can feel his fingers digging in, even through your jacket. My toes prickle, feet itching to run as he leans further over the fence, his breath close enough to move the hair next to my ear.

"Or are you on your own?" The hand moves down from my shoulder, fingers stroking, kneading at the fabric of your jacket. "Cuz I could keep you company."

I jerk away. "Splinter!" I don't turn to see if Splints is following, I run. I know he'll catch up. He always has one eye on me. I drag my heavy legs across the grass and down the path and don't look back till I reach the road, where I stop so suddenly a ball of dog barrels into the back of my thighs. It almost pushes both of us into the street. I catch us as a car horn blares, an angry face twisting through the window. I grab Splints's collar and stumble to the top of our street, dragging him beside me. My wobbly legs get me round the corner before giving out, dropping me onto the gravel of the car park, bruising my bum. Splinter licks my face, his warm dog breath soft and bone-y. It tickles the hair next to my ear. My eyes sting. I push my fingers into my eyelids, pushing the wetness back around my lashes and into the damp corners of my nose. Splints pushes his face closer into mine, breathing his breath into my breath, licking the salt off my cheeks.

I hate you.

I need you.

Please don't be gone.

SPLINTER OF THE limitless patience. He waits for my breath to steady, for my hands to stop shaking, his big warm body leaning into my side. When we're sitting, he's taller than me. His big dog head looks over mine back to the park. My bum's cold and numb but his gentle panting rocks me, the motion warming. I sink my hand into the fur on his back, defrosting my fingers. His skin feels hot.

I don't know if I can stand; my legs are impersonating sacks of water. I could use a nosy woman on a bike offering me a ride round about now, but the street stays stubbornly dark. I shove myself up and we head home. No one but us in the streetlights.

EVERY NOISE MAKES me jump. I imagine the man coming. Hear the sound of his heavy boots behind me. Hear him breathing in the bushes. Then the noises in the bushes take on the sounds of smaller bodies, smaller furry bodies, with teeth. Do I smell like you? Can people smell it on me? Do they know? Animals know. I imagine their sharp whiskery faces twitching behind us. The smell of me making them salivate. Who would notice if I disappeared? Splinter keeps himself pressed into my hip, flicking glances at my face. I scratch his ear and he licks his nose and huffs a sigh, satisfied. We're back on the paved footpath now, the shadows of parked trucks replaced by the solid outlines of warehouses and the lights of proper houses up ahead. I count. From the corner it should be about fifty-seven steps to our front door. I'm up to forty-two when a voice to my left makes me skitter into Splints.

"Bit late for walking the dog, isn't it?"

It's the old woman from next door, the one you called a *funny old goat*. Out on her porch again.

I loosen my grip on Splints's lead and continue counting steps in my head, *forty-three, forty-four, forty-five.*

"Didn't your mother teach you not to ignore people when they're speaking to you?"

Fifty, fifty-one, fifty-two, fifty-three, fifty-four, fifty-five, fifty-six—

"Rude little bugger."

Fifty-seven.

"No manners these days. That's the problem. Unsupervised, mannerless kids running wild." She's pretending to talk to herself. But talking loud enough for me to hear.

I shove the key in the lock. "Nosy old goat." I mutter it, not quite under my breath.

"I heard that!"

I ignore her and slam the front door shut behind us.

The smell of you greets me. The vaporizers need topping up. I forgot. I lean back against the door with the dark and the smells. The smell of you, the smell of the man in the park, and a new one, my smell, the smell of my fear.

I lock the door and grab a chair from the kitchen to sit under the handle. I check the back door, top up the vaporizers. Make sure the curtains are shut.

Splints and I sleep on the couch, lights on, TV on, sound off so I can hear. I put the subtitles on and read about home makeovers in Britain.

Splinter rests his head on my lap. His ears are down, his eyes closed.

I concentrate on relaxing my jaw.

DAY 31

TUESDAY

WHEN I WAKE the sun's creeping across the floor. I'm gonna be late.

I dress quickly. If I don't make the first fifteen minutes of class I'll be marked absent. They'll call you. You sound so normal on your voicemail. Like a regular grown-up. Would they just leave a message? Would they call your work? Where does work think you are? Your phone's next to the empty fruit bowl on the kitchen bench. I plug it in every couple of days but no one calls. Not once in thirty-one days.

I grab a banana and check the clock: 8:47. I should be on my way to school already. I tip some food in Splinter's bowl and hold the back door open while he runs out for a wee. I light some more incense sticks on the back porch. Refill the vaporizers. He slinks back in and I slam the door behind him, grab the parent-teacher notice off the bench—leaving several pages of failed signatures behind—and bang out the front door. My backpack thumps in rhythm with my running feet and the voice in my head counting me to school.

I WONDER IF I'm a hologram. A kid laughs at something I say but I can't remember what it was. I move the right way and nobody notices that there's something not quite solid about me. A teacher ruffles my hair.

The parent-teacher notice is heavy in my bag. I can't wait to get rid of it; I don't want to get rid of it. That cold thickness sits at the bottom of my throat. I want to get lost in the day but I can't with that piece of paper in my bag.

When the bell goes I can't swallow.

IT SITS IN a pile on the edge of Ms. Pham's desk, looking just like all the others. The numbers on the page in front of me keep getting tangled. I don't look as she scoops all the notices off the side of her desk and starts to go through them.

"Rae?"

The chest-rat starts trying to push its way out. I fight with it till I can get a breath.

"Yes?"

"Isn't Mum coming this term?"

"She's got a work thing."

Ms. Pham frowns. "Let her know she can call to make another time if she needs, okay?"

"She said she'll let you know if she has any questions." It comes out squeaky.

"Okay. Good." She gives me a smile and moves on to the next

notice. I bite my tongue on the traitor who wants to tell her you won't call. And why. And what that means about me.

I look down at the worksheet in front of me.

The only people who realize I'm alone are the people who see why. That woman who knew I was a thief, the man in the park who knew I was nothing. The people that make my insides stop.

SCHOOL'S NOT HELPING today. All morning I expect Ms. Pham to take a closer look at the form, to call me up to her desk. But the pile stays where it is and then after lunch it's gone.

We have creative reading and writing in the afternoon. We've been studying genre this year. We've looked at comedy, adventure, mystery. Now we're looking at ghost stories. Ms. Pham's been reading *The Turnkey*, about a ghost in charge of a cemetery during the war. She reads for twenty minutes, and everyone's quiet. I love it when she reads. It's my favorite part of school. I like to watch her feet. When it's scary, or tense, she curls her toes up in her shoes, and if it's really exciting she wraps one leg around the other and squeezes her knees together. She always picks books that everyone loves, including this one. It's a historical novel, which made some people groan, but it's also about ghosts, which made some people a little scared, but it's also about a twelve-year-old girl. And somehow everyone's loving it, even the kids who don't like ghost stories, or history, or books about girls. At the end of the twenty minutes she asks us to write something. Last week it was something set in the past. This week, she asks us to write something scary, and there's a lot more excitement about this than there was last time. To start she asks us to *think about something that scares you*. I stare at the exercise book on my desk. The other kids start talking almost immediately. There's a lot of laughter and chatter about vampires and ghosts. Ms. Pham shushes the chatter and then it's just the whisper of pens across paper. We have twenty minutes. *What scares you?* I squeeze my eyes shut. *What scares you?* I grip my pen and open my eyes. I don't see the page in front of me. I see shadows, the shadows running behind you. The scratch of pens becomes the scratch of small things that climb and scrabble. My guts tighten to a hard lump. I swallow, but that just pushes more of me down, making the ball in my guts heavier, weighting me, dragging at muscle and bone. Sinking me into a cold mass that used to be warm blood and breath, so heavy I should be pushing through the chair and the floor, falling to the center of everything.

"Rae?"

I'm cold stone, fingers heavy and frozen. My breath pushes inside a hard shell, moving nothing. The chair holds, supporting my impossible weight.

"Rae?"

There's quiet laughter. I drag my eyes up from the desk. Smiling faces. The kids in my class are nice, mostly. We took a pledge at the start of the year to give everyone the benefit of the doubt. That means we have to assume the best first. Even the teacher.

"Rae, do you have something to share? You were lost in thought there, what did you write about?"

I look down at the blank paper and wonder if my lips will move or if they'll crack and crumble off my mouth. I try. "I . . ." My voice comes out dusty. I swallow and try again. "I didn't finish."

"That's okay, why don't you read us what you've got." Ms. Pham smiles at me.

I breathe the gravel off my chest. "I didn't start."

"Oh. Okay. Why don't you tell us what you were thinking about, then?"

"I turned into stone. And nobody noticed."

"Oh! What an interesting idea. A statue. That would be pretty frightening, being trapped like that. What does everyone else think?"

People call out: "You'd never be able to scratch if you got itchy" and "Birds would poo on you!" There's laughter, a bit too high and a bit too loud. The room's buzzing, electric with approved silliness. My legs sink further into my chair.

Ms. Pham claps her hands to get everyone's attention, to bring them down a bit. "Okay, then. Zaha, what did you come up with?"

The attention moves on.

I turn back into stone.

THREE HUNDRED FORTY-TWO heavy footsteps home. I think I like being stone. It's better than having a sharp-toothed rat in my chest. I check the letter box. Nothing.

I step over the weeds growing through the front path and check over my shoulder to make sure that kid Oscar's not planning another visit. He's nowhere in sight. I'm glad. My fingers play with the key in my pocket. Splints snuffles at the front door. The front mat's covered in leaves. I pick it up and bang it over the side of the porch into the garden, put it back down, straighten it so it lines up with the doorframe. I slide the key into the lock and check up the street again. Still empty. The front path's covered in a slime of old leaves. Some of them have melted into stains. The porch looks good, but the garden looks straggly. Abandoned. It was always neat, once. Our house always looked well cared for from the street.

I step back onto the path and look at the weeds, the dead, unwatered plants lying wrinkled and desperate. It hasn't rained for ages.

Watering the garden was your thing. You'd clip that old metal spray fitting onto the hose and stand, moving a soft arc of spray from plant to plant, while I sat on the front step and watched. On good days you'd flick the spray at me and the droplets would land on my eyelashes, and you'd call me *Princess Rae* and spray an arc of water into the sun so it made rainbows over my head. *See that, Rae? See those colors? See what makes up a ray of sunshine? All those colors, that's what your name means.* And I'd grin with my whole face, blinking at you till the droplets ran off my lashes and down my cheeks. Other times, the hose would run till the garden was soaked and the water ran down the path, spilling under the gate and into the street, washing our garden away until I turned off the tap, took the hose from your hand and led you inside.

I drop my bag inside the front door and get the stiff broom from the cupboard. Splints bursts out the door, bouncing around the dead and dying plants like Tigger. I let him shadow me. Soon I'm sweating in my school jumper but the leaf slime's gone, the path's clear, and the whole front's watered and looks loved again, not just the porch. It's gloomy now, that gloomy gray that means the sun's on the way out and it'll start getting dark soon. Splints stands next to the front door, eyebrows raised.

"Hungry?"

He steps from foot to foot and gives me a *come on* whine.

I glance at the tidy yard, the empty street. "Okay. In we go." I stop. There's something. I'm not sure I'm hearing something real. It's a low sound. Faint. A ghosting moan that could be someone's TV turned to low. Except I'm outside. I turn my head, that rat nipping at my guts. It sounds like it's coming up the side path, from the back of the house. I walk stiff-legged to the side gate and listen.

It's coming from the old goat's house.

I STAND WITH my feet crushing weedy violets and my ear pressed up against the side of her house. From the outside it's just like ours, so probably my ear's pressed to the wall of her front bedroom. I wonder if the plaster in her place is cracked too, with the same long dark veins creeping out across the walls.

It's hard to hear over Splinter's tail thumping the weatherboards. I shush him with a look and he sits, tail swishing, at my feet. The press of my ear against the wall creates an echoey space in my head. I can hear the shooshing flow of my blood and the whistle of breath around a bit of snot in my nose. And something else.

I pull back a little, so my ear's close but not touching the weatherboard. The something else is clearer now. A groan. A word?

I tap gently on the wall.

It stops.

I tap again. *One, two, three.*

There's a faint bumping sound. Then two more.

I swing my legs over the fence and onto the old goat's porch. Splints tries to scramble after me and nearly skewers himself on the pickets. I lift his big paws onto my shoulders and he scrabbles up onto the fence rails, digs his nails in me and launches himself up and over. We land on the porch. Me winded, him licking my face, tail waving. I roll onto my side and try not to puke. I have dog saliva up my nostrils. When I can breathe without wanting to cry or vomit I roll up onto my knees. Splinter flicks his eyebrows at me and sits, head cocked to one side.

"We should've used the gate."

He huffs.

"Should I knock?" He doesn't answer. "I kinda feel like I already did that." Now that I've got this far I just want to go home. What do I think's going on here? The old goat doesn't like me. And I don't need her nosing around after she gets snippy with me for being on her porch.

I bite my lip. There was something not right about that noise. And she's pretty old.

I press my finger to the doorbell.

Nothing.

Before I can think about it I lift the letter flap and peer in. The smell hits me before my eyes can adjust to the gloom. I let the flap go and it snaps shut. I sit back on my heels, eyes watering.

Splinter sniffs at the bottom of the door.

Not again. The blood rushing to my feet pulls my bum onto the decking. And that rat's back, chewing away at the inside of my ribs. "I think we should go." My legs don't move.

The groan again. There's someone in there.

I force myself up, take a deep breath and push open the letter flap, breathing through my mouth this time. It's not better. "Hello?"

There it is again. It's a word. It's *help*.

I look at the street, at our house, at Splinter's steady eyes.

I get up off my knees and swing my leg to climb back over the fence. Splinter readies himself to follow. Nix that. I walk us both out her front gate and back through ours. I unlock our side gate and we walk down the side of the houses until we reach the fence between our backyard and the old goat's. There's the lingering scent of incense. And something else. I grip on to the top of the fence as Splints yaps.

"Stay here." I ignore my racing heart and heave myself over to fall in a heap on the other side.

The backyard's a mess. Piles of pots and old buckets all over the place. Broken chairs and a three-legged table resting on its side. And an overflowing shed, mirror to ours, only the door to this one doesn't close: I can see the dying garden equipment inside, rusting and tangled, pots scattered like broken birds' eggs out of an old nest. My focus lingers on that shed. I blink, cutting my brain off. That's not why I'm here.

I stand up and stare at the back of her house. Not that much different to ours. Same peeling weatherboard. Same square windows. I squint at them in the gloom. There's a gap at the bottom of one. I stand on tiptoes and give it a wiggle; it lifts. I haul myself up and scramble through. There's something piled up on the inside so there's not far to drop, more of a roll-in, really. The smell's worse, even though I'm expecting it. Sour, sweet and earthy all at once, a scalpy smell that I can taste at the back of my nostrils. And something rotten, like the fridge smell, like the—

I put my head between my knees. *Stop.*

I breathe through my mouth and try not to gag. Mouth breathing doesn't help. I can still smell it, creeping up the back of my throat, coating my tongue. I snap my lips shut. My nose picks up a new sickly top layer. Air freshener, a baby-pink smell that makes a spot between my eyes ache. I take short shallow sips of air and try to remember why I came in. The *help*.

"Hello?" I wait.

A muffled sound from near the front of the house. I wonder if whoever it is can hear my heartbeat.

I move carefully; after the first near trip I slide rather than step my feet along the uneven floor in the dark. I call out again. "Hello?"

"In here."

There are piles of stuff everywhere. On, beside, under. The floor is soft and I look down. I'm not walking on the floor. I'm walking on mounds of stuff. It's all shadows. I can't see the walls. I make a vague guess where the doorway should be.

Everything screams at me to get out. It's dark, it stinks, piles of shadow tower over me. The shadows, the smell, I feel something skitter across my foot. I can't look down. I can't look up. There's something hanging from the ceiling. I can't breathe.

There's something hanging from the ceiling.

The alarm *chik chik chik* of a blackbird explodes in my ears, too loud and too sharp. I can hear the grass growing. I crouch down, my fingers pressing into the earth.

I can't breathe. I grip on to the grass. But it's not grass that my fingers are gripping. It's hard things. And soft papery things. And something wet and sticky.

There's something hanging from the ceiling.

The door in my head slams shut. I'm back in this strange house. This like-ours-but-not-ours house. And there's something hanging above my head.

I try to stand and almost fall backward and my heart explodes against the inside of my chest. I can't move my feet. There's only one thought left in my head: *Get out.* I reach into the dark, trying to breathe, trying to be slow; if I run I'll fall. I really want to run. I dig my fingers into my palms, eyes squeezed shut.

"Help." It's from behind me.

I stop. Eyes still closed, trying to hear above the rushing blood in my ears.

"Please."

It's not you. There's someone in here.

"Help."

Someone who needs me. I open my eyes. I suck in slow mouthfuls of air, ignoring the stench and the taste on my tongue. I try not to gag. *Focus.* The walls become walls again and the piles of stuff relax into books, magazines, boxes filled with egg cartons and—what is that, a half-buried bike? Hanging from the ceiling there's an old chandelier and masses of flypaper, strip after strip. Even in the gloom I can see the dirt-gray age of them. *Focus.*

"Hello?" It comes out in a squeak. I want to grab onto something for support but I'm scared if I touch anything I'll set off an avalanche. I push my feet into the stuff on the floor, taking my time to find something solid beneath me before I risk the next step. I clear my throat. "Where are you?"

"I'm in here."

I find a doorway and make my way to the voice. There's a movement in the shadows. My heart hammers and my ears ring as my gut liquefies and I think I'm going to shit myself. I clench, sweat covering my skin, half-glad of the distraction from the moving thing in front of me. It shifts again and I make out a hand in the gloom, then an arm that's attached to . . . a semi-familiar person. I grab onto something—a doorway?—and breathe, the sweat drying to cold. I peer more closely into the dark.

The old goat's trapped under something. A bookshelf? There's hardly any daylight left, and the piles of stuff in front of the window aren't letting in much of what there is. I can't see the walls. I wouldn't even know where to start to look for a light switch.

"Are you okay?" My voice is close to steady.

"I'm stuck."

I make my way over to her. Put my shaking hands under the uppermost corner of the bookshelf and lift. It's so heavy I can't shift it. She's lucky there's so much stuff on the floor or it would've crushed her. As it is, she's probably just made a goat-shaped dent. I swallow a giggle at that and my hands stop trembling.

She's lying there in the dark, just watching me. I crouch in the stinking mess and try to think.

Okay. What about a tunnel? I leave a pile of what might be newspapers under one end of the bookcase and start to shovel stuff out from under the other side. She gets what I'm doing and tries to wiggle her way out. It takes some time. I'm sweating again when she finally pulls her whole body out.

She sits on the floor in front of me, panting. All that deep breathing . . . I guess she's used to the smell.

"Thank you."

I shrug, relieved to have someone next to me even if it's her.

"Let me get you a drink and something to eat." She pushes to her feet and stumbles off toward the kitchen like nothing unusual's happened and this is just a normal old house, not one stuffed to the gills with—I look around. Books, magazines, bottles, clothes; I can see a milk crate full of corks, a plastic tub of dolls—everything.

I pick my way after her, stepping over what I hope's a matted old toy and around jars with liquid in them. I don't look too close.

The kitchen is . . . well, if it wasn't the same layout as our house, I don't think I'd know it was a kitchen. She fusses around and pulls an old tin from somewhere.

"Aha. Here. Have a biscuit."

I know enough about germs to know that's a bad idea.

"Umm. If you're okay, I think I'm gonna go." I make my way back to the sloping pile of papers I slid down to get in.

"Don't be silly."

I look at her. Ready to run.

"Don't go out the window." She waves her arm toward the hall. "You can go out the front door."

I follow her down a passage, my shoulders brushing the piles of stuff on either side. She has to walk sideways to squeeze through.

Stepping out the front door's like being reborn. I suck in a lungful of air.

She flicks on the porch light. I'm surprised to see the front of her house still looks normal. The same as yesterday: two armchairs and a small chest that acts as a coffee table with a collection of mugs. No hint of the chaos inside.

She gestures me to a seat, getting her breath back. "That was a bit of a scare. I don't know what I'd have done if you hadn't heard me."

I sit, not sure where to look. I want to ask about the house but I don't know where to start. "Has . . . has your house always been like that?"

She stares at me. I look at her hands. She arranges the mugs on the chest into a neat row. "No. I was tidy once. If you can believe it. Organized."

Organized isn't a word I'd use for that place.

Or is it? The piles, the boxes. Maybe it would be organized if there wasn't so much of it. It must have taken her years. I look at her face. Not so mean as yesterday. I swallow and ask what I'm pretty sure is a rude question. "How—?" I wave vaguely at the house.

She shrugs. "How does anything happen? Suddenly and slowly all at the same time. Inevitable as the tide." She rubs at a spot on her hand. "And just as hard to push back."

I think about the things I've collected since you've been gone. The way I search them out and place them carefully on the porch. Collecting something to fill the space. To mark it.

"I had all these things. I know it's silly." She looks down at the bruises pushing out of her veiny shin. "Dangerous. But I couldn't let go. And everything new that came in, well, that had to stay too. Then there's so much stuff, where would I start? Even if I could throw it away." She shakes her head and sniffs, changes her face back to the one I recognize, the old-goat face. "Anyway. I don't know what I'm doing telling you. What are you, nine?"

I'm not having this. "Ten." I say. "Ten and a half, and I just pulled you out from under a bookshelf and probably stopped you from being eaten alive by rats." The word catches in my throat.

Splinter starts to pound at the side gate.

I stand up. "So, you're welcome."

"Lettie." The old-goat face is gone; the one that replaces it's almost nice.

"What?"

"I'm Lettie. And thank you."

"Oh." I swallow. "I'm Rae. And that's okay." I'm standing half facing her, not sure what to do with my hands. Splinter barks. "I'd better get home."

"Sure, sure." She nods me off her porch.

DAY 32

WEDNESDAY

THE LETTIE SMELL stayed in my nose for most of the night, despite a shower till the hot water ran out, and the last of your shower gel. It's stuck up in my sinuses, still here when I wake. Must be a brain smell. Not really in my nose, just in my head.

It's horrible, this musky, scalpy, thick smell of a living person's filth. It's a relief.

I lean down and bury my face in Splints's furry back. He lifts his head and cracks me with his skull. I take the cue and roll off the couch.

The kitchen's dusty. There're crumbs on the counter from last night's ham and cheese toastie. Splinter's missed some dried food that's rolled over near the bin. I sniff. The bin needs emptying. It's 8:35. I wipe the bench, sweep the floor, pull on my uniform and kick Splints outside for a quick wee. I don't look at the length of the grass out the back. I'm not ready to deal with that.

Breakfast. I grab a banana. I wait for Splints to do his thing and then lock him in and head for the door. The gas bill's sitting on the table, next to the pages of practice signatures. I pick it up. The envelope's tinted pink—I know what that means. The shadow-rat gives me a nip and I drop the bill back on the table. I'll deal with it after school.

I MANAGE A fairly normal day. No unwanted attention. I do well on a math quiz. I get home unbothered by that annoying kid Oscar. I clean the kitchen. The house is heavy and silent. You would have had music or the TV on; you'd talk while we cooked dinner. I'd listen to you replaying arguments with people who weren't here. Even your silent was noisy. You'd sigh, tap things, breathe. Whisper my ear with your finger as you walked past. There was always something. You moving around, living; the sound-print of someone else existing nearby. I could pretend you were just in the next room if it wasn't for the silence.

I bang a bucket into the sink and watch hot water mix with cleaning fluid to make steaming soap bubbles. The warm oily smell of fake lemons billows around my face, and the hair against my cheek curls in the mist. I slop the bucket to the floor, spilling suds onto the tiles. I add some bleach to the mix, the smell eye-stingingly strong. I start with long slow sweeps and work my way in. I focus on the floor and the darker lines of clean I create and not on the footprints I'm mopping away.

THE WASHING MACHINE'S hissing away in the laundry when I sit down at the table with your laptop. I pull out your diary with all the passwords helpfully written in the back. I'm just a kid and even

I know that's a dopey thing to do; useful for me, though. Your attempt at a code isn't hard to work out. I've seen you flip to the back of your diary often enough to know what they're for.

BAun: bank account user name

BApw: bank account password

I log in. You've even favorited the log-in page. I pay the gas bill. The money's going down. I scan over the numbers. A few weeks ago out went one big whack with *Rent* next to it and *Automatic payment*. I thank your crappy memory for that too. I look at what's left and do some calculations. If the last month is about normal for spending and bills, I have enough left for about a month, maybe. I look at the amount on the gas bill. Hopefully. I stare at the cursor. I don't think about the *then what*. I'll think about that when I have an answer. I snap the computer shut and finish cleaning the house.

The bathroom sparkles and vacuuming has made the house warm. It feels better warm. Safer. I let Splints out of your room and shut the curtains. I turn the heater to low, shutting all the doors so it only has to heat the lounge. Splinter hates it; he sits near the door panting with a face that asks what he's done to deserve *the heater*. I think of the money in the bank, turn it off and pull on another jumper.

WHEN IT'S DARK I put on your jacket and take Splinter out. We walk past the old goat—Lettie.

She nods at me.

I nod back.

Splinter and I stick to the lit streets now. The ones with cars and buses. No more dark parks or trees or bike paths. Or people's front yards. If he's disappointed, Splints doesn't show it. He's happy to be walking next to me, to be with me. The thought bruise-aches. I press on it again; I'm enough for him, at least.

On the way home past Lettie's she calls out to me. "Might want to check your letter box."

I do. There's a book. I squint at it in the streetlight. Oscar Wilde. I look around. There's no one in the street.

"From that kid up the road."

I nod. I figured.

"Sweet on you, is he?"

The question annoys me. "No. He's just got no friends."

She laughs at that, which makes me more annoyed.

"Bit like you," I mutter just loud enough for her to hear. I shut the door before she can reply.

HOME'S KINDER TONIGHT. Maybe it's the leftover vacuuming warmth and the soft smell of heated dust. It reminds me of Sunday afternoons. The bathroom door's shut to keep the cleaning fumes contained. I could pretend you're in there. I could. I throw the book on the couch and head into the kitchen.

Cheese on toast, with tomato this time. Better get to the supermarket soon. There's no fruit or veggies left. I wipe the kitchen down carefully when I'm done. Do the dishes. The quiet rushes back when I turn off the tap. The cold creeps in through the curtains.

I sit on the couch with Splinter's head heavy on my lap, TV on. More doom. Something pokes into my bum. The book. I pick it up. Fairy tales?

I read it anyway.

DAY 33

THURSDAY

THERE'S PRICKLY COUCH fabric pushing into my cheek. Splinter's snoring on the floor, my pillow across his paws. I'm awake, sharp awake, but only in my head. I imagine wiggling my toes. They ignore me. I close my eyes. The heavy of my body soaks my brain. *Get up*, I think, but I don't mean it. The words with all the power are *For what?*

The light changes. I'm pretty sure I should be leaving for school now. The thoughts come slowly. The idea that not being at school could be a *bad idea*. That there might be *consequences*. My brain chews on that word for a bit; it was a favorite of yours. I roll it around my head. I should do something. Sleep tugs at me.

Online absentee form. That jolts me awake. I keep my eyes squeezed shut, thinking. It would be easy to cheat. The school app automatically logs in. I've seen you use it.

Magically my body works again. I'm up and in the kitchen and logging in to the school portal.

I mark myself sick. No alarms go off. It's done. Completely legit.

I put your phone back on the bench.

The floor's cold. My toes ache. The kitchen clock ticks. I have a day.

I sit on the couch and reread Oscar's book of fairy tales.

It's not as easy as I expected. It's not that the words are hard, but how they're put together is different from what I'm used to. For this second read I drag our big blue dictionary up onto the cushion next to me to check some of the words and I skip the bits that drag. But I like how it feels. It's kind of sad but not a scary sad, not a sad that hurts. It's the sadness of an old painting, all shadowy and soft with warm-blanket colors.

I stop when I get hungry, but there's no food left. Just the crusts of a stale loaf and some butter. I toast and eat them, dropping crumbs all over the bench. I write a list.

It's time to do a proper shop that's not from the gas station round the corner. I grab the green bags from the cupboard. Splinter's got that happy twitch to him. He knows when I'm getting ready to go outside. I tickle his ears and lean my face into his, then throw some dried food to scatter across the kitchen floor. He hustles after it, excited. I shut the door on him. I feel bad but I'm not taking him with me. I don't like tying him up outside the supermarket—last time I came out, a drunk man was blowing smoke into his face and, I'm pretty sure, untying his lead.

He's all I have. He's staying home.

I'D KIND OF forgotten how much stuff there is in the supermarket.

I look at my list and stroll around, chucking things into the little half trolley. No one pays me any attention, other than to give me an annoyed face if I'm standing where they want to be. If I get more than a glance I just find another adult to pull my cart up next to and look at the same stuff they are. People assume I belong to them and wander off and the person next to me assumes I'm with someone else. Kids in supermarkets are annoying. It's only kids outdoors that people seem to worry about.

Carrots, tomatoes, baby spinach, mushrooms, eggs, cheese, yogurt, bananas, apples, mandarins. Dog food. Incense. Mosquito coils. Essential oils. Bread. Butter. Ham. Eucalyptus spray. Bleach. Some milk. Muesli. Loo paper. Noodles. I stick to the discounted stuff, but the essential oils are expensive.

I buy some soup in cans and a microwave lasagna thing. I check the calculator on your phone, that's $98.04. I look at my full trolley. I think I can make it last. I walk down the chocolate aisle to the self-serve checkout. There's Kit Kats on special. A family block for $1.95. You don't eat Nestlé, you say they kill orangutans. All the other chocolate's more expensive, even the smaller bars.

I take myself through the self-checkout: $99.99.

I tap your card.

LUGGING THE BAGS home is hard work. It's heavy, especially the milk and bleach. I have to keep stopping to swap the bags around. If I carry them with my hands the handles dig into my fingers and the bags bang against my legs. If I hook them in my elbows they make my arms ache and my fingers tingle. The toast feels like hours ago.

I'm a sweaty mess by the time I get to the front gate.

A movement next door catches my eye.

Lettie.

"Shouldn't you be at school?"

I'm hot and pissed off and hungry and I want to get inside and make myself a sandwich. With fresh tomato and ham that I don't have to give a sniff test. Who does she think she is? The cops?

I give her a look. "Shouldn't you be at work?"

She lobs the look right back. "Does your mother know you're wagging school?"

Fuck you. I yell it in my head. Not brave or silly enough to say the words out loud. A muscle in my jaw twitches. She has no right to lecture me about anything. I glare at her. "Does the council know you live in a dump?"

She stares back. "You're one rude kid."

I huff the bags through the gate and stomp up onto the porch, not looking at her. I swing my arm up and shove the key in the lock, banging the bags against the door. The bottom of one gives out, the one with the eggs. I close my eyes. *One, two, three, four, five, six, seven, eight—*

"This what kids do when they wag these days, huh? The shopping." She's leaning over the side fence now.

I give her a dirty look. In my mind I'm throwing the eggs at her.

She smiles. She's different when she smiles. Nice. An acid prick stings the back of my eyes. I blink, trying to maintain the glare.

A warm, wet, treacherous thing slides down my nose. I lean down, angling my face away and furiously shoving the stuff from the broken bag into the others.

"Hey—" Her voice is kind.

I leave the cracked eggs on the mat and drag the bags through the door. She's still saying something and I don't want to hear it.

I kick the door shut behind me.

DAY 34

FRIDAY

SICK TWO DAYS in a row will get questions asked. I've got a good lunch packed: sandwiches bursting with spinach, cheese and tomato; fresh fruit, even some yogurt in a little reusable container with a spoon. I'm a well-looked-after kid. My hair's washed and brushed. My shoes are clean. My breath's minty fresh. I sit at the kitchen table, Splints's head in my lap, packed schoolbag at my feet, until the clock shows eight forty-five. As the second hand ticks up to the twelve, I stand and shove Splints gently toward the back door. I don't have to show him twice: he's been miserable locked inside and I need him to do some chasing. I can't have another night awake to the scratching and scrabbling from out there. I'm done with sharp-toothed dreams and I want them gone. I fill his water bowl and shut the back door. Three hundred forty-two steps to school; I should be there by 8:50, allowing for time to wait at the crossing. I stop my foot just in time; it lands awkwardly off the doormat. I stand half inside, half on the porch, my legs straddling the mat. The broken eggs are gone; in their place is a green bag.

I step over it and look inside. An egg carton.

I look across at Lettie's house. The porch is empty.

I lift the carton out of the bag and give it a sniff, remembering the piles of egg cartons in her house. It smells okay. I check the date on it: the use-by's two weeks away.

I put it gently back into the green bag and look across at her empty porch again. I can't take them with me. I place them inside the front door, shut it quietly and head for school.

I don't think about what they might mean.

SCHOOL'S A RELIEF. We have art today. The usual art teacher's sick but Ms. Pham says it'd be a shame to miss it, so she takes us into the art room and gets all the paints and brushes out. *Paint what you like*, she says. *Just do something that feels good to you.*

I use lots of yellows, oranges and browns. Light and warm in the center and dark at the edges. I paint how I felt sitting on the couch, Splinter next to me, reading Oscar's book, TV on silent and the lamps making the room a warm color.

"That's nice, Rae. What do you call that?"

I stare at its center. "A mirage."

I LENGTHEN MY strides on the way home. Big deliberate steps that jar on landing. It takes 123 of them to get to our gate.

I'm watching my feet, so his voice catches me off guard.

"What are you pretending to be?"

I glance at his face. "Nothing."

"I thought maybe you were being a selfish giant or something."

"I'm not six, I don't act out stories."

He grins like I'm not being mean. "You read it, then?"

"Yeah, I read it."

"What did you think?"

I shrug. "Okay, I guess."

"Which story did you like best?"

"I dunno."

"C'mon. You must have a favorite."

I do, but I'm not telling him. He looks way too pleased I even said they were okay. And if I keep talking to him, he might think we're having a conversation.

I brush past him to step through the gate.

"You must have an opinion. Everyone has an opinion." *Everyone has an opinion*—I can hear you mimicking him in my head, trying to get me to laugh at him, to make him small.

I look at his face. His eyes remind me of Splinter. He smiles, waiting.

I turn my back and check the letter box. "They're a bit God-y."

He takes a big breath; I can feel the excitement behind me. He wants to *talk* about it. I hope he's not one of those Christians you used to slam the door on. Is that why he gave me the book? The thought weighs in my chest. I talk over the top of him. "It made me uncomfortable. Like he wasn't telling me the story to tell me a story. Like he was trying to make me see his way."

Oscar stops talking. I flick a glance at him. He's frowning. "I hadn't thought about it like that."

"I like them apart from that, though." I don't know why I want the frown to go. Maybe it's the Splinter eyes. I mentally shake myself. He's not Splinter. He's just a kid who's bothering me and standing in my front yard too close to the door.

"Right. Bye, then." I turn and walk away.

"So you've finished it?"

"Yep." I don't turn around.

"Can I have it back, then?"

That stops me. "Oh. Okay. I'll drop it in your letter box." I slip the key in the lock.

"I'm here, just give it to me now."

My fingers slip on the key. I should have just dropped it in his letter box this morning. Why didn't I just get rid of it? I can feel him standing behind me, sense him bouncing up and down on the balls of his feet.

"Fine. I'll get it." I step through the door, nearly tripping over the eggs. I pick them up and give the house a quick sniff. I turn to tell him to wait but he's followed me in. "What are you doing?"

"What?"

How do I answer that? Is this normal? Is this what people do? Do normal kids wander into other people's houses after school? Too late now anyway, he's already sitting on the couch.

"Make yourself at home." I do your best vinegar voice but it's lost on him.

"Thanks." He smiles.

I hand him the book. He takes it and stays sitting on the couch.

"Okay. You can go now."

He looks around. "You know, our houses aren't that different. We've got the kitchen on the other side, and an extra room at the front, but otherwise they're kind of the same."

I shrug and wait for him to go.

"What's with all the vaporizers?" I keep my face still, shrug again. "Is it because of—" He angles his chin to the backyard.

The entire weight of my body sinks into my feet, taking most of my blood with it. I make my lips move, fight to breathe like a normal person. "What?"

"You know—" He makes the movement again. "Because of her?"

My lips don't move right. I force the words out around them. "You know about her?"

"Everyone knows about her."

I can hear a rushing sound, static. I struggle to focus. "What?" It comes out a whisper. I dig my fingers into the back of the couch, hanging on, forcing myself to stay upright.

Oscar peers at me funny. "Are you okay?"

"I'm fine." The words echo in my head. *Fine fine fine fine fine fine fine fine.*

"It's the smell, right? Everyone knows she's a hoarder."

Lettie. The relief makes me want to vomit. "Yes. The smell's from Lettie's house." My voice is thick in my head like my ears are blocked.

He nods and stands. "Well, duh." I walk him to the front door. When I get there he's not behind me. I spin around; he's in the kitchen, staring out the back. My stomach falls away. I watch him, my head as small as a pin, as he squashes his face against the window and looks out. Splinter launches himself at the glass, paws smacking the pane in line with Oscar's head. He jumps back, laughing.

"What's your dog's name? Can I meet him?"

I remember to breathe. "Splinter. And no."

"Why not?"

The blood rushes back into my fingers, tingly and hot. I tuck them under my armpits. "I've got homework to do. And my mum'll be home soon." My voice sounds a long way off.

"Come on. Just for a few minutes?"

He rests his hand on the back door. I think frantically for an excuse. *He's not good with people*? Splinter's licking at the glass, his face a goofy mess of tongue. Oscar pushes his face closer to the pane.

My pulse vibrates in my arms and legs; sweat pricks at my pits and top lip. I want to grab Oscar and throw him out the front door. My feet don't work. The rat's back, nipping at my guts. Oscar's rattling the handle. Splinter's barking outside. *Nip nip nip*. "Your backyard's a bit of a mess. Don't you have a mower?"

I can't think. I need to get him out.

"You can walk him with me if you like."

THIS IS HOW we end up out the front, Splinter on the lead between us, and Lettie smirking at me from her porch.

I ignore her but Oscar gives her a long stare. "That house is a breeding ground for rats."

"What?"

"Mum dropped round once to offer her some veggies. Not long after we moved in. An older woman on her own; Mum thought it'd be a nice thing to do." I can hear someone else's voice in the words. "She got a quick look inside when the door was open and she said it stank. Plus"—he glances over—"she was really rude."

Lettie's smells. Everyone knows about it. A little muscle below my left shoulder relaxes a bit. "Yeah," I agree quietly, "it's pretty ripe." I think of the eggs on the front step. "She's all right, though."

"She's a public health hazard is what she is." There's that other voice again. "It's pretty strong even at your house, especially near the back door. Funny it's not so bad at the front of her place, must be worse out the back." He cranes his neck like he's trying to peer between our houses. "Maybe it's those office buildings behind you guys, boxing the stink in."

"I'm not deaf, you know." Lettie's face is all angles, like a hawk that's spotted a nice rippable bunny.

Oscar pretends not to hear, but I can see his cheeks going pink. It makes me smile.

Lettie catches my eye and gives me a wink. I nod back. She glances at Oscar and says to me, "What are you doing with that, then?"

It's a good question. Splinter's hustling after him, his lead pulling at my arm; he knows a walk when it's on offer. I ignore Lettie's question and let Splints drag me along. Oscar's talking again, his face angled just enough so I can catch his words but not so much that he has to look back toward Lettie. I follow, wondering how I'll get rid of him now. He's chatting on about something that doesn't involve input from me. I hold in a sigh. At least having another kid with me means no one will look twice.

We go to the dog park—Splints loves it here, but we haven't been since Monday, since the man—and we walk around the fence line. I don't need to talk because Oscar really does not stop. His family, his teachers, what he's watching and reading. But it's what he doesn't talk about that tells me the most. He doesn't say anything about friends.

Not that I care.

It must be hard for a person like him to have no one to talk to. He's talking about gardening now. The backyard he designed himself. "My parents helped, of course. But I planned it out. You should come see it."

I don't want to see his garden. I'm only walking with him to keep him from—

"I could help you with yours, if you like? No offense, but it's a real mess. And you've got a really nice old shed there and a lovely brick wall that would be perfect for climbing plants. A bit of trellis—"

I stumble.

"Rae, what's wrong?"

"Nothing. I stubbed my toe."

He looks at the path. "But there's nothing there."

"I gotta go, okay? See you round." I whistle for Splinter and we run, and leave Oscar standing there on the edge of the park.

LETTIE'S SITTING ON her front porch like I knew she would be. I brace for the comments but she just waves as I scurry past with Splints. I fall through the front door and just make it to the kitchen sink in time to vomit.

I'm sweaty and my jaw aches. Maybe I am sick.

I know that's not it. I shouldn't have let him in.

I concentrate on breathing, counting in for five, out for five, like in mindfulness at school. Like we used to practice together outside in the sun, the grass crushed beneath us. *In—two, three, four, five. Out—two, three, four, five.* I can feel your hand in mine. I can see your hands clenched into fists, your feet off the ground. I shake my head and stare at the kitchen floor. *Concentrate on what you* can *do.* I focus on what I've done. The house is clean. The porch is clean.

I lift my head and look out the back. He's right. It's starting to look as bad as Lettie's. It's the only thing that doesn't fit.

I sniff and tip some eucalyptus on a tea towel and leave it sitting folded next to the sink. No more smells and death. I glance at the eggs on the kitchen bench.

I am not her.

I need to fix the backyard.

DAY 35

SATURDAY

SPLINTS OPENS AN eye as I step over him. It's not quite light but not dark enough to be night anymore. I stand in the bathroom under the heat lamps and stare at my face in the mirror. There are dark shadows under my eyes, matching three-quarter moons. I look like you. I flick the lights off and head for the kitchen.

Splinter wanders out at the smell of toast. He licks my toes and twitches his eyebrows at me. I hold out the crust and he takes it gently from my fingers, his lips smacking softly as he chomps down. His tail swings in a circle of happy; he's never been a side-to-side wagger. You'd say, joking, *He's too lazy to even wag properly*, but the circle always makes me smile, his helicopter tail. Sometimes I imagine if I could just make him happy enough he'd fly. I give him the rest of my toast.

I STARE AT the back. Sleeping Beauty's garden. The grass is growing higher around the back shed. The grass is growing higher full stop. If I don't get out there soon I won't even be able to open the door to the little metal toolshed. I light more mosquito coils and the incense that makes Splinter sneeze, and stick them in some jars and slide them out the back. I close the door again and go sit on the front porch. Splints leans against me with a sigh.

The plant in the hanging pot I stole is dying. I forgot to water it. I look out across the yard. Most of the plants look half-dead again. We've had no rain in weeks and the whole space looks wilted. Everything needs watering and weeding. Things need to be tended to be kept alive, even in winter. I look at the chair next to me: the cushion looks dusty. It's not even been a week since I tidied up out here but everything's looking tired, like it's too exhausted to keep up the lie.

I water it all again anyway.

SATURDAY. THE WASHING'S done. The front yard's clean and watered.

Saturdays used to be fun. Sometimes. Those nights when you'd change your clothes, slip your feet into *inappropriate shoes* and we'd head straight down Cowper, you laughing as we dashed across Napier Street, with your high heels threatening to snap, and down the lane to the pizza place. We always sat upstairs, taking the booth closest to the fire in winter. We'd both have pizza and you'd have a cocktail.

I liked the less fun nights too. Just me and Splints. We'd call ahead so the pizza was waiting. When it was Rafa with the neck tattoo working downstairs he always let me bring Splints in while I paid. The same order every week wherever we ate it: one margherita with olives and a salami special.

I haven't had pizza in a while. The whole pizza-every-Saturday thing was more fun when I wasn't in charge of all the money. And doing stuff that we used to isn't fun anymore.

But it's Saturday. The house is clean, and I've eaten pretty much the same two things for dinner for thirty-four nights in a row. I want someone else to feed me.

"Come on Splints, we're getting pizza."

THE SMILE RAFA gives me as I poke my head round the door makes me forget my nerves.

"Hello, stranger, we've missed you! I was beginning to think you'd dumped us for some other pizza place!"

I smile.

"You didn't call ahead tonight. The usual?"

I nod.

"Alrighty! Two pizzas for Rae coming up!"

"Oh, just the margherita . . ."

"What? Just one?" He peers at the door. "Where's that lovely mum of yours?"

"She, ah, she's not feeling that well." It's not a lie.

He tips his head to the side. "You sure that's it?"

My mouth dries. "What?"

"You sure that's it?" He stares, arching an eyebrow so it wrinkles like a fat hairy caterpillar. "You sure she hasn't gone and found herself another pizza man?" He winces. "I don't think my heart could bear it."

My laughter sounds too loud. "No! She asked for a—" I pick a random name off the menu board. "She asked for a vulcano this time."

"Really?" He's surprised.

I nod.

"Alrighty, then."

I guess I've got lunch for tomorrow as well. I perch up on the stool closest to the door to be closer to Splints. Rafa finishes what he's doing and wanders over.

"Where's that dog of yours, then?" He glances about and winks at me. "Nobody but us and Gus in the kitchen." He rubs his hands together. "Let's get him in for a bit of a rumble!" He raises his voice and yells toward the kitchen. "You won't tell, will ya, Gus?"

A woman pops her head around the partition. "If I see nothing, then nothing's happening."

Rafa grins and opens the door. "Come on, buddy!"

Splinter can't believe his luck. He tumbles in and throws himself into the pizza-smelling arms held out to him. He gets a good ear ruffling and a wrestle in return.

"What a dog! Master Splinter! We've missed you, oh yes we have."

"What's all the noise?" Gus wanders out of the kitchen. "If I didn't know better, I'd think there was a dog in here." She bends down and gives Splints a scratch behind the ear. She grins at me. I smile back, but the edges feel tight. These two adults, with their cool hair and tats, are talking to me like I belong here.

"How've you been?" She asks it like I'm interesting.

I nod. I don't know how to answer. How does anyone answer—do they tell the truth? Does she really want to know? Is it rude to lie?

Rafa's talking now. "You guys been away? It's been so long we thought you mighta moved."

I shake my head, still smiling. The tightness making its way to my eyes, like my hair's pulled back too hard. Why are they still talking to me? My body feels like it's forgotten how to stand, my arms don't hang right.

"You don't say much, huh?" He smiles at me, right into my eyes.

My lip trembles.

"S'okay. I was pretty shy when I was your age too." Gus hands me a lemonade and winks. "The good ones always are."

I focus on opening the bottle and putting the paper straw in.

They let us wait in the function room with the lights and heaters on and bring in the pizzas when they're ready. They give me them two for the price of one, and I wave as I bundle Splints out the door, pizza boxes balanced in one hand.

It's cold outside. The wind in the alley makes my eyes water.

I STAND ON the front step for a while. Splinter sits at my feet. I've left the porch light and the inside lights on. It's like a hundred other Saturday nights.

No it's not.

"Pizza night, is it?" A voice cuts through the dark air from next door.

I look at the two boxes in my hands. "I bought one for you." The words are out before I've realized. I'm sick of eating alone. I glance at her.

"What?"

I shrug. "For the eggs the other day."

She waves it away, my thank-you an irritation.

"Oh." I'm surprised how disappointed I feel. I turn back to the door.

"Come on." Her voice is rough, like she hasn't spoken much

today. She clears her throat. "I was just being polite. Bring that pizza and your oversized fleabag over here."

I'm on her porch before she can change her mind. Or before I can. I stand there awkwardly and try not to look at her front door. I don't want to go inside again; once was enough.

She gestures to the seat. "Take a load off, Rae."

She reaches behind her seat and pulls out a bottle of ginger beer. "You buy me pizza, the least I can do is offer you a drink to go with it."

I take it and sit down. I hand over a pizza box. She cocks her head like it just occurred to her: "Your mum won't mind, will she? Should you be getting home?"

I open the box on my lap. "Nope. It's okay. She had to go out." Splinter makes himself at home, bum placed squarely between the chairs. Maximum crust-action positioning.

Lettie gives me a bird eye, her head tipped to the side. But she drops the subject. "Great, then. I won't look a gift pizza in the mouth." She flips the lid of her box open and sniffs. "Chili?"

I nod.

She smacks her lips together. "Excellent."

LETTIE'S HALFWAY THROUGH the pizza before she says anything. I don't mind. It's a comfortable silence. I give the ginger beer a try. It's warming, sweet and spicy on my tongue even as the coldness of it sliding down my throat makes me shiver slightly. I pull your coat around me a bit tighter. I've got pizza on the sleeve; they only roll up so far, and every time I reach in for another slice they drag in the cheese. It doesn't upset me like it usually would.

"So, you're friends with that kid up the street, are you?" Her voice is casual in a way that makes it clear she doesn't like him.

I shrug. "Not really."

"You met his mum?"

"No."

She grunts and drops some cheese into her mouth. "She's a busybody, that one." She gives me her bird eye again, sharp as a magpie. "Got her face up in everyone else's business."

I nod, thinking about what Oscar said about Lettie.

Lettie's eyes glisten in the porch light, more owl than magpie now, and I think of the dark inside her house. Makes sense.

"Did he say something to you? About me?" She leans forward, watching my face.

Oscar's not my friend. I'm not sure what Lettie is. But I'm sitting on her front porch eating pizza, and Splinter's head is resting on her foot. I've been around people enough to know that telling anyone something someone else said never works out well. Lettie's still watching me with those bird eyes. She leans forward. "He did, didn't he?"

I say nothing.

She leans back and nods. "I knew it." She drops her crust in the box and the sound makes Splinter pop his head up, ears lifted. She gives it to him. He scoops it out of her hand with his tongue, and when he's done chomping he gives her fingers a good licking too. She doesn't even notice. Her gaze is turned down the street, face all pointy like it used to be when we first started talking.

"Say something about my house, did he? Call it a health hazard or some bullsh—" She looks at me. "Nonsense."

The return of the old-goat face reminds me it's cold and dark and your jacket's a bit uncomfortable under the arms when I sit in it, the way the extra fabric bunches up. And it's Saturday. It's been four Saturdays now. Not counting that day.

"Well?"

"I don't know." Maybe it's time to go. I shut the lid of the pizza box. I can feel her looking at me. Splinter rests his head in my lap and I give his ears a scratch.

"You want a hot drink?" The sharp voice is gone. I flick a glance at her face. She raises an eyebrow at me. "Well? I can make you a hot chocolate if you like. It's getting a bit cold out here."

The thought of drinking milk from her house worries me. I turn my head to look through the front window. It's dark in there. Not like a house at night, but like it's filled with solid dark: a giant wooden kid's block decorated to look like a house with the windows painted on in black. Except it doesn't smell like wood in there.

"Relax. I'm not going to make you go inside." She leans over and slides the pizza boxes off the table between us, but it's not a table, it's a chest. She lifts out a kettle and a plastic jar of instant hot chocolate powder.

"Here." She shoves the kettle at me. "Go fill that up from the tap round the side."

I look in the chest as I stand up. It's shop-neat. A green and white tea towel folded into a sharp square, four clean cups stacked in pairs, a tall glass with some shiny teaspoons standing in it, three glass jars filled with tea bags, and a small bowl with those little tiny milk things you peel the lid off, like the ones in that doctor's waiting room with the tea and coffee you used to slap my fingers away from. I wonder how often Lettie has visitors over for hot chocolate. I've never seen anyone else here. When I bring the kettle back she leans down and plugs it into one of those outdoor power points that's hidden behind her chair. I watch as she spoons the hot chocolate powder into the mugs.

"It says two heaped spoons. But I always think it tastes better with three."

We wait for the kettle to boil.

IT'S GOOD HOT chocolate. The mug's just a little too hot to wrap my fingers around. I hold on to the handle with the fingers of one hand and rest the fingers of the other around the rim, warming the tips. I lean my face into the chocolaty steam.

Lettie takes a loud sip of her drink and sits back with a sigh.

I wonder if she spends every night out here.

We finish our drinks without saying much of anything. When I'm done, I place the cup carefully onto the chest next to Lettie's. She picks them up and disappears around the side. I hear the tap running. She comes back and takes the green and white tea towel out of the chest, carefully dries each cup, stacks them, folds the tea towel back into its tight square, places it next to the empty kettle and shuts the lid.

She runs her hand over the top of the chest. "There. All clean."

I stand up and gather the empty pizza boxes off the ground.

"Okay. I'd better get home."

Lettie nods. "Sure. Sure."

I whistle Splinter up from his spot between us and head for the gate. I'm facing away from her when she speaks again.

"Your mum away for the weekend, then?"

The rat jerks awake from its pizza and chocolate coma and stabs its claws into my chest. I swallow. Lettie basically lives on her porch. Why not let her think she knows what's going on? People don't look closely when they think they've figured stuff out. I clear my throat. "Yeah." I glance at her.

She nods. "Let me know if you need anything."

"Okay." I think of the chaos of her house compared to ours and wonder what she could possibly help me with. "Thanks."

DAY 36

SUNDAY

I WAKE TO quiet nothing. Calm.

Oscar hangs out in the street. I ignore him. I pull out *The Wee Free Men* from my bookshelf and read it again.

The house is quiet.

It's nice.

Mostly.

DAY 37

MONDAY

IT'S A HALF day today, teacher development or something. We get let out at lunch.

I come home to Lettie standing on her front porch yelling at someone, her voice tight and high, and Splinter barking from behind the side gate.

I duck inside with her voice pressing into my ears.

I can still hear her from the back of the house, though not what she's saying. The sound makes my chest tighten on the rat, pinching it so it nips at my belly. I let Splints in. He weaves around me cat-tight, nearly knocking me over. I run my hand over his back, tap his forehead between his eyes the way he likes, but he keeps weaving. He can't settle.

It's the sound of her voice. The feel of it, too much like you on a storm cloud day. The feel of you is pushing into my ears from Lettie's porch and it makes you more here and less here at the same time. Are these sound waves crashing into your ears too? I think of the shadows, *Do you still have ears?* and my yogurt from recess lurches into my throat and I move away from the back door, from the back of the house. I can't think about that. I can't. I focus on Lettie's voice and what it's saying, trying to find the words in the noise to trap my thoughts, keep them still and stop them going somewhere else.

I sneak into your room and peer out through the curtains; they smell of damp and not so much of you. I'm not here for you. I press my cheek against the glass and try to see across to Lettie's porch.

I can see half another person. A woman, cuffed sleeves and a neat-looking cardigan. A business cardigan, you'd call it, the sort you see on bank tellers and doctors' receptionists. She's gesturing, but gently. Like someone trying not to startle a small animal. I wonder if the small animal's Lettie. I hear a bleat and a screech, and the hand comes out from the business-cardigan cuff, the one not holding a clipboard, and smooths the air, palm facing down. Lettie's voice settles to a high whimper. Of course the animal's Lettie. I think of her sitting, watching everything from her dark porch. A night goat, definitely.

After a while the woman leaves. I see neat hair, glasses on a fine chain and sensible pleated pants. She gives Lettie a little wave as she pulls the gate closed behind her. I can't hear what Lettie mutters but it isn't a polite bye-bye.

I wait for the car to drive off. I don't know if I should go over. She's not my friend. She's not *not* my friend either. Strange women in cardigans are never good news. My breath fogs the window, my cheek aching from pressing against the cold glass. I look at Splints. He's facing me, panting, his eager outside face on. He gives his tail a swish. I bite my lip. He barks.

"You can come out now, nosey parker. The witch is gone." Lettie's voice launches from her porch, familiar again.

I consider pretending I'm not here. For all she knows I'm inside watching telly. Splints shifts his weight and wiggles his eyebrows, bark brewing. I go to shush him but he's up, bum in the air, forelegs spread on the floor between us. He barks again, three short shouts, loud enough to make my ears hurt, his tail spinning like a flag behind him.

"Yep. I can hear that too."

I stay where I am.

"Suit yourself."

Splints stares up at me and whines.

I pull a face at him. "Fine." He races to the front door.

LETTIE'S SITTING WITH her back to me. She doesn't move when I step onto our porch. She doesn't move when I walk out our gate and over to hers. She doesn't move when I open the latch, my fingers holding on to the same spot as that cardigan-cuffed hand.

Splinter pushes past and rushes over. She gives his ear a scratch.

"Biscuit?" She holds out a tin.

I stare at her.

She shrugs. "Suit yourself." She takes one out and eats it. It looks good. It looks really good. My tummy growls, reminding me I haven't had lunch. "Bought them today. From that fancy shop in Seddon." She waves the tin again.

I take one and sit down. It is good. Really good.

She smiles and holds out the tin. I take another. I watch her as I chew, crumbs falling down my front. I feel like I should say something.

"Are you . . ." Crumbs fly out of my mouth. She bird-eyes me. I clap my hand over my lips and finish chewing. The biscuit's turned to clag. I swallow it and try not to gag.

"Am I what?"

"Okay." It comes out in a croak. "Are you okay?"

She scratches Splints and gives him a biscuit. "I'm all right."

"Who was that?"

Lettie pushes the lid back on the tin and places it carefully at her feet. Splinter gives it a good sniff and she shoves his nose away gently with her toes. She lifts the lid of the chest and takes out the kettle. "Hot chocolate?"

I nod. Lettie hands me the kettle to fill.

SHE HEAPS TEASPOONS of mixture into each cup, stirring quickly as she pours the water, spoon chiming against the side. She hands mine over but puts hers down on the chest and pulls a small bottle from inside her jacket. In a quick movement she cracks the lid and empties the bottle into her cup before putting the cap back on and slipping it carefully back into her pocket. She lifts her drink, takes a small gulp and smiles at me over the rim.

"Sometimes you just need a little something extra. It's been that kind of day."

I recognize the smell. "Whiskey?" Splinter huffs out his nose and shifts his muzzle to rest on my foot.

"I don't usually, not during the day. But today's been particularly shi—trying."

I think about going home. Is it rude to leave before I've finished my drink? She sits back in her chair and sighs, her cup resting in her palms. A currawong calls over the distant rumble of the docks. It was only a little bottle. I wonder if she's got more in her pocket.

"She was from the council. She wanted to see inside my house." Lettie's voice makes me jump. Hot chocolate sploshes out of my cup to land hot and wet on my leg. I rub at it, picturing the inside of Lettie's house.

"Did you let her?"

"No."

We sip at our hot chocolate.

"Why?"

"What?"

"Why did she want to see inside your house?"

"Someone reported me." Lettie glares down the street as she says it.

"Reported you for what?"

"Environmental health and fire risk, apparently."

"What does that mean?"

"That someone thinks my house is a health and fire hazard."

I focus on swirling the hot chocolate in my cup.

Lettie clears her throat. "Yeah, all right. Be quiet."

"I didn't—"

"You didn't have to."

I think of the cardigan sleeve, the official-looking clipboard. The council car. "Will she be back?"

"Yes."

I chew my lip. "What will she do?"

"Stick her nose in where it's not wanted, no doubt."

You can see our backyard from Lettie's backyard. I can smell Lettie's from ours. I know what that means. "Can she make you let her in?"

"Probably."

"What did she say?"

"Gave me a form to fill out to *help me see there's an issue.*" The voice she imitates pronounces issue with an *e* sound. *Eeshew*, like a sneeze. I wonder if Lettie knows what color her carpet is. Or even if she has carpet.

Lettie gives me a side-eye. "Your silences are really annoying, you know that?"

"Yeah. I've heard that before."

Her side-eye turns to a stare, and I lean down and wiggle my toes under Splinter till he sits up, his big head blocking her gaze. "If you fill in the form, will she leave you alone?"

I catch a movement from the corner of my eye. Lettie shrugs. "Depends."

"On what?"

"What my answers are, I suppose."

I think of that council car again, of people poking around Lettie's place, looking over the fence. Getting rid of all her smells. "Maybe you should do it, so she leaves you alone." I adjust Splinter's collar, spinning it so the tag hangs down straight.

I can feel Lettie watching me. She clears her throat. "Yeah. Maybe. We don't want people like that poking around, do we?" She reaches down for the biscuit tin and holds it out. "Don't worry, kiddo. I'll sort it out."

I ignore the biscuits. I'm not hungry anymore. "When do you have to finish the form by?"

"She said she'd be back in a couple of days."

Wednesday, then. If they come at the same time I'll be at school. I have time to make sure the back's tidy, perhaps I could hang out some freshly washed sheets before school. Light a mosquito coil, or four. I feel myself relax a little. "I could help. If you like."

Lettie pokes the tin at me again; I take it from her and concentrate on getting the lid off, choosing a biscuit, taking a bite. She picks another one for herself. "Sure. Why not."

Lettie's sitting on the pages. She shifts her bum and pulls them out. They're folded at odd angles and she smooths them on her leg, making them crackle. She peers at them one at a time. I catch the titles on a couple: *Clutter image rating scale* and *Hoarding behavior rating scale.* I focus on my cup.

She digs in her jacket again, her hand reaching through her pockets. Well, what did I expect? I start thinking of an excuse to leave, but it's only a pair of glasses she pulls out. They're bright yellow. I sit back again as she rests them on her nose and reads.

"Well?"

Lettie reads aloud. *"Look at image and circle which one matches best."* She stares at the pages, her face wooden. "Here, you do it." She thrusts them at me. "You've been inside."

The kitchen. There are nine images of a kitchen, the first tidy and the others progressively messier. I study them. Number one is neat and tidy and nine is, well, nine doesn't even look like it's a room. It's just a pile of junk. I wonder if they took the images with the kitchen clean and then made it messier, or took them from when it was messy and tidied it. Either way it looks like a massive job.

I bite my lip, thinking about Lettie's kitchen. Well, you wouldn't be able to walk in picture nine, and I managed to get through the window and walk out of the room, so hers isn't a nine. And you could see the window, so not an eight because you can't see any walls or anything else vertical in that one. I hover the pen between the six and the seven . . . probably more a seven, but we don't want Cardigan Lady coming back . . . I circle the six.

The next images are the bedroom. "You'll have to do this one."

"Why?"

"I haven't been in your bedroom."

"Yes, you have."

"No, I haven't."

"Yes, you have. That's where you found me."

That was a bedroom? She *sleeps* there? I concentrate on the page in front of me without seeing any of the pictures.

"What, can't you decide?"

I force my eyes to examine the photos. Well, she was under a bookshelf, so there had to be enough space for it to fall; that means nine is out. It was pretty gloomy in there . . . just because I didn't see the bed or walls doesn't mean they weren't visible. I imagine the room again, the dark, the heavy smell of human, the flypaper hanging from the ceiling. I bite the inside of my mouth and focus on the pictures, and circle six.

"The living room's next. I didn't go in there."

"You walked past it, it was the room on the right on the way out."

"The door was shut."

"The door doesn't shut."

"But there was—" Oh. I look at the images, and nine is a wall of clutter: no room visible. My hand hovers. It was dark inside and I wasn't really looking . . . I circle eight.

That's it for the images. I read the bit down the bottom. *A rating of 4 or above for any room is indicative of a problem with clutter of clinical significance.*

Lettie's watching me from her chair. "How'd I do?"

I look from the sixes and eight I circled to the word *clinical.* "We've still got the other one to do yet."

There are five questions. I look at the first two. *How would you rate the level of difficulty you experience using the rooms in your home because of the amount of clutter or belongings? How would you rate the level of difficulty you experience in throwing away, selling or recycling things that others would discard?*

"You need to answer these. They're about you."

"Read them out, then."

I clear my throat. The shadow-rat's starting up a sharp nip and nibble beneath my bottom left rib. I take a deep breath and read. *"Answering from one to nine, one being not difficult at all, nine being extremely difficult . . ."*

The first question, after consideration, she gives a six. "Because I'm used to it, aren't I? And you got around okay, didn't you?"

I think of the pile of things waiting to fall on me as I balanced my way across the unsteady rubble on the floor. "Uh, well . . ."

"Okay, seven. And that's my final offer."

I write it down.

The discarding question she gives a five, then changes it to a six. I glance at her pocket, where she put the empty bottle from before. Despite the fact the recycling bin is sitting behind her chair. She's watching me. I see her fingers twitch toward the little bottle sitting snugly at her hip. Her cheeks go redder. "Seven, then."

I write it down carefully, putting a little line through the stem of the seven and a full stop after it.

I don't look up as I read the next two questions. *"On a scale from one to nine, one being no difficulty and nine being extreme difficulty, how would you rate the difficulty you experience in NOT collecting, keeping or purchasing more things than you can use, need or afford?"*

"Five." I start to write it down. Lettie coughs. "Six." I cross out the five and write a six neatly next to it. I need to clean my fingernails. It's funny how when you don't look at someone you become more aware of their movement than when you're looking straight at them. I can feel Lettie breathing.

"On a scale from one to nine, one being no distress and nine being extreme distress, how would you rate the emotional distress you experience caused by the amount of things you acquire that you are unable to get rid of and/or the clutter in your home?"

She's quiet. But I don't look up. I sit, pen hovering over the paper, focus on the question mark and wait. My ear itches. I ignore it.

"Eight." Her voice is quiet. I write it down, gently looping the top and bottom of the number. Going over it again to make it darker. The last question's waiting.

"On a scale from one to nine, how would you currently rate the negative effects on your life (financial, social and family relationships; employment or study; daily routine, etc.) caused by clutter and/or your need to acquire and/or the difficulty you experience in discarding things?" Does Lettie have family? I flick a glance at her. She is staring at her hands clasped in her lap, the fingers squeezing through each other like desperate worms. The fingertips are dark pink but the nails are white.

She takes a deep breath. "Nine." The answer's so quiet I wonder if I willed my ears to hear something that's not there. Nine would be bad. It can't be nine. It would be obvious if her life was a nine. I think of you. I think of me since you've been gone. I write down the nine.

I read the wording under the questions.

"So? How'd I do?" Lettie's voice sounds dusty.

I don't want to answer.

"Well? Spit it out. I'm not made of porcelain."

My tongue's heavy. *"Scoring indicating clinically significant hoarding . . ."*

"Well? Get on with it."

I look at her answers: seven, seven, six, eight, nine. *"A score of four or above for questions one, two and three, in addition to a score of four or above for question four and/or question five."*

Lettie sits back. I don't know where to look, so I look at her feet. Her shoes look comfortable, even though I can see the shape of her toes through the sides of them.

"Well. I'm stuffed, then."

I look up at her and she gives me a half smile. "Come on, it's not such a surprise, really. You think I don't know what my own house is like? I know that's not normal. Granted, I'd perhaps been kidding myself it's not as bad as all that"—she waves at the pages with the rating pictures on them—"but I know it's got out of control." She shifts in her seat. "Why do you think I spend so much time out here?"

I shrug. "I just thought you were nosy." She lets out a loud snort, making Splints jump; I swallow a laugh and keep my face serious. "Or a perv or something."

I can see the dark fillings in her teeth as she throws her head back; her laugh scares the pigeons off the footpath. I grin. The laughter rolls into a crackling, bubbling cough. Her eyes are wet and her face's going from pink to red. I'm not sure if she's laughing, coughing or crying. My grin's gone. I'm a bit worried she might die. I grab a cup out of the chest and fill it from the tap. She takes it from me, sucking wheezy breaths in through her mouth and breathing out bubbly coughs, and, despite my fear, I realize I've never seen her eyes twinkle like that before. And I don't think it's entirely due to choking. She grabs the cup, spilling a fair bit, but eventually manages a few slow gulps. I sit down again.

She wipes her eyes. "You're all right, kiddo."

"It's Rae," I remind her.

She pulls a face. "I know that. I was being nice. It's a nickname. A term of endearment."

"Oh. Okay." I wonder if I should reciprocate. What do you say to an old lady who likes to refer to you as a baby goat?

"Thanks. Goat-o."

DAY 38

TUESDAY

I DON'T SLEEP well. For once the thoughts aren't all about me, or you. I keep thinking about Lettie's house. It's bigger now, breathing, crouched next to ours like a great, hulking, maimed creature. I think about Lettie. Where does she sleep in there, in the belly of that sad thing where there's barely room to stand? Not outside, right? She must go inside to sleep. *How* does she sleep in there with all that smell? It's too cold to sleep outside in winter. I think of the room I found her in. Which part of it's for sleeping? That lady's going to come back on Wednesday and Lettie's going to give her that paper that says she's a nine. My left eyelid keeps twitching, flickering my lashes, letting the TV light into my closed eye. I fall asleep eventually. I know because I wake up with the inside lights dimming against the dawn and the solution in my head.

We'll clean up before Cardigan comes back. We'll just fix the problem. It doesn't have to be perfect, just enough to show she can take care of it herself, just enough to make them go away.

* * *

THE MORNING LIGHT'S a sharp yellow, spiking between the buildings across the street as I knock on her door. She's not on the porch so I guess she does sleep inside. It can't be that bad, then. I shift my bucket of cleaning stuff to my other hand and knock again.

"Go away." The voice is loud and mean.

I remind myself it's just Lettie and keep knocking.

The door flies open, or it would have if there wasn't so much stuff on the floor. In reality, it flies open about a face-width before it crashes into something soft and unmoving, which I'm guessing is the pile of newspapers I squeezed past to get out. Lettie's face pokes through the gap.

"Oh. It's you." She peers at the bucket in my hand. "What do you want?"

"We're going to clean your house. Then that busybody can just leave you alone."

Lettie pinches at the bridge of her nose between her eyes and sighs. "Shouldn't you be at school?"

"It's six forty-five. School's not for two hours." I don't bother to tell her I've already marked myself absent.

"Can't clean this mess in two hours, kiddo."

"We don't have to do all of it." She raises an eyebrow at me; I ignore her and continue. "Just some of it, to show you can take care of it yourself."

She snorts. "And which bits do you propose we do, then?"

I've been thinking about this. "The hallway, kitchen and bathroom. The first thing she'll see, where you need to eat and how you keep clean."

Lettie just stares at me. So I give her the best fact. "And the smallest rooms." She doesn't move. "So they'll be the quickest."

"Yep. I got that."

"Well?" I lift up the bucket and wave it.

"Look, I don't think—"

But I'm not listening. I push past her into the dark.

I trip over almost immediately. The smell's a living thing, pushing its way up my nostrils and into my mouth, making my eyes water. It's decay and filth and rot and the smells of *living*. The gloom and the stench and the lumpy things under my legs press in on me, making it hard to focus. The sliver of light from the front door starts to narrow.

"No! Leave it open."

"You okay?"

"Yep. I just tripped over." I haul myself to my feet, coughing, trying to keep my gaze on that crack of light from the door.

Lettie disappears into the dark. I fumble around for my bucket, trying not to imagine all the things I'm touching. Perhaps I should have brought two rolls of garbage bags.

"Here." Lettie shoves something at me in the gloom.

"What's that?"

"Vicks. Rub it under your nose."

"Why?"

"It'll help with the smell." Her voice is gruff. So she does know it smells, then. I'm glad I can't see her face clearly.

"Do you use it?"

"No, I'm used to it." I stick my finger into the pot and wipe the Vicks under my nostrils. It makes them burn and my eyes water, but it helps. I stand up.

"Still want to help?" she says.

"Yep."

"So where do we start, mastermind?"

"The hall."

"First place first, makes sense."

I nod, not bothering to tell her the only reason I want to start here is to be closer to the door. "We'll start with this." I tap the pile of papers heaped up against the wall.

HER RECYCLING BIN is full in less than twenty minutes. Or it would be, if Lettie didn't keep going and pulling the papers back out to check she doesn't need them. I go over to grab our recycling bin, and in the time it takes me to bring it back she's emptied half of them back onto her porch.

"Lettie! You can't keep doing that. We're never going to get it done."

She barely raises her head from what she's doing. "I'm just checking you're not throwing out something I need."

"They're old newspapers. You don't even know what's in them!"

"Exactly."

I'm beginning to think this'd be quicker if she was somewhere else. I snatch a paper out of her hands and shove it back into the bin.

"They're newspapers. There all online anyway."

"Not these ones, they're old."

"Exactly! They're old and moldy and *useless*. Just throw them out!"

"But what if—"

I grab the next one out of her hands. "Look it up online, they have archives and stuff. Even *I* know that and I'm *ten*."

She tries to grab it back off me. "Don't tell me what I can and can't do! You can't come in here and tell me what's important. You don't know." She beady-eyes me, like *I'm* the one with the problem. The sun's fully up now. The day's ticking away, and if this hall's an indication, we'll be lucky to get the first meter cleared. It'll never pass as manageable. Lettie rips the paper back out of my hands. "Who do you think you are anyway?"

I snatch it back. "Someone who's trying to *help* you." I yell it at her, right in her face. She steps back like I've hit her.

We stare at each other. I *want* to hit her.

Lettie slumps onto a pile of crap. "I'm yelling at a ten-year-old. About newspapers." The hardness slides off her face, taking her cheeks with it. She reminds me of the plants in the front yard before I watered them.

I sit next to her. "They're just newspapers, Lettie."

"I know."

"I can help you look up anything in them online. If we throw them out, all the information and stuff, we can still find it."

"I don't have a computer."

"You can get one." I think of all the stuff already in her house. "You can use mine," I add quickly.

Lettie nods. "That's sensible." But her hands are still pressing into the pile of papers in front of her. I lift them off; her skin's dry and soft, like one of her old newspapers.

I remember the time you told me I had to get rid of all my old toys. You dumped a big cardboard box in my room and told me I had to fill it up, or you would. *You don't even play with them anyway.* And that was true enough. I barely even saw them. But when I went to put them in the box, it wasn't like I was throwing toys out; it was like I was throwing my memories away. That silly orange carrot I won at the show. Only one eye left, smooth in places, the fuzz all worn off, and I never used to really play with it anyway. But it sat next to the top of my bed and reminded me of the day I won it, when we went on all the rides I was tall enough for and you bought me three bags of candy and I ate so much fairy floss that I got a headache and nearly vomited on the tram ride home. And you let me lie with my head in your lap while you stroked my hair and you bought me bubbly water from the gas station. And the big-eared rabbit I've had since forever, Bunny-Nenee, who was so old and grotty I didn't like to keep her on my bed anymore because she smelled like sneezes and looked like she might have fleas. But that time I dropped her we walked for a whole day round the neighborhood looking for her. I don't even remember finding her, just that when I got too tired to walk you carried me and even though you were swearing, it was quiet and not at me. And when I woke up the next day, not remembering going to bed, there she was, tucked in next to me. She lived in the cupboard and I never looked at her anymore but I couldn't put her in the box. You said we were moving and I couldn't take all that *stuff.* But I couldn't chuck it away. So I left the box in the middle of the room and one day I came home and the box was gone. And so were the books I was too old for, my old drawings I'd stuck on the walls, the carrot and my favorite shoes that didn't fit anymore. They were all gone, except for Bunny-Nenee, who you washed and left on my bed. I was sad, especially about the books, but also relieved that I didn't have to do the throwing away. I just came home to a room without them, and I could pretend that they'd never even been there, so there was nothing to miss.

"Lettie?"

"Hmm."

"If I promise to throw out only the newspapers we can find online and nothing else, would that be okay?"

She gives me her best bird eye. "Only the newspapers?"

"Only the newspapers."

She nods. "Okay." Her hands are resting on the papers in front of her again. I ease one out. She watches me as I bin it but doesn't get up and take it out again. I think of the box that wasn't there when I got home from school.

"We're going to need some more garbage bags. Can you go and get some while I sort all the newspapers?"

Lettie gives me a half smile and gets slowly to her feet. "You're a crafty old soul, kiddo. Anyone ever tell you that?"

"Not as old as you, Goat-o."

She swats at me, but she's smiling when she does it. "Only the papers."

"Only the papers."

And she goes.

I FILL ALL her bins, recycling and rubbish and all the bags, working quickly to get as much done as possible before Lettie gets back. Despite my promise, after the first pile I'm not really looking through it. The stacks are heavy and dirty and I can't see anything inside them would be worth saving. If she asks, I'll lie. She doesn't need to know.

By the time she gets back I can see wall and the front door opens fully. Lettie stands in the doorway looking in.

"Huh."

"What?"

"I forgot how ugly that wallpaper is." She hands me the garbage bags: five packs, the heavy-duty ones.

"All you got rid of was newspapers?" She sounds slightly suspicious and also a bit amazed. Like she can't believe getting rid of just one type of thing could make such a difference. And it has made a difference. The light from the front door travels all the way back to the kitchen. Though I'm not sure that's such a great thing. You still can't see the floor, except where the piles were sitting. And the light means you can see everything else more clearly. Like the bathroom. She must wash under the tap at the side of the house as well as fill the kettle there. You can also see how much there is left to do. I look back at the wallpaper. It's visible all the way to the living room door. If I can clear the hall completely it'll make a difference.

I hand Lettie a bag.

"Just newspapers?"

"Just newspapers."

We get to work.

I WORK FASTER than Lettie. She keeps stopping to look at things. Or she puts a paper in the bag, then takes it out and looks at it, puts it back in, takes it out again, puts some others in, repeats. I leave her to her slow pile and power down the hall, making sure my body's blocking her view at all times so she can't see the other things I'm sneaking in: magazines, tissues, collapsed cereal boxes, plastic packaging. If I hear her get up, I shove newspapers on top of it all so when she looks in the bag, that's all she can see. I fill another twenty bags. Lettie does one. I'm down to the last pile of papers. I dump them in, one armload at a time, then drag the bags out the front. Her little front yard is full. I hadn't thought of this. How do we get rid of it all before the woman comes tomorrow? Would it be better or worse to have it lined up out the front when she comes? It would show Lettie's fixing it herself. But it would also show her how bad it all is. And I still need to clean the floor. My tummy rumbles. I've had nothing since breakfast and I've been lugging piles of papers all day. My arms ache, my back hurts, and my mouth feels like an animal crawled up in it and died. I can't get the smell out of my sinuses. Lettie drags her one bag out and places it neatly next to the others.

"There."

"Lettie, we need to clean the floor."

She sinks into her chair on the porch. "I think we need a cold drink and a rest first." She hands me one of the ginger beers from behind her chair. All I can think is where are we going to put the bottle when it's empty? All the bins are full.

"You need some food. How about we go get some lunch?"

"I'm not dense. I can tell you're procrastinating."

"That's a big word for a ten-year-old."

I know what she's doing. "Don't change the subject."

"We still need to eat."

"Well, go and get some food, then. I'm not stopping you." I collapse into the chair next to her, giving my best exhausted sigh. I close my eyes for good measure.

I can feel Lettie watching me. "You need to eat too."

"You could get me something too." I stretch my legs out. "I'll just have a rest for a bit."

Lettie's still for a minute. I resist the urge to peek at her. She clears her throat. "Right. Okay. So, we'll have a break, eat and do some more after lunch."

"Sounds good."

"And you're just going to wait here?"

"Yep."

"Okay." She stands up. "I won't be long."

"Good, I'm pretty hungry."

She stands, her shadow falling across my face. I can almost hear the thought occur to her. "Shouldn't you be at school?"

I keep my eyes closed. I thought this would come up again a lot earlier. "Teacher development day."

"Huh. You didn't say that before."

"I needed you to let me in."

She snorts. I stay where I am. I hear her fiddling around with some things then leave the porch and shut the gate behind her. I count slowly to thirty, then open my eyes. She's gone. I move fast: jump the side fence and push past Splints straight to our little metal toolshed. I grab the shovel, the green-waste bin and our wheelie bin. There's only one way that floor's going to get clean, and I don't have a lot of time.

IF I THOUGHT my body hurt before, it's nothing like how it feels after shoveling half her hallway. I can't stop, though. She'll be as quick as she can, and if she gets back before I'm done, there's no way I'll get it finished today. She's going to want to look at every little thing before I can throw it out, so it needs to be thrown out before she gets here. I try not to focus on what I'm shoveling. I'd assumed having the front door open would help with the smell, but weirdly it's having the opposite effect. It's like the movement of air is encouraging new smells to wake up, or maybe it's all the stuff I'm disturbing with the shovel. I needn't have worried about making it too fresh; I think the smell might be part of the house. I wipe some more Vicks under my nose and keep going. I use the shovel to push everything in the bin down, trying to make more room, and keep shoveling. I don't think about what I'm moving; don't allow myself to look at what I'm seeing. There are floorboards under it all. I keep going, ignoring the blister on my hand and the sting in my leg from something that scratched me. The bin's full. I drag it back to our place and get started on the green-waste bin. The last shovel goes in. It's done. I drag that bin home too and park them both on the curb in front of our place, as far away from Lettie's as possible, then go back with the shovel to have a go at the flypaper. I'm swatting away at it when I hear her behind me.

"What have you done?" Her voice is low and angry. A familiar tone that kicks your rat into action, ripping at my stomach, spilling acid into my guts.

I swallow. "I cleaned the hallway."

"Where is everything?" She pronounces each word carefully, like I'm hard of hearing.

"It was all rubbish."

"You don't know what it was."

I'm tired and hot and dirty, I haven't eaten since 6:32 a.m. and I just cleaned forty-three shovel loads of rubbish out of her hallway. And I'm *helping* her.

"I do know what it was. It was *crap*." The word's hard. Yelling it at her makes my heart beat a little harder but I can't stop now. "It was *rotten* stuff, and empty jars and bags of used tissues and dirty old rags and half-eaten cushions and broken bits of plastic and bottles and takeaway containers and plastic spoons and plastic bags and junk mail and dead spiders and rubber bands and broken pens and chopsticks and moldy fruit and what I'm pretty sure was rat poo and something dead that I think was a cat squashed at the bottom of it all. A *cat*, Lettie." My voice cracks as that rat tears away beneath my ribs; I swallow the acid and keep yelling. "A squashed, leathery, manky-furred cat with a paper plate on top of it." My shouting's getting higher and squeaky in a way I don't recognize. "That's not what you keep in a house. That's *crazy*!"

"A cat?"

"A dead cat!" My breathing sounds funny. "Dead. A dead thing. Dead." I can't stop saying the word. I need to stop saying that. "Dead." I push past her, shaking, biting my tongue to stop my mouth from betraying me further. I need to sit down.

"You found my cat?"

I'm sitting with my head in my hands. Not thinking about the shed. Not thinking about the leathery cat body. This was a mistake. I've been working all day and all I've managed to do is clean a hallway. And the crazy old cat-smothering goat isn't even thankful. As soon as I can get to my feet I'm going home. She can deal with the council and get kicked out of her house and I'm going to stay the hell away from it all. They'll be so preoccupied with this pile of shit they probably won't even *look* at my yard. It's not like you can smell *anything* else when you're inside her house. I shouldn't have got involved in the first place. She's nothing to me. I don't need her or her stinking house and definitely not all the trouble she's about to bring with her.

"You found my cat?" She drops a plastic bag—it looks like it's got banh mi in it—on the chest and sits on the porch in front of me. I glance at her face. Her eyes are huge. Her cheeks are so pale the little red veins near her nose look drawn on with pen. "You found Sylvester?"

"Who?"

"My cat. I thought he ran away. He was . . ." She looks horrified.

I don't know what to say. I glance over to our yard, at the bin where I dumped the stiff, leathery, hole-filled carcass. I remember the sparkle I focused on as I shoveled the body off the floor. "Did he have a collar with jewels on it?"

She puts her head in her hands. "Oh god."

I hover my hand near her head, then pull it back and slip it into my pocket. There are tissues in there. I kneel in front of her and offer her one. She takes it, holds it in her hand, nods. And we sit there like that, just the two of us and a yard full of rubbish bags.

"Hey, what's going on? You having a hard rubbish or something?"

That kid. Oscar's standing at the front gate with his shiny green bike and a look on his face like he wants to be in on a joke.

"None of your business." Lettie and I snap it at him together.

He looks hurt. "I was just asking."

"What are you doing here anyway, shouldn't you be at school?"

"It's nearly four o'clock. No one's at school."

What? It'll be getting dark in an hour and we haven't sorted how we're going to get rid of all the bags yet. I look at my bucket of untouched cleaning supplies sitting next to the front door. We haven't even cleaned the windows.

I stand up.

He points at me. "What happened to you?"

"What?"

"Your leg."

"What about it?"

"It's bleeding?" He says it like a question. Like I'm thick for having to ask.

I look down. He's right. My trackies are soaked in blood from below the knee down.

Lettie pulls me gently back into the chair. "I told you not to touch that jar of beetroot. That stain'll never come out."

I look at her in confusion. She frowns at me and flicks her eyes toward Oscar. "Oh. Yeah. Sorry." I look at his annoying concerned face. "I'm not hurt, Oscar. But we were having a private conversation. So . . ."

"Yeah. Right." He wheels his bike back down the street. Lettie and I sit on the porch not moving until he's out of sight. Then Lettie kneels in front of me and gently rolls up my pants. There's a gash just below my knee; it's not very long but there's quite a bit of blood oozing out of it. As I watch, the pain in the back of my mind gets a bit sharper, and hotter.

"Oh shit." Lettie looks worried. That just makes it hurt more. "How did you do that and not notice?"

"I was busy. I was trying to get everything done before you got back." My breathing sounds funny.

"I think that's going to need a doctor, kiddo."

"No."

She sits back on her heels, looks at my face. "It's going to need disinfecting at least." She looks toward her house. "And I don't think I can help you with that."

"I can. I've got Betadine and stuff. I'll fix it." I stand up.

"Okay, come on, I'll help you."

"No. I'm fine. It's just a little scratch. It's fine." I step toward the garbage bags lined up in front of us like an army of sad. The hall's clear but it's not clean, the other rooms are still solid eights and the smell, with the door open, is strong where we're standing. How did I think we could fix this in a day? I gesture at the bags. "You need to sort this stuff out for tomorrow."

"Rae."

"I'm fine, Lettie. Really. Will you be okay to do all this without me? It's bin night tonight."

"Of course. Don't worry about that. Don't worry about me. You go sort that out, okay?" She pats at the air near my shoulder, her hand all fluttery.

I nod and move away.

"And, Rae . . ." She clears her throat, glances at me and away again. "Thanks, kiddo. I'm sorry about . . ." She waves her hand. I'm not sure at what, the dead cat? The mess? Herself? I get it, though. I understand.

"It's fine." I step off the porch.

"Are we okay?"

She sounds worried. I smile at her this time. "We're okay."

Her hand hovers over my arm. "Thanks, kiddo, for all . . ." She waves her hand at everything. "For your help."

"You're welcome, Goat-o."

She gives me a smile and I limp back home. I look up the street as I open the gate. Oscar's standing outside his place, watching. I ignore him.

THE STING OF it gets worse the closer I get to the front door, like the hurt's been saving itself up. It takes three goes to get the key in the lock. I know Lettie's watching. I'm pretty sure nosy Oscar is too. I keep my back straight, my arm relaxed; it's just my fingers that won't cooperate. I can hear Splinter barking from the back as the door swings wide; I close it gently behind me and look down. The blood's soaked my shoe. It's dark and red, and the more I stare at it the more it hurts. It's worse than the time I sliced my ankle open on that piece of wire from the fence. When you sat next to me and held me while I cried and told me you didn't think we'd have to amputate the whole thing but perhaps I should just show you to be on the safe side. And you picked me up and carried me inside even though I was nearly as tall as you, and you fixed it all up, disinfectant, Band-Aids, ice pack and a stool to put my foot on. Hot sweet tea to finish.

I'm thirsty and tired. I've not eaten since breakfast and I'm probably bleeding to death, alone. I slide down the wall so I can gently pull off my shoe. It hurts.

I want. I want hot sweet tea and someone to carry me into the bathroom and fix my leg. I want the lights and heating on and food that I didn't have to cook. I want someone to tell me I'm not bleeding to death by myself in the hall. I want. Want. Want. I want you. I want you to do those things, to come in and tell me it'll have to come off, the whole leg not just the shoe, and then carry me into the bathroom and fix me up.

The hall stays gloomy. Splinter bangs at the back door. The pain stings like hot bees in my veins, making stillness impossible. I throw my shoe at the wall. Even in the fading light I can see the bloody lace prints it leaves. More mess for me to clean up. I throw the other one too; it disappears into the kitchen, crashing into something. I throw your boots, my school shoes and Splinter's lead, not caring where they go. I'm still in here bleeding on the floor. And none of it matters to you. I kick my heels on the floorboards, flashing white-hot pain up my shin and into my head. I do it again and again and again till I can't move my legs and my breath's ragged.

You're still not here.

I lean my head against the wall. It's getting dark now; I watch till I can't see the shoe print. Splints whines at the back door. I heave myself to my feet and limp into the bathroom, leaving a trail of blood drips.

I wonder if I've lost enough blood to affect my brain. Calm breaks then—waves of it washing those bees out, smoothing the pain into a background hum. The hand that opens the sink cupboard and lifts out the Betadine is shaking . . . which seems silly because my mind's so calm. I swallow a giggle. My arms and legs tingle like they've licked a battery, but my heart's beating slow and steady, pulsing through the cut and vibrating in my chest and fingers. My head carries on clear and unbothered. I sit on the edge of the bath with my leg over the side, dripping blood onto the enamel. I try to slide the leg of my trackies up but it's heavy with blood, it keeps slipping down. They'll have to come off. I lift my bum up and slide the cut pant leg and then the other off and drop them in the bath with a wet plop. They're going to need soaking. The smell of Lettie's is still stuck up the back of my nose, but there's another smell there too, a damp animal smell, thick and sleepy. The smell of my insides, I guess.

I pull the showerhead down and spray my leg. It brings the bees swarming back and I suck air in through my teeth. The water takes the blood. I watch it swirl and drain away till it catches the trackies, pushing them closer to the plughole. When I snag them and slide them up closer they leave a red streak on the enamel. There's less blood now, though the cut's still seeping. I put the showerhead down carefully and bring my eyes closer to the cut. I place a finger either side and pull it apart. The sting of it makes my ears ring. The inside of my leg's pinker than I'd imagined and smaller, for something causing so much pain. It looks clean but I know what I need to do. I pick up the showerhead and spray water into it. I shrink into a little spot on my leg, nothing but pain, till my fingers give out. There's blood in my mouth. *Nearly done.* I feel you sitting on the bath next to me as I turn off the water. I feel your fingers, gentle on my back. I'm breathing slowly through my nose and I pick up the Betadine and take off the cap. With one hand I tease apart the cut and with the other I pour the contents of the bottle in.

When my thoughts come back, I'm sitting in the bath, undies wet, the bloody trackies beneath me, the empty Betadine bottle still gripped in my fingers and my leg stained orangey red. My shin throbs in a sharp beat. With shaking fingers I grab a hand towel and mop the wetness off my leg, making sure not to get too close to the wound. It's clean now. It winces back at me, edges gaping. I've watched enough *Operation Ouch!* to realize it probably needs stitches. I consider doing it myself—for about three seconds. Then I heave my bruised self out of the bath and pull the first aid kit out from under the sink.

I find what I'm looking for: butterfly strips. I used them on you that time. That was in the bath too. You said I did a good job. The scar faded to something so thin and silvery you could only see it peeking out from under your watch if you knew it was there. *A good job.* Just not good enough. I pull the strips out of the box and the sterile wrapping and stick the edges of my leg back together. I use five, so it's completely covered. It hurts less when I can't see it. It's more a deep ache now. It's done. I sit back. It looks okay. Better than okay, it looks unremarkable.

I stare at the mess around me. At least most of the carnage has been contained to the bath. I fill it up and leave the trackies to soak. I use the hand towel to mop the drips off the floor, the hall, the wall, then I dump that in the bath too. Cleaning done, I let Splints in, feed him, then collapse on the couch. My back aches. My everything aches, my eyes are scratchy. I let them close.

DAY 39

WEDNESDAY

I SLEEP THROUGH the alarm, through Splinter licking my face, through the start of school. Through the cutoff for the online absentee form. I know it's late when I wake. The room is midmorning light.

Your phone rings. The sound jolts through me, kicking my heart, making it thump into my ribs.

It's still on the charger where I left it. Blinking away. Waiting patiently.

My stomach twists and my tongue swells too thick and pushes clumsily against my bony, too-large teeth. My mouth's shrunk, all teeth and tongue. I stumble into the bathroom just as my throat opens and spray acidy vomit at the toilet.

I want my mum.

The phone stops. The vomiting stops. I rest my head on the seat.

The plastic's cool against my cheek. My breathing slows. My hands stop shaking.

The house is quiet. I can feel every room, empty. A hollow shell house. Then there's the click of Splints's claws on the tiles and his nose huffing wetly in my ear.

I sit back and rest against him. His panting rocks me.

It hasn't rung before. Fully charged for thirty-nine days and it hasn't rung. Not once.

I'm the only person who knows you're gone.

Aren't I?

But it's rung now. Somebody wants to speak to you. I've managed everything else, but I don't know what to do about this.

I wash my face, mop the vomit from around the toilet, pull on some clothes, feed Splints, get some breakfast, all the while keeping myself as far as possible from that phone. I can hear you teasing: *What? You think it'll bite?*

The clock shows ten. I can *feel* the phone flashing on the table.

I edge closer. The little light on the side blinks at me. I lean over and touch the screen on. One missed call.

Rae School.

The silence echoes.

I stare at the words some more.

The screen flicks to black.

Splinter licks my ankle.

Lettie. The answer's firm. Lettie will help me. I brush my hair. Wash my face again and calm-face myself in the mirror. *Cool, calm, collected.* It's your voice in my ear. I straighten my shoulders, slip your phone into my pocket.

Lettie will help.

* * *

THE GARBAGE BAGS are still in the front yard, but the porch is empty and the front door's half-open. It can open. At the sight of it the acid bubbles in my chest soften into something more warm and glimmery. *I did that.*

"Lettie!" I'm almost smiling when I step around the door, straight into the back of someone. The back smells like roses. Not Lettie, then.

"Oh!" The back turns to show a slightly familiar face—and a very familiar cardigan. She lifts the glasses off her nose and lets them drop onto the chain around her neck as she peers at me. It's not an unkind face. It's round and a bit soft-looking with deep creases that run like brackets along either side of her mouth, separating her cheeks from her lips. The lips are pursed now, making the creases frowny.

"Hello. Who are you?" She smiles and her face folds up into her eyes in a way that makes me think she might smile a lot.

I step back into the doorjamb, bruising my shoulder, my heart kicking up again. I pull my hands behind my back and pinch my fingers, hard. I need to focus.

"Where's Lettie?" My voice squeaks at the end.

"Lettie's right here." She steps out of the gloom.

"And this is?" The councilwoman looks from me to Lettie, an eyebrow raised.

"This is Rae. From next door. She and her mother keep an eye on me." She turns and gives me her best bird eye. "Don't you, Rae?"

"I—"

"Saw the door was open, did you? Came for a stickybeak?" She softens the mean words with a smile. But her eyes are still sharp on me. I'm familiar with this situation; I know how to play.

But before I can say anything the councilwoman interrupts. "You didn't help clean this up, did you?" I don't miss the glance at my legs. *Oscar.*

A surge of panic stretches time, giving me room to think. I meet the woman's eyes. "Are you kidding me? Lettie doesn't let anyone in here." I don't look at Lettie, I keep my gaze on the councilwoman but I can feel Lettie relax slightly to my side.

"Damn straight." I catch the look Lettie shoots at the councilwoman, but the official's gaze is still focused on me.

"Shouldn't you be at school?"

"I'm sick."

"You don't look sick."

"I'm getting over a cold."

"How old are you? Where are your parents?"

"I'm twelve." The lie's easy. "Mum had to go to a meeting. She's been home all week with me already. She told me to ask Lettie if I need anything before she gets back. Didn't she talk to you before she left, Lettie?" I give her my own bird eye. She owes me.

Lettie waves her arm. "Sure, sure. Said you'd be asleep all morning, though, not gallivanting about on my veranda. You seem well enough for school to me." She looks me up and down, frowning. "Perhaps I should give her a call?"

"No, I just popped over 'cause we're out of tissues and I thought you might have some." I let my eyes wander around the hall, hoping my face is getting across a suitable amount of shock. I glance at the councilwoman and back to Lettie. "Guess you're busy, though. I'll just call Mum and ask her to bring some home." I turn to go.

The councilwoman starts to say something, but Lettie steamrolls over her. "Off to watch TV, no doubt. Kids today! Home with a bloody sniffle. Her mother's too gentle with her. Runs her round to three sporting activities too, can you believe it? Three! Bloody helicopter parenting. Raising a generation of wusses."

I keep walking to the gate. I'd smile at her using the old-goat voice if it wasn't for the phone in my pocket and the time ticking closer to the next unavoidable call. She's still going on as I shut the front door; the council lady's trying to interrupt her with questions about booking a date for something, but she's not getting a word in.

I DON'T KNOW what to do. I put Splints out the back for a pee and lie on the couch waiting for him to scratch to be let back in. He takes his time. When he's done, we sit under the window in your room and wait.

I can hear murmuring, then the gate opening, then the slam of a car door and a car leaving, and I know the councilwoman's gone. I squish my face into the window, trying to catch sight of Lettie's front porch.

Her face looms out over the side fence, making me jump, and she gives me a grin. "You can come back now, kiddo, she's gone."

I pull on your jacket and head over, Splinter on my heels. I drag our bins in, then grab hers from the curb, parking them where I can find space among the bags.

"What was that about?" I lift my chin in the direction the car went.

"I am getting some assistance. Whether I like it or not."

"Do you?"

"What? Like it?"

I nod.

Lettie tips her head to the side, eyes on the rubbish bags piled against her front fence. "Yes. And no. Mostly no. Except for the part that's yes."

I nod. I get it.

"Not sure I can cope with having more of that wallpaper revealed, though."

I don't bother to smile.

"So what do you need, then?" Lettie sits herself down into her chair on the porch.

"What?"

"The look on your face when you skedaddled out of here was more than just understandable relief to be out of the presence of the council."

"I wasn't—"

"We neither of us want much of that attention." I look away from her bird eye. "I'm stuck with it and didn't need more for contributing to the injury of a kid. How is it, anyway?" I shrug. "See. You don't like attention either." She peers at me, all magpie eyes. "Except you came over here looking for something before you got scared off. I'm wondering what."

I think I need to sit down. I wrap my fingers around your phone in my pocket. I feel a little sick and I think it's because my body's leaning into the wait, expecting it to ring, here, in front of Lettie before I've had a chance to—what? Convince her? Lie to her? I'm not sure what to say. I just thought the words would come and now I can't decide if I should even sit down.

"Sit. You're making me nervous."

I sit. Splints rests his head in my lap, his brown eyes focused on my face. He waggles his eyebrows at me. I feel a tiny bit less sick.

"Spit it out."

"I need you to make a call for me." I try to meet her gaze but my eyes keep sliding off. I focus on the spot between Splints's eyebrows instead and give it a scratch; he licks my wrist. I clear my throat, start again. "I need you to call the school and tell them I'm sick."

"You don't look sick."

"I'm not. I slept in." I consider telling her about the vomiting, or playing the leg card, but decide against it. "I missed the online absentee time and you need a parent to sign you out or call you in sick after that."

I can feel Lettie watching me. "And you need me to do that."

I nod.

She swallows loudly and leans back in her chair, making it creak. She crosses her ankles then uncrosses them again.

Why did I think this'd be a good idea? I stand quickly, making Splints skitter backward. I don't look beyond her feet. "Never mind." I turn to the gate.

"Who would I say I was?"

I stop. "What?"

"Who would I say I was, if I made this call?"

I shrug.

"Well, this doesn't strike me as a particularly good plan."

I knew this was a bad idea. I step away.

"I mean, I need to know who I'm pretending to be, if I'm to do this. Convincingly."

I stop. "You'll do it?"

"Well. I figure I owe you for the manual labor yesterday. And I could probably do with an insurance plan, in case that cut of yours gets infected and you have to have an amputation. A bit of leverage can't hurt my cause." I risk a look at her face. The smug old goat's smiling. Not one of the mean smiles.

I look at my blurry shoes, trying not to sniff. "You'll call?" It comes out croaky.

She digs around in her jacket and brings out a phone. "You've got the number?"

I stare at her.

"Well?"

I shove your phone into her hands. "Better if you use this."

SHE'S GOOD. SHE'S more you than you.

. . . *Very sorry, we've been up all night and then at the doctor's all morning, I completely forgot to call . . . Just a twenty-four-hour thing, apparently. I think I'll give her another day tomorrow just to be on the safe side, it's knocked her around a bit. Okay, thanks. Bye now.*

She hands me back your phone with a wink. "Shut your mouth. The flies'll get in." She points to the kettle. "Pop some water in that. I could do with a nice warm cuppa." She grins at me. "And you need to keep your fluids up."

THE HOT CHOCOLATE warm seeps slowly into me, relaxing the knot in my belly. I stare past Lettie to our front porch. The bright pink and yellow cushions look ridiculous today. And the potted plants need watering again; they're starting to droop. They look tired, like their job's wearing them down.

"So, where's your mum?" She's super casual as she says it. Like she's asking about the weather. Except for her eyes, they don't leave my face. I should have prepared for this. Of course she was going to ask. What ten-year-old asks the grumpy old goat next door to call in sick for them? She gives me a look. "I'm not blind."

I wonder what she already thinks she knows, living next door. She's probably noticed you've not been coming and going. No early-morning work starts, no evening walks back from the station. I need to give her enough for it to sound truthy. I meet her gaze. "She had to go away for work."

Lettie looks unsurprised. "Doesn't she have someone who can come and keep an eye on you?"

I consider the possible replies and settle for the most honest. "No."

"Hmm." She nods. Takes a sip of her drink. "She's been gone awhile." She's keeping her voice casual, like I'm the little spooked animal in this situation. I watch as she adds some more sugar to her tea. I keep my breathing even and my fingers relaxed around the cup as I watch her lips. I have to watch her lips because the sound of my heartbeat's so loud in my ears I don't think I'd hear if she spoke.

I make myself take another sip; it takes a couple of goes to swallow. I force myself to ask what I don't think I want to know. "Are you going to tell?"

She snorts into her cup. "Who would I tell? You think I want the council poking around here again?"

The relief makes my head dizzy. I place my cup gently on the chest between us and sit on my hands. Splinter shifts over and sits his furry bum on my toes. His huffing masks my shaking limbs. I hope.

"You know where I am if you need me. Can't say I approve, leaving a nine-yea—"

"Ten."

"Right. Sorry. Leaving a *ten*-year-old alone. Lord knows being a single parent isn't easy."

Pretty sure you'd agree with that. I slam the door on where that wants to take me and grab onto something else. "Why'd you give me an extra day? Off school, I mean."

Lettie gives me a smile over the rim of her teacup. "You look like you could do with a mental health day."

I focus on swallowing. Splints shoves his head onto my lap, nudging at my arm. I take my hand out from under my bum and give his nose a scratch. I can feel Lettie waiting for a reply. I think of filling another day when the rest of this one's already stretching out endlessly in front of me. "Thanks."

"You don't sound pleased."

"I like school."

"Maybe you should have got up earlier, then." Her face is sharp again. I've offended her.

I reach for my cup and take another gulp of my drink; it burns my throat. I cough, eyes stinging.

Lettie picks up a spoon and stirs her cup some more. I concentrate on the sound of metal against china; it's annoyingly cheery. She flicks the tea off the spoon and wipes it on the hem of her jacket before placing it carefully back into its jar. She leans back in her chair again. "Anyway, won't do you any harm to keep off that leg for a bit."

"It's fine."

"Well, I don't want to get into trouble for breaking a child. So give it another day, okay?"

It's not like I've got much choice. I glance at her face and keep that thought to myself. I take a smaller sip of hot chocolate and shrug agreement.

"We could go somewhere. Get out of the city. A bit of fresh air."

I imagine hiking through some muddy paddock with the old goat in the cold. I'm not filled with enthusiasm.

"Your Splinter can come too."

"How?"

"I'll drive."

"You have a car?"

"Yes. I have a car."

I know she doesn't have a garage. "Where is it?"

"The white one." She points across the road.

I look into the street. There's a red SUV and an old white bomb of a van and a few normal cars.

"The old van?"

"I said car."

The only white car is a very shiny-looking Prius.

"That's yours?" I'd assumed it belonged to one of the other neighbors.

"Why are you so surprised?"

"Because it's so . . . shiny."

"It is, isn't it." She looks pleased. "My son bought it for me."

She has a *son*? I try not to sound surprised. "What's his name?"

"Christopher. So, you've got nothing on tomorrow, I'm planning on not being here to answer the door, and your big hound here'll fit in the back seat. What do you say we go for a drive?"

She grins at me.

The idea doesn't fill me with dread. I smile back.

Lettie finishes her tea in a gulp and bangs the cup down on the chest. "It's a date, then."

Looks like I'm going on a road trip.

DAY 40

THURSDAY

INSIDE THE CAR is ridiculously clean, as different from Lettie's house as you can get. It even smells clean. I stand with the back door open, wondering if I should let Splints jump in.

"Well, come on!" Lettie's behind the wheel, seat belt on.

Splints looks at me and wags his tail. I hesitate. Maybe I should put a towel down or something.

"What?" Lettie twists around, gives me her best bird eye.

"It's so . . . clean."

"No need to act so shocked. Put him in and let's go!"

Splinter hops up and settles himself in the middle, his head poking between the front seats.

I climb in beside Lettie. She brings a hint of her house with her, wafting out of her clothes. I guess I'm getting used to it. It doesn't make my stomach churn like it used to. She waits for me to do up my seat belt, checks her mirrors and we're off, the car doing its quiet electric hum as we head toward the West Gate.

We're out of the city before I think to ask where we're going.

"Surprise." Lettie gives me a side smile, her eyes all crinkly.

"Is it far?"

"Hmm, it'll take us a couple of hours."

She clocks my glance at Splints in the back. "Don't worry, we'll stop a few times for dog-face here." She flips on the radio: something classical. "We're taking a scenic route, so sit back and relax."

Classical music. I'm not used to it. It's nice. I stare out the window. Lettie stares ahead, concentrating. With no one watching me I've nothing to do. I watch the paddocks go by and zone out.

THE CAR SLOWING wakes me. "Where are we?"

"Geelong. I need a coffee. You want something?"

I shake my head.

"Stay here, then." The door bangs. I'm vaguely aware of her coming back and letting Splints out. I crack my eyes open to see him wee against a small tree.

My door opens.

"Out."

"What?"

"This dog of yours can ride next to me and you can lie down in the back."

I don't argue. It feels nice to lie down. I sink into a proper sleep. Not a listening-out sleep but a heavy, rocked, safe sleep.

I WAKE AS we're driving into green. I sit up muzzy-headed and stare out at wet trees. Splints is sitting in the front with the seat belt on. He turns his head and waggles his eyebrows at me like this is the most normal day in the world.

"Good sleep?"

"Yeah."

"Excellent."

I rub the crust out of my eyes. "Where are we?"

"About half an hour from Lorne."

"No." I gesture at the green out the window. "Where *are* we?"

Lettie smiles. "The Otway rain forest."

"We're in a *rain forest*?" Don't they belong in hot, tropical places? Places that aren't less than two hours' drive from our house . . .

I stare out the window. It's so dark. Not nighttime dark but a close dark: trees and giant ferns, rotting things and living things all tangling up to the sky. The road's small next to this looming green. This must be how fish feel swimming through kelp forests. The car's warm but the damp shadows press through the windows, trailing cool-fingered through the glass.

I catch the end of something Lettie says.

"Huh?"

"Haven't you seen a rain forest before?"

I shake my head.

"Kiddo, you're going to have to speak up. This road needs both my eyes."

She's not kidding. We're heading downhill now, the road narrow and tight with corners that stop my breath. How did I get here? In this tiny eco-car with my dog and a cranky old goat in a rain forest that blocks the sky? It's beautiful. It's wonderful. It's terrifying. I want to stick my head out the window and breathe in the smell of it, the full version of the cool, woody, rotten, green, wet smell I'm getting hints of through the air vents. I want to ask Lettie to stop. But the road's so narrow and windy I'm pretty sure we'd be killed by an oncoming car, from either direction, if we did. I sit on my hands and stare.

"So," Lettie prompts, "first time, then?"

"Yes."

"Like it?"

"Yes." My cheeks hurt. I wonder how long I've been smiling.

THE FOREST ENDS as abruptly as it started and we're at the top of a street overlooking the water. There are houses on either side now, but my eyes are on the blue as it slips in and out of sight behind corners as we descend. Then we're on a road with a strip of green between us and the water. Cafés, apartments and houses jostle for space on the hillside. Lettie pulls a last-minute swerve that has Splints and me half-strangled by seat belts. She turns to face me, glee turning her into an American movie grandma.

"How's that for a car park?" She rolls the window down and the breeze hustles in. The drizzle's stopped and the sun's having a crack at pushing through the clouds. I can smell sea. And not that damp, slightly eggy sea smell you get at home when a sea breeze blows up from the bay. This is proper sea; the smell's alive, tangy and a little bit fishy with a fat, salty touch on my skin.

The radio goes quiet, and the windows glide up again. Lettie raises her eyebrow at me. "Lunch?"

My tummy growls and Lettie nods. "Sounds like a yes." She undoes Splinter's seat belt. Swats him away as he sneaks in a lick to the top of her head. "Right, then. Let's go find a café where we can sit outside, so boofhead can come too."

* * *

I PANIC A little as we get to the café. I didn't think about lunch. I didn't bring any money. Didn't bring anything except Splinter and his lead. I look at the menu. The cheapest thing is fifteen dollars.

"What looks good, kiddo?"

"Umm . . ." I wonder if I should just say I'm not hungry. My tummy growls again. I shift in the seat, pretending to consider the menu. I can feel a flush spreading up my neck to my cheeks.

A waiter wanders over. "Ready to order?"

I bend down and adjust Splinter's lead.

"Well, I'm starving." Lettie gives him her best smile.

I look back down to my hand again and give the lead a tug.

Lettie orders the schnitzel. "Well?" She raises an eyebrow at me. Both she and the waiter are staring now.

"I'm not—"

"My treat. I've been wanting to come down here for ages but I hate driving down on my own. So it's my thank-you. Okay?"

I want to agree. I'm hungry. But—

"Anyway. I still owe you a pizza."

I'd forgotten about that. "Okay."

Lettie shrugs.

"Thanks," I add. I order the pizza, a large one, and eat it all. Even the crusts.

I'M ON THE verge of uncomfortably full but free food is free food. Lettie suggests a takeaway hot drink and a walk when we're done. A walk sounds like a good idea; I'm so stuffed if I don't move soon my next stop's going to be a food coma. Lettie whips out a couple of keep cups from her bag. I wonder what else she's got in there. It's a big straw thing with leather straps, the type of bag a TV mum would take to the beach. Lettie gets a coffee for her and a hot chocolate for me and we head to the foreshore. There's barely anyone else around so I let Splinter off the lead. The ache in my leg gets deeper the further we walk. I stop and pretend to adjust my shoes and check the dressing, and there's no blood, it's just a bit sore. Lettie clocks me looking at it.

"How's the leg?"

"Okay."

"Don't mess around with cuts, kiddo."

"No, really. It's fine, just aching. Must be the walking." She looks at me. I look right back.

"Righto. Let's go sit down, then. This dog can run about and we'll take in the view. What do you think?"

"Sounds good."

We sit on a pile of rocks that cuts down the center of the beach to the water and watch the ocean. If I'd thought about this, I would've thought it would be awkward. Hanging out with an old lady I don't really know in a town a long way from home. Especially as she just bought me lunch. And a hot chocolate. I'd expect to be racking my brain to come up with some polite, boring conversation. About the weather, or what a nice town it is, or how I like her shoes. But Lettie says nothing. And I say nothing. And Splints perches between us and we drink our drinks and watch the water and my mind's not racing for things to say. Or not to say.

Lettie stretches her legs out.

I feel my mouth start to twitch. I hadn't noticed her shoes. They're ugly. *Ugly* ugly. I can't stop looking at them. I want to. I feel like I'm being obvious. I'm trying not to laugh and not to look. I can feel Lettie turning her gaze to my face.

"What?"

I shake my head. Take a sip of my drink.

She wiggles her toes. I inhale and cough; a trickle of hot chocolate dribbles painfully out my left nostril. The inside of my nose is on fire.

Lettie bangs me on the back. "You 'right?"

I nod, blinking and pinching my nostrils.

"Serves you right for laughing at my shoes." She's smiling, though.

"Those're some ugly shoes."

"Ugliest ones in the shop," she agrees.

"So why . . . ?"

She shrugs. "I felt sorry for them, I guess. Poor ugly bastards. No one wanted them. Even on sale." She tips her foot to the side, examining the instep. "Anyway, I like purple."

"And green?"

"Green too."

"And velvet?"

"Yep."

"And frogs?"

"Important sentinel species, frogs."

"And sparkly flowers?"

"All right, you've made your point. They're hideous."

"So why?"

"I don't know, I guess I wanted something silly in my life, okay? Sometimes it's nice to look down and see something absurd." She crosses her ankles and looks back out at the water. "They made you smile, didn't they?"

I like that. I look at my own sneakers. There's a hole forming near the left big toe. I wiggle my feet in them. They're getting tight—soon I'll need new ones. I've never bought shoes on my own.

Lettie's shoe-happy evaporates.

"So . . ." I look back toward the car park. "Is your son who gave you the car your only kid?" I've resorted to conversation-fluff to smooth the ripples inside.

I am interested in Lettie's family, though. In Lettie. This woman who takes me on a car trip to buy me lunch at the beach but lived quietly next door for years with her cat dried out like a giant raisin squashed in a pile of crap beneath her.

"No. I have two children. One son and a daughter."

"Do they visit?"

"Oh, not so much." She puts the lid carefully back on her cup. "My daughter died. When she was eleven."

I don't know what to say. Lettie goes on, "And Christopher, well, he's all grown-up with his own busy life."

I peek sideways at Lettie, not sure how to word my next question. "Does he know . . . ?"

Lettie's face sets. "No. And that's the way I like it."

The hot chocolate curdles in my stomach, the thick of it making my guts twist. Mothers hide things from their children. I glance back at Lettie's face. Hers is set, but not sharp like usual. More fragile than sharp. Something about the stillness of her cheeks and the press of her lips. It occurs to me that maybe she's ashamed of her house, ashamed of hiding it from her son. It's so big and swallowing and she keeps it a secret.

I've been in there, though.

The woman from the council's been in there.

But her son's not allowed. She keeps *him* out.

The shadow-rat nips at my insides.

"Doesn't he visit at all?" My voice comes out small; the wind catches it and twists it away. I clear my throat to try again.

Lettie speaks. "No."

"Do you see him?"

"Sure, I go to him. Or we meet up, sometimes."

I think of how I see her sitting on the porch most days.

"When?"

"Sometimes."

The sparkling clean of the car makes sense now. She must go to visit him in it. He must have given it to her for that. I wonder how much he knows. How much he pretends he doesn't.

"He's allergic to cats, so it's better that I visit him."

"You don't have cats."

"I used to."

Neither of us mentions the cat in the bin.

"So he hasn't seen—"

"No."

My drink's finished. I pop off the lid and peer at the chocolaty foam stuck in the bottom. "Would you invite him over if it were, if the house was more, I mean less—"

"I'm not sure that'd matter." Her face is set again.

I push at the dressing on my shin. "It's looking better, though, right? Your house?"

"Sure, sure it is." Lettie stands up and stretches. "Come on. We'll give this hound of yours a run and a pee and then it'll be time to start thinking about heading back. I don't want to be driving in the dark."

* * *

SPLINTER'S CONKED OUT on the back seat before we've even left Lorne. Lettie peers at him in the rearview mirror.

"Looks like someone's had a good day."

Splinter lets out a long fart and sighs. Pizza and Splints never ends well. We roll down the windows, heading out of town on a different road to the one we came in on. We pass some tourist signs. "Is this the Great Ocean Road?"

"Yep."

I look at the two single lanes of traffic and the long line of cars in front of us. "Pretty small for a great road."

"I think the *great* refers to the ocean rather than the road."

I stare at the water to my right. "Makes sense."

Lettie flicks on the stereo, not classical this time, something I vaguely recognize. Not what I'd expect from someone like Lettie. She catches me looking at her and flicks her gaze back at the road again, a half smile rounding her cheeks. I get a glimpse of what she would have looked like before she got old. It's unnerving. Like seeing someone step out of her face. I stare back out the window.

"I wasn't always this age, you know. I was a music obsessive once. Young and so cool it hurt."

I look at her hands gripping the steering wheel. The skin's thin and loose with twisting veins and splotches like coffee and plum juice splattered from wrists to fingers, like the paper we aged at school to make pirate maps. She has pirate-map hands. I look at mine and wonder if hers once looked the same.

"You like?"

What, her hands?

"The music."

"Yep. The Beatles, isn't it?" I guess.

She laughs. "Not every song from my generation is the Beatles." She turns it up a bit. "This, my girl, is Pink Floyd." She pulls a CD cover out of the pocket in her door and flips it into my lap. "There. Sit back and listen."

So I do. And we drive on. Lettie turns it up and the sounds of it push into my head and my chest. I want to turn it off and I want it to play forever. I want to close my eyes and listen but I'm afraid to shut them. I'm scared of the sound. I don't want it to stop.

I glance at Lettie. She's giving me a few glances herself. "You okay?"

I nod.

"First time you've heard *Dark Side of the Moon*?"

I nod.

"It's a bit intense." Her hand reaches out to the stereo.

I put my hand over the off button. "It's perfect."

I close my eyes.

WHEN THE ALBUM finishes, our soundtrack becomes the airy hum of the car tires on bitumen and wind rushing past the side mirrors. The closer we get to Melbourne the less real the day feels.

The familiar tightening squeezes my belly as the towers of the CBD rise grayly in front of us. I'm thirsty and the angle of the headrest's making my neck ache. I think about the house, waiting, the tick of the clock echoing in the kitchen.

A silver car cuts in front of us and Lettie swears. "Bugger this. I'm hungry. And cranky. Fancy something to eat? My treat. We'll grab some takeaway and eat it at Williamstown Beach. What d'you reckon?"

I wonder if she feels like I do about going back, now that so much of her home sits in bags on her front lawn.

"Sounds good."

She changes into the far lane and speeds up before swerving across to the exit, cutting the silver car off as she goes. There's honking behind us. Lettie raises her middle finger, waves it cheerfully in the rearview mirror and cackles.

WILLIAMSTOWN BEACH IS empty. And cold. We sit on the wall and try to ignore the seagulls stalking us, Splinter sitting on the sand in front. It's fish and chips from the kiosk. They're warm and greasy and just hot enough to make you eat with your mouth open.

The nearness of home looms behind me, almost touching my shoulder, blurring with the afternoon shadows. A low hiss of tomorrow. Of everything. I bang my heels against the wall.

Lettie's chewing slowly in a way that reminds me of walking home from school. I don't feel like thinking about our house, so I ask about hers. "So what's going to happen, Lettie? With your house?"

She shrugs.

"Are they going to go throw everything out?" *Are they going to go out the back?*

Lettie digs into her jacket pocket, pulls out a crumpled notice and hands it over.

I stare at it. It makes no sense to me.

"What does this mean?"

"*Enforced clean*. They're going to organize some *very nice, understanding* people to come over with a skip and take my stuff away."

"They can't just come and take all your stuff. Can they?"

Lettie nods at the notice. "Apparently they can."

I look at it again. *Fire risk, health hazard, public endangerment.*

"Public endangerment?"

"Apparently there was an anonymous tip-off that a local child had been injured in the house."

Even the shadow-rat freezes.

"What?"

Lettie shoves some chips in her mouth, flicks one at Splints. She speaks around the potato, her voice moist and thick. "You heard me."

I put the notice on the wall between us. The breeze catches it, flipping it onto the sand. We watch it tumble toward the water.

"Chip?" Lettie holds the box out.

"Ta." It's glue in my mouth. I work on chewing, then swallowing. The pain of it moving down my esophagus makes my eyes water. I cough.

Lettie thumps me on the back. "You all right?"

I nod, my breath scraping out of my throat. "Odynophagia."

"What?"

"Odynophagia. The pain when you swallow something that's dry."

Lettie snorts. "Learn that at school, did you?"

"No. From the dictionary."

"You read the dictionary?"

"Sometimes."

Lettie nods. "Good for you." She shoves another chip in her mouth. "It's a good word. Much better than 'that pain you get in your food pipe when you swallow something too heavy.'"

I lean across her and grab another chip. "Esophagus."

"What?"

"It's your esophagus, not your food pipe."

"I was playing for laughs. You're a tough crowd, kiddo. Anyone ever tell you correcting people is really annoying?"

I drop my chip back into the box. "Yes." It comes out quiet. Lettie hears, though. She puts down the box of chips and sighs.

The seagulls edge closer.

"How's that leg anyway?"

"It's okay."

"Not hot? Or red? Or oozing anything we should be worried about?"

"Nope."

I pull my pants leg up a bit so she can see the dressing. It's been bleeding a little, but the skin around it looks good. "Just a little sore still."

"Right." She looks off down the beach. "Because that councilwoman was asking some questions. About you. And your mum."

My arms and legs go heavy, my edges blurring with the cold bluestone of the wall.

"She asked for your mum's number."

My torso solidifies to join my arms and legs.

"Don't worry. I gave her a firm what for about involving other people in my private business. Privacy and confidentiality are very big these days." There's movement on the wall next to me. Lettie thrusts something in front of my face. "She gave me a card to pass on to your mum."

I stare at the crisp white rectangle, impressed that something so pristine came out of Lettie's pocket. I think she wants me to take it, but my hands have melded with the wall, joining my stone legs and arms. She drops it in my lap. I stare down at it, willing the wind to take it away.

Lettie sighs. "You can't ignore this, kiddo. That council lady will make *enquiries*."

The wind is not cooperating.

Lettie picks the card up out of my lap. "You'd better call her, Rae."

"The council lady?"

"Rae." That look. I don't need to see her face. I can feel it. *Rae*. Why do people always use your name when it's serious? Makes you not like hearing it. "Your mum. You need to call her."

"She's working." I mumble it to the wind.

I can feel those beady eyes on my face. "I'm not an idiot. Call her. Tell her she needs to come and sort this out. Before someone who'll make it their business finds out you're at home alone."

The shadow-rat vomits freezing acid into my veins. It makes my fingers twitch. I watch them. "I can't."

"Why not?"

"She's not contactable."

"What?"

I don't answer.

Lettie leans forward to peer up into my face. Her eyes have speckles in them and veins in the whites that make them look yellow. "Do you even know where she is?"

"Yes." It's not a lie.

"But you can't contact her?"

"No."

"Some kind of retreat, is it?" She sits back.

Retreat. It's as good a word as any. I nod.

"Bloody hippy-dippy parents. I'm all for kids standing on their own two feet, but to go out of contact . . ." She shakes her head.

The acid's in my eyes now. I blink. They feel better closed. I keep them shut.

"Right." She sits the card back on my lap. I open my eyes and look at it. "I'll do it. But I'm having words with your mum when she gets home." Her voice gets muttery: "Twice in less than twenty-four hours. I keep doing this I'm going to go all Daniel Day-Lewis on you."

I've got no idea what she's talking about. She sighs, digs out her phone and hands it to me. I turn it over. She has her phone number stuck on one of those printed labels on the back. I stare at the numbers. "You kids know about phones. Hide the caller ID and give it back."

I watch as she dials. She squints at the screen and pecks out the numbers with her fingers. I feel sick rising. But, again, when she speaks the old lady disappears and the voice that comes out is not hers. I watch, fascinated. She's sharp; she speaks like a reporter on the news. Uses words like *inappropriate*, *confidentiality* and *harassment* and then *community-minded*, *neighborly* and *civic duty*. After five minutes I hear the other person apologizing and thanking her for her call.

I watch, openmouthed.

"How did you do that?"

"I keep telling you. I wasn't always a sad old goat in a house full of junk. I was someone, once."

"RIGHT." LETTIE DROPS me at the front gate. She leans over the handbrake as I coax Splinter out of the back. "You all right, then?"

I nod.

"Good. I'm off to get the car washed and vacuumed. No offense to fleabag here. But if I leave anything for too long . . ." She trails off. Neither of us look at her house.

I wave her off, and as Lettie pulls out from the curb Oscar walks toward me, a hand raised in greeting.

I stare at him. "You've got a nerve."

He stops, his palm still up.

"What?"

"As if you don't know." I gesture at Lettie's car, at her house.

"I'm not sure what you—"

"Don't bother." I pull Splinter back from sniffing at his foot and walk through our gate, shutting it firmly behind us. Oscar speaks to my back.

"It wasn't me. It was my mum. She didn't do it to be mean." He points at Lettie's house. "She's got a problem. She needs help. People can help her."

"Maybe she doesn't want help."

"It doesn't matter if she wants it; she needs it. You can smell her house from the street. I could smell it from *your* house." He sniffs. "Reckon I can smell it from here." His nose wrinkles. "It's like there's something dead in there."

Something inside me goes very still. Not scared still, still like *he* needs to be scared still. I turn and face him, the closed gate between us. "You don't know what you're talking about. You don't know much about anything at all." He blinks at me. "You act all clever and smart and talk about other people like you know their lives, but all you really know how to do is repeat what you hear your mum say and pretend like the thoughts are yours." He steps back from the gate. I glare into his cow-brown eyes. "I doubt you have any thoughts of your own, do you, Oscar? Just like you don't have any friends. So piss off back to your own house, friendless, and leave us alone."

I don't look at his face with his cheeks pink like I slapped him and his eyes wide like he's going to cry. I don't look at him at all. I walk up the path, get my key out and open the front door, stalk through and slam it behind us.

I FILL ALL the oil vaporizers inside. I've been gone all day and they've dried up. I wait till he's gone before I go back out the front to water the sad hanging pots and stick a mosquito coil or two on the front porch.

Lettie's back on her chair. Splints hustles over to the side fence in the hope of an ear scratch.

"All right, Rae?"

"Yep." I keep watering.

"Want a hot drink?"

I keep doing what I'm doing, lean down and pull out some weed-looking plants. Fill up the watering can again. If Splinter wasn't so obviously tired from his beach run we'd be out walking. I'd rather be out walking. The thought of sitting on a porch makes my feet itch.

"Nah. Thanks."

"Sure. Okay." She gets out of her seat and leans over the fence to give Splinter a scratch. "I saw you having a go at that nosy kid as I drove off."

"So?"

"So, you don't have to look out for me, okay?"

I think about my leg, the way the councilwoman looked at me, the aches still in my body from hauling all that shit outside Lettie's house. I pull one of the plants out of the ground and drop it on the path and squash its little roots under my foot.

Lettie sighs. "Look, kiddo, I'm not ungrateful for what you've done. What you tried to do. But look at this." She waves at the house. "It isn't normal, is it?"

I don't answer.

"In case you hadn't noticed, I'm not great with throwing things out." I give her a half laugh for that one. "They reckon they can help sort it out. So I'll see. I'll just talk to them and see."

I'm not delusional, I know they're coming; you can't score eights and nines and pretend there's not a problem. But I'd thought maybe, just maybe, if the house wasn't too bad, just a little bad and a little smelly, Lettie'd be able to convince them she could take care of it herself and they'd stay away.

Of course that was never going to work. I was foolish to think it. People don't come through, that only happens in movies.

"'S'okay, Lettie. I've gotta go. I've got stuff to do."

DAY 41

FRIDAY

I'M STILL ON the couch when I hear it, the *beep-beep* of a truck reversing and the boom of heavy metal landing in the street. I peer out your window. A scraped old container, once blue, possibly orange before that, now just a dirty, rusty bang of a skip, rests in front of Lettie's. The truck it was dumped off is already halfway down the street.

The cleaners.

I didn't think they'd be here this soon. I thought I'd have a week or so, a few days at the very least. I pull on my school gear and hurry to the kitchen. I grab mosquito coils from under the sink, the purple lighter from the drawer next to the stove and step out the back. My thumb keeps slipping off the lighter. By the time I manage to get each ring smoldering my fingers are aching. I place one on the table next to the door, one on the pavers and one in a mosquito-coil tin near your shed. The coils smoke and the heavy scent pushing into my sinuses makes my eye sockets ache. I breathe in through my nose, long and deep. It's still there, underneath, sweetly sour, a sharp sinking rotten that catches at the back of the throat and forces my feet back. I light another coil and place it near the fence line. Splinter sneezes and shakes his head. I loop my fingers through his collar and step us both inside. He might bark and I don't want anyone popping their face over the fence. I cut the tape and open the windows from the kitchen so I can drop incense sticks in jars on the outer ledge, half a packet in each. I light them and pull the windows mostly shut, hoping to keep the smell on the outside. Overkill? Maybe. It'll give me a few hours, at best. What else can I do?

I leave early. Lettie's in her front yard scowling at four people in white jumpsuits piling out of a van. It has one of those cage trailers attached at the back. They wave at her. She stands next to the skip and glares at them. Another truck with a skip on the back appears around the corner. Good luck to whoever thinks they'll be filling that thing. My shoulders relax a little. There's no way they'll get through the house today, they won't make it to the backyard for ages.

"Who do you think you're waving at? We're not friends." Lettie's angry voice cuts through the morning chill.

I smile.

SCHOOL'S NOT THE relief it usually is. Ms. Pham asks if I'm okay and tells me I have some extra homework to catch up on, then we get a notice for school camp. A trip to the old gold mines in Ballarat. It costs eighty-nine dollars. The rest of the day jumps through moments: I'm performing coherent actions I don't remember starting or finishing.

What if I pay? That's enough to feed me and Splints for more than a week. I don't taste the sandwich in my mouth, the bread's stale. What if I don't go? That's *attention*. I stare at the numbers in front of me, half the problems already solved. *Everybody* goes. I get paints out in the art room. I could ask for help to pay. I'm washing paint off my hands. But that means forms and more attention and involvement of parents and the school welfare officer. I'm in the bathroom, there are younger kids splashing each other at the sink. I have to go. It's the only unremarkable option. I'm reciting something in Chinese in the language room with the rest of the class. Who'll look after Splints? It's only two nights. I'm sitting back at my desk. It's two months away. Money's due in a few weeks. I'm copying something off the whiteboard. A little voice asks if I even need to worry. By the time the camp rolls around we'll be out of money anyway. My pen makes a hole in the paper in front of me. The end gouges into the desk. *I don't know what to do.*

"What was that, Rae?"

I look up. I'm talking out loud now.

My neck's hot.

"Are you okay? You look a bit flushed."

"I'm fine." It croaks out, my throat the size of a twenty-cent coin. I swallow and try again. "Just getting over that bug a bit still."

Ms. Pham's giving me one of her looks, the one she reserves for *What's going on here?* "Do you want to go to sick bay?"

"No!" Everyone is looking now. "No." Quieter this time. "No, I'm fine." The set of her lips tells me she's not convinced. I throw her a bone: "But can I go and get a drink, please? My throat's still a bit scratchy." I flutter my fingers around that little dip in my neck at the base of my throat, hoping she can't see how fast my pulse is banging around beneath it. She straightens slightly, the subtle lean toward me no longer needed. She was right, there was a problem, I needed a drink. Intuition satisfied.

"Of course, Rae. Off you go."

I don't waste any time.

I FORCE ATTENTION for the rest of the afternoon. The worry stumbling around behind everything. It's tangled my insides into a tight knotty ball.

I walk home with a sharp pain sitting behind my left eyebrow and my limbs weighted like I've run cross-country, twice.

I'm too tired for words. Too tired to count. I just want to close my eyes and sleep.

"Stop that!" Lettie's voice cuts through the fug. She's on her front path. Blocking someone with an armful of—what? I squint; it looks like a huge jar of bath plugs.

"I said stop." It's a voice I haven't heard from her before; it's tight and high. It's not the voice that lacerated the councilwoman about privacy, or told me off for being rude, it's not the confident impersonator of other people's parents. Its edges are frayed and it speaks to the me that wants to hide in the corner of my room and cry. It's the voice of little-girl Lettie, and she's scared. I stand frozen at the front gate.

One of them looks at me over their face mask. I bend down and check the letter box, then push through the gate and walk carefully to the front door. I keep my gaze locked in front, slip inside and close the door gently behind me. I go into the lounge, tailed by Splinter, and switch on the TV, then head to your room. I prop the window open slightly and sit under it to listen.

Anxiety vibrates through Lettie's voice. I know what she's doing, more of that grabbing out of bins and demanding to check everything. These people seem practiced, their voices soothing, unhurried, like they've done it before. They serenely discuss whether she really needs five toilet brushes when she only has one toilet and slowly convince her to keep only two, the new ones, still in their plastic wrapping. Their calm logic wins, but I can hear in the anxious goat footsteps moving from the porch down the hall and back that she's not okay with it. I hear two of them talking near our fence, then they peel off, one of the voices asking Lettie to come into the backyard to help her sort through which pots to keep. That does the trick. I hear Lettie's voice moving through the house after her.

"What do you mean which to keep? They're all good pots. All useful, I'm not getting rid of any of them."

I can't hear what the white-suited person says, only the sound of her voice. But I hear Lettie's replies clear enough.

"You leave my pots alone. You leave my shed alone. What do you mean smell? There's nothing dead out here! There are no dead rats or possums or anything smelly in my shed, only my *things*! Just leave it alone. You're already taking everything from my house! The council said nothing about my shed! You have no *right*!"

The calm murmuring continues. I hear them moving back inside . . . something about going through the kitchen instead for now.

I sit frozen under the window as the cleaning noises intensify from the front. The speed of the crashing—piles of Lettie being thrown into the skips—picks up significantly without her there.

For now.

They'll work their way through her house. Then they will go out the back. My throat's making it hard to swallow. Splinter pushes his nose into my face, licks my ear. I shove him away, angry at my stupidity. There are no mosquito coils left.

He whines and clicks his nails on the floor. He's right: we can't just sit here and wait.

I stay where I am, listening.

They don't keep her away from the bins for long. Pretty soon I hear her running up and down the hallway, her shoes banging on the floorboards I uncovered. Her voice pinches at my chest. The pacing and anxiety, the running out to check everything they take, trying to sneak it back in. The sound of her need tickles up the anxiety in my head. She needs those things to keep her head full. If all that's taken away, there's nothing. Nothing to stop her seeing what's gone. I don't let my thoughts go there. I don't think of all the words, numbers, homework and shopping, the plants and cushions and bills to pay, the keeping normal, the TV blaring . . . or what would be left without them. Of where thinking goes when it has nothing to distract it.

I can't stay crouched under your window all afternoon. I wait till the voices disappear deep into her house and then Splints and I make a run for it. I don't get far: Lettie spots me trying to dash past her fence.

"Rae!" she yells around the white-suited people standing in her hallway in paper masks. She pushes past them to the gate. "They've been here since seven thirty." I stare at her. "They're going to take all my stuff."

I don't recognize her. She's old-old, and weak and reaching out to hold on to my arm like I have some way of protecting her. The face masks look on with interest. Splinter tries to lick her through the gate. I shake off her fingers.

"You asked them in."

Her hands drop away; I yank Splinter's lead and turn and run, past our gate, past Oscar gawping from his front fence.

"Hey! Rae!"

I ignore him and keep running toward the river. The rage ball in me fueling my feet. *His fault.* I can feel those eyes on my back. He'll keep.

WE DON'T STAY by the river, too many people on bikes and Splinter wants to chase them all. We veer up, cut through Footscray and Seddon and into Yarraville. We walk the streets, getting ideas, waiting for the sun to set.

Then, as the sun sinks, we steal some plants. Flowering ones, lush ones. I pull them out of the parks—pansies, violets, begonias—out of front gardens, from pots, soil still clinging to their roots. I drop those in the nylon bag you keep screwed up in your jacket. Others I drop straight into the long pockets of your coat, folding their leaves gently into the edges. I work methodically, staying away from houses with lights on in the front. I find something that might be broccoli in a communal veggie patch on a nature strip, and rainbow chard too—the only thing we grew successfully with our neglect-based method. I think even that might be dead now. I shove the chard in the nylon bag with the rest. I check out Yarraville Gardens; they always have new plantings. I don't go to the dog area, though Splinter wants to. I stay in the dark part of the park, uprooting plants in the shadows. I squat in the soil and dig out geraniums with my fingers.

"Hey! What are you doing?" The voice behind me is loud and angry. "This isn't a nursery! I've had enough of people stealing from this park whenever they feel like it."

I look up from where I'm squatting, my fingers on the plant in front of me, my heart kicking into my chest. An old guy with white hair is standing at the edge of the garden bed clutching a dog lead, hands on hips and a face like a cartoon general. The type to grab children by their shoulders and march them home to let their parents know what they've been up to.

I give the only answer I can think of. "I'm doing a wee."

He steps around from behind me to stand on the path in front, eyes on my face.

I squat closer to the dirt and try again. "I'm doing a wee." I wait a beat. My voice wobbles. "And you're watching me."

He steps back ever so slightly.

His mouth opens, then closes. "No, I . . ." He still looks mad but there's a flash of uncertainty. He shoots a whip-fast glance toward my legs and bum.

"You are!" I squat down further, counting on the gloom and your long jacket to hide my lie. Splinter steps out from a bush behind me, head lowered. I see my way out. "You're perving on me!" I let my voice get louder.

"No, I—" He steps back, hands raised, and shoots a glance down toward the dog park.

I stay squatting where I am, a frightened kid caught with her pants down. Even in the gloom I can see the crease between his eyes. He's pretty sure I'm lying. But not sure enough. He looks down to my hands, still clasped around a small geranium.

"You're still looking!"

Splinter growls, a low rumble at my back.

I raise my voice, increasing the volume with each word. "You're still doing it. You're still watching." I make my voice high and tight.

It's not such a stretch. "Stop it. Stop looking at me!" I take a big obvious breath, ready to scream.

"You should be at home." But he scampers.

I finish pulling up the geraniums, being careful with the roots.

I don't push my luck. When I'm done we head home, the plants tucked gently around me.

Lettie's not on her porch. The skips are gone from the front of her place. I don't look too closely at her house. We sneak in quietly. The TV's still on. I put the plug in the bath and run in some cold water before gently taking the plants out of the bag and your pockets and placing them in to soak. It's too late to cook. I tip some food in Splints's bowl and turn the kettle on. Pot noodles again. I sit on the couch wrapped in your duvet and eat.

I can't get warm.

The windows to the backyard are still ajar.

You fill the house.

DAY 42

SATURDAY

MY MIND'S AWAKE before I am. It's been planning in my sleep. I've got two days, I reckon. Two days at most before the cleaners get through the mountain of stink inside Lettie's and make their way out the back. I don't think about Lettie's dark porch last night, or her sleeping in that house. Or what I said to her.

I get up instead.

I make tea, Russian Caravan with milk and honey, like you'd make on cold Sunday afternoons before sitting on the couch to read. It's smoky and sweet. I drink it slowly, then make another. I stand with the cup at my chin, warm smokiness curling up my nose as I stare out the back window at the Sleeping Beauty garden. The sun's not up yet, it's just pushing light into the sky so all the colors are a version of gray. The weeds are up half the height of your shed door now. I watch for insects. They're not up yet either but I know there's less than before—they're in quiescence now. I learned about that the first week. I was worried about flies. And what came after: little things that eat. I was worried about you, I guess. So I googled *insects in winter* and I learned *quiescence.* It settled over me like a blanket. It was me too, before I started talking to Lettie. Before the outside started creeping in like meltwater through the cracks. The grass is touching the bottom of the washing. One of the towels is gone.

I can only put it off so long. I pull on my old trackies, last year's school jumper and my gum boots. I'm as ready as I can be. I open the back door and step out. Splinter pushes past and bounces through the grass, his tail waving like a tatty flag in the gloom.

My eyes water. The white-suited woman was right. It smells. Still. *Focus on what you can do.* I can't stop it smelling. But maybe I can try to make it seem like it doesn't . . . or, even better, like it's got a good reason to. A not-worthy-of-attention reason. I don't look at the grass and thistles growing in front of your shed door. I look at my feet. *Focus.*

A movement catches my eye, the towel flicking on the clothesline. The same towel you hung. Another thing you left. The shadow-rat turns, eyes sharp as it sinks its teeth into my belly, the burning heat of it pushing me forward. I stalk across the grass, ignoring the squelch of dog shit and the spike of old bones stabbing into boot rubber and yank the towel off the clothesline. It's stiff and gritty under my fingers. The fibers crack and scratch as I wrestle to fold it. It makes a demented towel-tent in my hands. I try again. I use my leg to push against it, but it stubbornly holds its line-hung shape. I throw it at the back door. It doesn't even make it halfway before falling stiffly on the grass. Probably in some dog shit.

My hands are on fire. My skin is on fire. The shadow-rat surges up from below, pushing a gasp from my lungs as it forces its way up into my head to stare out my eyes, rabid, furious. This yard, this mess, this house.

You.

A howl surges, belly deep, rip-roaring mad, clawing at my throat as it tears out. Splints stops dead in his tracks. It builds again, another heaving sound-vomit, molten and electric. I plant my feet, suck the gray air into my lungs and let it spew out, my face twisting, my cheeks hurting like sunburn. My throat tears, my head swims, and then it's over. The silence rushes in and I stand panting in the grass. The shadow-rat falls back into my belly where my insides are raw, torn.

I kick at the fallen towel. The swing of my leg hurts my knee and my boot flies off. It thumps into the back of the house and I fall on my arse in the grass. The only sound now is my breathing and a scrabbling at the side fence. Real rats. I press my palms into my eyes until lights bloom in my head. I sit and push everything in until it's a little pinprick. Something small enough to swallow and forget.

Splinter snuffles warm into my ear. I drop my hands. Everything's quiet. He licks my cheek and lowers his bum onto the ground next to me. We sit, probably in poo, and stare at the back of the house. I'm too tired to move. Splints leans against me and sighs.

THE GRAYS SLOWLY become green and brown. My trackies are damp from the ground. I don't think—I know what needs to be done. First, the grass needs cutting. I can't do that with bones and dog shit everywhere so I get a bucket and shovel from the little metal toolshed. Bend, scoop, drop. I fill the bucket. I dump it in the bin at the side of the house. I fill the bucket again. I move in a grid from one side to the other, making my way toward the back fence. I avoid your shed.

Ground clear, I wrestle the old lawn mower out of the toolshed, ignoring the hulking figure of the other, with its dark spidery windows and the roof you said was probably *fucking asbestos.*

I was never very good at starting the mower; my arm aches and the rope's heavy; I can't pull fast enough to make it cough. I clench my teeth, put my foot on top of the engine, grip hard and throw myself backward into the grass. The motor growls to life. Splinter runs around barking.

I mow stripes in the grass. It's not a big yard. It doesn't take long.

I leave the grass and thistles around your shed. Maybe it'll just disappear like Briar Rose's castle. Splinter keeps running over to sniff at it. I call him away, glad of the petrol fumes from the mower, glad of the noise. I tell myself it's because of the redbacks that hide in there to keep warm over winter. What do redbacks eat? I saw a YouTube video of one with a bit of raw chicken once. I drag my mind away, let the mower die and wrestle it back into the toolshed.

In the quiet I can hear voices from the front of Lettie's. The rumble and crash of new skips being delivered. The cleaners are back.

I collect the gardening trowel and some gloves, checking that the bag of blood and bone is still there. It's sitting where you left it when we were going to grow our own veggies before it became clear how much work that involved.

I get the plants from the bath and dig each one a small hole. I sit them gently in place, ease the soil around and smooth it flat. I water them in. I do some in front of the toolshed too. If you looked over from Lettie's you'd see them easily. A freshly planted garden bed: flowers, broccoli and rainbow chard. They look a bit wilty, but it's protected from the wind out here and the soil's nice and damp. They should survive for a few days. Long enough.

I go in and open the bag of blood and bone. It stinks, stick-in-the-back-of-your-throat stinks. And it's heavy. I drag it out. Splinter shoves his nose into the bag; I try to push him away but he's having none of it. He snuffles and snorts like a pig until a giant sneeze forces his head out. He's almost cross-eyed with pleasure. I tip the bag up, spilling the lot into a stinky pile next to the fence. I leave Splinter pushing his back through it and get the rake from the toolshed. I rake it around the flowers and plants, pushing the excess across the grass, covering as much of the yard as I can. Splinter's nearly melting in excitement. I water it in—I've given up trying to keep Splints dry—then pack the tools away and shut the small shed door.

I stand on the back step and look at what I've done. The flowers look freshly planted, the soil all turned over. The place stinks of fertilizer. It's clean. No poo, no bones. Grass mowed. I grab Splints away from his back-rolling, drag him inside and shut the door.

Just a normal backyard.

SPLINTER TRIES TO head for the couch but he reeks and he's wet and covered in mud. I hold on to his collar and wrestle him into the bathroom, shutting the door behind us. I strip off because there's no way I'll stay dry through any of this, grab him round his chest and force him into the bath as he splays his legs out, scrabbling at the enamel. I use my knees and elbows to knock his paws down and climb in after him. I stand legs wide to keep upright, one hand on his collar. I can see in his eyes he knows what's coming. I turn on the shower and he jerks like it's acid. I go down, my elbow hitting the side of the tub. The pain of it takes my breath but I don't let go. I wrestle him, keeping him in. His claws catch my arm, my shin, one sinks into my thigh. I hang on.

The water warms up. He eventually stops struggling. The steam mists the mirror. I use your expensive shampoo on both of us, the one that smells like real flowers and herbs. It takes the whole bottle. A lot of it ends up on the floor.

By the end the hairy git looks like he's enjoying it. He sits, panting quietly, the full warm spray pummeling into his back as I massage the bubbles into him. He lies down with a sigh. I rinse myself off, pop the plug in and let him have a little soak. I rest my head on his neck. He smells like you. I sit on the bath mat and let the bathroom fill up with steam.

EVENTUALLY WE'RE DONE. There isn't a dry towel in the house, but he's never looked so shiny. Your hairbrush has never been so manky. I pull on some clothes and then I'm dressed and he's dry and there's nothing keeping us inside.

I can hear banging from next door, things being dumped into the skips at the front. I wonder if Lettie's on the porch. The thought makes my heart kick a little too high in my chest. I don't think about her face when I last saw her, or what I said. Splints licks my hand.

"We look so good, we should go for a walk, huh?"

He circles his tail in agreement. I snap his collar on and we go outside. I glance at Lettie's. She's not on the porch. I wonder if the twist in my stomach's relief or disappointment.

I'M NOT SURE where to go now we're outside. I glance back at Lettie's just as a couple of cleaners come out dragging black garbage bags. I turn the other way. I have to tug at Splinter to follow.

"You going for a walk?"

Oscar. He's leaning over his gate, watching. Does he just wait in his front yard for people to walk past? His chin's lifted as he looks at me, and I can see that his fingers gripping the fence are white.

I don't slow my pace. "Am I walking?"

"Yes." He shifts his weight on the gate and gives a half smile.

"Then what do you think?"

The smile droops slightly. "So, how's the cleaning going?"

That stops me. "What?" Has he been watching me?

"The cleaning. You know, the old—" He looks at me. "Ah, your next-door lady's house." His nose wrinkles, like he's smelling something bad.

Relief makes me careless. "Oh, that." He takes it as an invitation and swings out of his gate to stand in front of us. He stretches out his hand and Splinter gives his fingers a lick. I pull him away.

"You live next to it; you must be glad she's getting some help." He says it casually, but it's not. He's watching me as he says it; he wants me to tell him he's right. "I mean, you must be glad they're intervening." He holds out the word like a trophy. *Look how smart I am.*

"Heard that one from your mum, did you?"

His cheeks flush and I catch a little twitch below his eye, but he still meets my gaze. "It's terrible. She's a health hazard, the council should have stepped in ages ago. You can't deny it. It's dangerous. Mum says—"

"*Mum says,*" I mimic him in a high baby voice.

"It's true!" His whole face is pink now, he's forgotten about convincing me he's right and just wants to yell his opinion at me. His *mum's* opinion. Another adult who thinks they know what's best for everybody else. Someone who gets off on reporting people to a Melanie or a Tracy so they can knock on the doors of people they know nothing about and lecture on *well-being* and *safety* while forcing parents to twist themselves through checkboxes like circus animals. People who always think they know best.

I watch Oscar, his eyes all shiny as he stabs his finger at Lettie's house and pretends it's about caring. "She's an adult, so not looking after herself is one thing, but when that affects other people that live here that's not okay. There's the smell and the fire hazard and the health risks." He stops, still looking at me. I stare back. "And the rats! They're everywhere! They're all through our backyard. It's irresponsible. And selfish and gross."

I think of Lettie buying me lunch. Making me hot drinks. Making phone calls for me. Taking me and Splints on a trip to the rainforest. I remember her face when we did the councilwoman's test. How she tried to let me help, and her eyes when she asked me for help and I told her what was happening was all her fault.

Oscar's still going. Using words like *unstable* and *dangerous. Sick.*

I tighten my grip on Splinter's lead. "You don't know what you're talking about."

"Yes, I do! She's a danger."

"She's not. She was doing perfectly fine before you showed up."

"Just look at what happened to you." He gestures at my leg.

"What?" I feel very still as I stare at him. "What did you say?"

"Your leg." He points again. "You hurt it in her house."

"You don't know what you're talking about."

"Yes, I do! I saw it and when I told Mum—" He says it like it's nothing.

"You told on me?"

He looks confused. His confusion makes me want to punch him in the face. "No, I didn't tell on *you*, I told on *her*."

"This is *your* fault."

"What's my fault? That a smelly old woman who lives in a dump is getting some help? That place was a health hazard, even you can't say it wasn't. People like that don't deserve houses. I could even smell it from inside your place!"

My hand's shot forward before I'm aware of what it's doing. It takes me a second to connect him holding his nose and the feeling in my knuckles. I look down at them, they're red. I look back at Oscar. He takes his hand away from his face; there's blood on his fingers.

"You hit me." His voice sounds like he's watched me turn into a rabbit.

He looks at the blood on his fingers again. "You hit me!" This one's less shocked and more outraged.

I'm not sorry. I'm also not stupid.

I run.

IT'S DUSKY BY the time we slink back home. We've walked the length of the river to the end of the trail and back; my legs are aching and Splinter's head's hanging low, his tongue out. Oscar's place is quiet; there are lights on inside as we walk past, quickly, careful not to look too close. There are no lights on at our place. The front yard still looks good, though. The cushions with their popping color and the mismatched stolen chairs make a respectable front yard, one that might belong to people who *garden* and *pay their bills on time*. Neat and tidy. Loved.

I wonder about the people who chose those cushions. What did they feel when they saw them sitting cheerfully on their front porch? I think about what it felt like when they came out to find them gone. They make our front porch look cared for, or . . . I search for the word. *Curated.* Like an Ikea catalog. I ignore the slightly wilting plants, I can take care of them tomorrow. There's something more important I need to do. I go in, grab your phone and go sit on Lettie's dark front porch.

The skip's gone from the front strip. I wonder when they'll deliver another one. Splints licks my hand with a dry tongue. I lead him to the tap at the side of her house and let him lap at the water as it splashes to the ground. I peer in the windows; the human animal smell still pushes into my nostrils through the glass. Lettie's house is as dark as ours but it sits more solidly. It's like a big wooden Splinter waiting patiently for her to get back. I lift the lid on the chest and pull out the kettle and a cup. When Splints has finished his slurping I fill it up and make myself a hot chocolate.

We settle, Splints in front of Lettie's seat. The dusk slips to dark. I sit on Lettie's chair, sipping my drink, watching the street. So this is Lettie. It's not so bad. Splinter snores. A figure moves down the street. I watch her and try not to tense up.

I wasn't prepared for the relief. And the shame.

"What're you up to, kiddo?"

"Just waiting for Goat-o."

Lettie snorts and settles into my chair, crossing her feet in front of her. "Well, you'd better get comfortable, we could be here for a while."

"What?"

"Never mind." She leans forward and touches the kettle with her fingers. "That still hot?" I shrug. "It'll do."

She makes herself a hot chocolate, actions she's done countless times before. I don't know why this time it makes my eyes fill. The sound of the spoon hitting the cup has Splinter up and licking her wrist. Lettie pushes his face away. "Heard you got into some trouble."

I take a sip and swallow before answering. "Yep." I keep my gaze on the ground.

The chair creaks as she shifts her weight in it. "Wouldn't have anything to do with me, would it?"

I watch the tear drip off my nose and disappear into the hot chocolate. You used to say salt made chocolate taste better. "I'm sorry, Lettie." It comes out quiet, but I can tell by the stillness in her that she heard. I clear my throat and glance at her chin. "About what I said to you."

She nods. "I know."

I look at her and she gives me a half smile.

"I was mean."

"Well, at least you didn't punch me in the nose."

I can't manage a smile. "How d'you know?"

"His mum came to see me when she couldn't get hold of anyone at your place. Seems you and I are seen as a bit of a team."

My stomach twists the hot chocolate into something sharp. I've really fucked up.

I swallow again, trying not to cry, but it leaks out the edges, making my lips wobble.

"His mum came looking for yours, I assume. And when she couldn't find anyone at your house she came knocking on my door. Demanded to know where you all were."

I inhale the tears and concentrate on my cup. "What did you tell her?"

"Told her you were both out. Ballet lessons." I look up and she gives me a wink. "No one ever thinks ballet kids are trouble."

I'm not sure what to say to this. "Thanks. I guess."

Lettie leans back and drinks her drink. Splinter settles his head in her lap with a sigh and she scratches him softly behind the ear. My brain's churning through the options, none of them great.

"She's dogged, that one," Lettie observes. "I know her type." This makes her smile, but there's not a lot of happy in it. "She'll be back, Rae." I can feel her looking at me. I watch her stroking Splinter's ear.

"Lettie, can you call her?" My fingers itch to slip into my pocket, but I keep them wrapped around my cup, leaving your phone where it is.

"I've already spoken to her."

"No, I mean—"

"I know what you mean."

"Well, can you?"

She sighs. "I know why you're asking. Seems logical after I've done it for you twice already." I nod, hopeful. "But I don't think it's a good idea this time, kiddo."

"Why not? You did it before, what's the difference?"

"I'm not so sure I should have done it before, to be honest." It's Lettie's turn not to look at me. "The difference is: that woman lives next door. She's not someone wanting their job done quickly over the phone."

"That's not fair. I helped you." I gesture at her house.

Lettie nods. "That's true. And I appreciate the help." I smile, relieved. "I also appreciate there may have been some extra motivation in the form of keeping the council away." She gives me her bird eye and the bottom drops out of my stomach. I'm losing her.

I point at my shin, my voice getting squeaky. "But I didn't tell anyone about my leg."

"I think that might have more to do with my previous point than loyalty to me . . ."

"But—"

". . . but I appreciated your sentiment."

"She's an interfering busybody, you said so yourself."

"True enough. But that's not a problem when there's nothing to hide, is it?"

The unfairness makes my hands shake. "Just because your house is clean now doesn't mean you're better than me. Doesn't mean I don't deserve some protection too."

She raises an eyebrow: a look that makes my pulse spike. "Protection from what?"

I slam my cup down. The sound of it cracking sits between us. I won't look at her. I hate this need. "Why won't you help me? I helped you."

"Oh, kiddo. I think you know what needs to be done here. And we both know me making that phone call is not it."

"Lettie, please—"

"Call your mum. She needs to sort this out."

I grab Splinter's lead and jerk him up. "Thanks for nothing."

Lettie just nods as I storm off. I slam her gate behind me, not caring that it makes a sound like the latch has been broken.

I DON'T THINK about Lettie, or Oscar and his interfering mum. I make noodles with a fried egg, feed Splinter and turn the heater on. It fills the house with the smell of burning dust. I turn it off again and finish cleaning the kitchen. The sink's all streaky. I wipe it, first with the dishcloth, then the tea towel. I pull one of those soft white foam sponges from under the sink and move it in circles against the stainless steel, turning the smudges into shine. A drop splatters from the tap, shattering water droplets over the clean. I twist the tap off harder, the metal digging into the flesh of my hand. I mop the drips and go back to the circle work, streaky to gleaming.

There's only so long you can polish a sink. The house sits hollow around me. I consider going to bed. I haven't slept in my bed in so long I reckon it'd be damp from the cold. Do sheets go moldy? I settle on the couch. The TV muffles into the corners and bounces too loud off the walls. I'd imagined sitting on the couch feeling satisfied and tired: job well done; crisis averted. But the house is more a stage than ever. The nothingness of it tickles at the back of my neck. I sink lower, pull up the duvet, turn up the TV. I stare at it: some adult in nice clothing being mean to someone for entertainment. I flick: whales dying from eating plastic. The old goat's right. If I wait for her to save me I'll be waiting forever. I've got used to her porch and warm drinks and it's made me forget I'm on my own. I'm the one who needs to fix this.

Splinter hops up next to me and lowers his head onto my hip. Your phone, still in my pocket, digs in to the bone. I pull it out. It's flat. Lettie couldn't have used it anyway. Splinter raises a furry eyebrow at me and I pat him between his big brown eyes. He's right. Why can't I do it? Just because Lettie won't help me doesn't mean I can't learn from her tactics. I can be somebody too.

DAY 43

SUNDAY

I'M UP EARLY and out the door. I shut it behind me with a firm click. Hair brushed and teeth cleaned, in my own winter coat and lace-up shoes. I'm even wearing a scarf. Splinter whines behind the door. I do up my coat buttons, pat my pocket and walk out the gate.

Their front yard's not as tidy as ours, but it's not-tidy in a way that suggests hard work. There's straw from under the plants scattered on the path and a trowel sticking out of a pot with a gardening glove over it, the other glove propped up on a small stake in the pot next to it. They wave at me as I walk past. I ignore them and step up to the door. I knock with intent.

"Hello." It's Oscar's mum. She doesn't smile but she isn't mean either. The warmth of their house spills out. I can smell toast, fried eggs and coffee.

"Hi, Ms.—" I can't remember her name. I dig my nail into my finger. I should've practiced this part.

"Lucy."

I thought it started with *G* for some reason. I clear my throat and start again. "Hi, Ms. Lucy."

She does smile now. "It's Lucy. Just Lucy." I watch as she pushes that smile away again. "What can I do for you, Rae?"

I straighten my shoulders. I prepared for *this*. "Is Oscar home? There's something I'd like to say to him."

Oscar steps out from behind the door. Sneaky little rat must've been there the whole time.

I give him a smile, but I don't let it go to the edge of my lips. It's a sad smile. An *I'm really sorry* smile. I make eye contact; his eyes go narrow.

"I'm very sorry that I hit you, Oscar." He says nothing. I wait. I thought he'd be better trained than this; I was expecting an immediate thank-you. But I'm not unprepared. I've practiced more than one outcome. I take a deep breath and double down on the eye contact. "What I did was wrong. Hitting is never okay, and I shouldn't have done it." I look down at my shoes to show his mum how bad I feel and to give Oscar time to accept my apology. He still says nothing. I peek up from under my eyelashes. His eyes are still narrowed at me and he's rubbing his nose. I glance at his mum. She's saying nothing. I'd hoped she'd be more the stepping-in type. I swallow my annoyance and reach into my pocket for the big guns.

"Why did you, then?"

I leave my hand where it is. "Huh?"

"Hit me. If you knew it was wrong and you shouldn't have done it, why did you?" He's jutting his chin at me. I know what I'd like to do to it. I ball my hand in my pocket, staring at him. This is not going as planned. I look at his mum again. She tips her head to the side and nods.

"It's a reasonable question, Rae. I think Oscar deserves an explanation."

I focus on keeping my face smooth, my eyes clear. I push the mad back, keeping it contained, hot and spitty, in the notch of my throat. I know what they want. *Because I can't control my temper, because I'm a bad kid, because my mum's not as good at being a mum as yours—*

"Because you were rude." It comes out more fiercely than I'd intended. Oscar takes half a step back. I like that.

I lean toward the door. "You were rude and mean about Lettie. You don't know anything about her, you've already caused her no end of trouble, and then you said horrible things on top of it." I catch myself and step back, shoot his mum a quick glance. She's looking a little embarrassed. I continue, deliberately keeping my voice down. "I know she's got problems, but she's always been good to me . . . and my mum." I stare his mum straight in the eyes. "And *my* mum says I should accept her as she is and respect her. That she's had a whole life that I know nothing about and she deserves my compassion. And you"—I point my finger at Oscar—"you called her old and filthy, and said she's a disgrace and a danger. You made fun of her and her house and complained about how it affected *you*. I saw those people come and go through her things and throw them out and I saw how upset it made her. How hard it was. How hard she tried to do the right thing and how much it hurt to do it. And you"—I point at his chest, pinning him, a little insect, while I methodically remove his wings—"you think it's nothing, that it's funny."

I meet his eyes; his chin isn't jutting out anymore. "And then I find out it was you who called them in the first place. You didn't talk to her, didn't offer any help, you *told* on her. You were the reason she was so upset. And when you said she was disgusting and unstable and dangerous, that she didn't even deserve to have a house, I got mad. And I hit you."

My heart's on fire. I catch my breath, remember why I'm here and stare at my feet again, willing my pulse to slow. Then I look at him. He's slumped, his shoulders disappearing into his arms like I've hit him all over again. It feels good. It also doesn't. I pinch myself through my pocket. I wish I'd brought Splinter. I make myself look at his face. "I'm ashamed of how I acted."

And it's true. He deserved it but I still feel bad. I look up and meet his mum's gaze and focus on why I'm here. *Keep to the script.* "Mum made me come. She said I had to own up and apologize and not hide because I was ashamed. And she's right." I look at Oscar again. His cheeks are pink and he's not meeting my eyes. "I'm sorry. I'm very sorry, Oscar. What I did was wrong and you didn't deserve it."

It's not entirely a lie. I reach back into my pocket and pull out my ace. "I brought you this." I hold out the book. "This is my way of showing how sorry I am. I want you to have it." I force myself to hand it over. "It's one of my favorites." That part, at least, is true.

Oscar takes the book and looks at it.

"And where is your mum?" Lucy looks down the street. "I thought she'd have come over herself."

"She said I had to do this on my own. That I needed to take full responsibility."

She nods thoughtfully, like she's taking mental notes. You've never been such a good mum. "And what else did she say?"

I bite my lip. "No ballet for a month. Which means I'll miss the recital." I look down at my feet.

Oscar's mum looks concerned. "Oh, well I'm sure that's not—"

"No. She's right. There are consequences."

"Oh." As I watch, a soft pinkness washes up her neck and into her cheeks. "Of course. Yes."

I swallow a smile and touch my nose. "I can't imagine how I would feel if Oscar had hit me." I look at him holding my book. "I really am sorry, Oscar."

Lucy gives me a bright smile. "Well, why don't you stay and play for a bit?"

I give her a serious face. "No. Mum says I have to help Lettie today. She says it keeps me out of trouble."

"Not in that house, I hope?"

She can't help herself. I see where Oscar gets it. I straighten my coat. "I'm reading to her. We mainly sit on the porch." I give her my best smile. "Her eyes aren't what they used to be." I imagine what Lettie would say if she could hear this, and I smile for real. Serves the old goat right.

"Well, okay, then. Maybe another time. What do you say, Oscar?"

"Sure. No worries." He's not convinced. But she is. I grin as I wave good-bye and then almost skip home. I'm opening the front door when it occurs to me. Now I have to spend the day with Lettie. I don't have to look over my shoulder to know Oscar's mum's still watching from her gate.

SPLINTS IS STUPIDLY pleased to see me. All sniffs and wiggles. I let him into the front yard and change into your jacket and a pair of sneakers.

Lettie's not on her porch. I head over anyway, careful not to look back up the street.

I'm not sure whether to knock or just take a seat and wait. She's usually outside by now. But there wasn't much of an inside to spend time in before; maybe she's an inside goat now. Splints lowers himself in front of her chair with a sigh.

I knock. The door swings open. Lettie. She doesn't smile but she doesn't not smile either. "Didn't think I'd see you this morning."

"Yeah. Well." I shrug.

"Nice to have someone so communicative come to visit."

I look at my feet and consider leaving.

"Shit." Lettie says it quietly, fingernails scratching away at the back of her head. She drops her hand and sighs. "Look, kiddo, I don't blame you for being mad at me. I might be too, in the same situation, but I'm doing what I think's right." She clears her throat. "And I'm doing it because I like you, not because I want to be a pill. Okay?"

"Yeah." I can't look at her.

"You're a good kid, Rae. Someone should be looking after you. Someone better than me."

"You're all right."

Lettie lets out a snorty laugh. "Thanks for the ringing endorsement." She bird-eyes me. "But I'm not letting those honeyed words distract me." I know what's coming. I give her my best blank face as she leans against the doorframe. "At the risk of you stomping off again, did you call your mother?"

"Yes."

This gets an eyebrow raise. "Really? You spoke to her?" She's skeptical: my middle name, you always said.

"Yes. I called her." Lettie's eyes are hard to stare into. It really is like staring into the eyes of a goat, except without the freaky sideways pupils; same level of intense, though. We used to see them at the children's farm. They were always the animals I liked best and least.

"You called her at the retreat?"

"Yep. Well, I called them. They got her to give me a call." She's not tripping me up. Lettie knows I've got Mum's phone. Anyway, people aren't allowed phones at retreats. I saw it on that luxury travel show on Netflix.

"So *she* called *you*." She gives me a hard look.

"Yep. I told her people were beginning to realize she wasn't here and she needed to come home."

"And?"

"She's on her way."

"When?"

"Next week."

"Next *week*?"

"Yes."

"Jesus. Better than never, I guess." She shakes her head. "I'm not happy about this." I've got her. I keep my face serious. "And if she's not back next week I'll bloody call child protection myself."

"She'll be here." It's not a lie.

Lettie straightens up. "She'd better be."

I force out a smile. Next week is next-week-me's problem. "In the meantime, I need to read to you."

"What the hell are you talking about? I can read perfectly fine on my own, thank you very much."

"Well, I apologized to Oscar and his mum. Told her Mum said I had to say sorry."

"And did she?"

"Well, she would have if I'd told her." Also not a lie.

"Huh. Color me unsurprised. What's that got to do with reading?"

"His mum wanted me to stay and play so I said I had to read to you"—I can barely stop my lips from twitching—"because your eyesight's failing."

"You what?"

"Blind as a bat."

"You cheeky little rat. Like she doesn't already think I'm useless." She gives me the stink eye. "You did that on purpose."

I smile sweetly. "Serves you right. Anyway, you're not mad at me."

She steps back and puts her hands on her hips. "Oh, I'm not?"

"No."

"How do you know that?"

"'Cause you're smiling."

"That's not you. That's just muscle memory. You remind me of someone."

"Who?"

"Never you mind." Lettie looks up the street and pulls a face. "You'd better come in, then. Seems the fences have eyes."

EVEN KNOWING WHAT the house was like before, I'm shocked at the damage, the smell, the awfulness uncovered by the cleaning. Lettie watches me as I step through.

"Guess this is the first time you've seen all the walls, then?"

I look at them. They're covered in a blotchy, swirling patterned wallpaper. I look more closely at what looks like growing things. Or maybe they aren't. I step over a cat-shaped stain, and Lettie watches me notice it. Distress scuds across her face. She waves her arm at the spaces and gaps that were towers of *stuff*, the imprinted ghosts of them still on the wallpaper, bits of baked-on dust making it look like they were vaporized rather than removed by people in white paper suits and face masks.

"They said they'll take that off, the wallpaper. Won't be sad to see that go. A coat of paint apparently will help too"—her hands flutter—"you know, to deal with the . . . It gets trapped in things apparently, the wallpaper, carpets, floorboards . . . so on." She stares at a particularly dark patch on the floor. "The smell, I mean. A sand back will fix it, they say. Then an acrylic-based polish to seal."

She swings from sad and embarrassed to factual and uncaring, the change so fast I can't tell which is real. Maybe they all are. She's an old flickering movie of herself.

Three bookcases still stand against one wall. I walk over to them. "Well, what should I read, then?"

Lettie shrugs. "They didn't leave me any magazines or newspapers."

I think about the condition of the ones I shoveled into bins. "I hope not."

She pulls a face at me and steps over to the first bookshelf. I wonder if it's the one that fell on her. I look at the chair under the window, the small coffee table next to it.

Lettie nods at the furniture. "New. From the cleaners. Well, secondhand new. Couldn't keep the old stuff."

I stare at them. "Wasn't this your bedroom?"

"It was and it wasn't."

"What does that mean?"

"It means I slept in here. When I ran out of room in the other one."

"Oh."

"Yeah. 'Oh.' The other one's cleared out now. They even got me a new bed."

"That's nice."

"Yep."

We stare at the bookcase. All the books are stacked neatly, all the spaces filled. She runs her finger over the spines while I look around the room some more. It's bigger than I thought. Though I guess that's not surprising.

Lettie pulls out some books, flips them over. She hands me one. "This should be all right for someone your age to read."

I look at it; it's old, but clearly a kids' book. There's a girl and a horse on the front cover. I wonder if it was her daughter's. I open and flick through it. The smell from the pages takes me back to the day I found Lettie under the bookshelf. An overwhelming animal smell, full of decay, oil and shit.

Lettie clocks my reaction. She looks sad. "I ruined them too. I kept these on the bookshelf to keep them safe."

"It's okay. They just need an air out, it'll be all right."

Lettie shakes her head. "No, it won't. Paper loves smell. That's there forever." She hooks her arm in behind a row of books. "They'll all need to go now, I guess." I wait for her to sweep them onto the floor. But she doesn't. She just stands there, her arm in behind like she's hugging them.

"We could try?" I suggest. "Take them out and give them some air? Maybe give them a spray with something? Some eucalyptus?"

Lettie sighs. "What's the point?"

I look at them. The only neat things in the house that aren't new. Kids' books. Girls' books. The things you keep when it's all you have. I feel your jacket big and warm around me.

"They are." I take an armful off the shelf. "Come on. No harm in having a go." I don't wait to see if she follows. I take them out onto the porch and arrange them on the boards, spines facing up, pages gently fanned out beneath like little legs to let the air in.

I have to tie Splints's lead up to Lettie's chair to stop him knocking the books over. They smell good to him, I guess. When we're done they take up most of the front porch. We leave a narrow path to the area with the chairs, which we also leave free. Reading from one's going to be bad enough; I don't want to be completely surrounded by them too.

The books sprawl across the boards like they've collapsed after a long hike. They wouldn't all rest spines-up on paper legs, so some are on their backs with pages blowing in the air, others standing open like a fan to the street. Some of the littler ones I had to get creative with, using the edges of hardbacks to hold open their pages. They look like a family of rectangular cats sleeping on each other, dusty old tails and whiskers twitching in the breeze.

"Not a bad job." Lettie sinks into her seat and turns to watch Oscar and his mum on their nature strip, gardening gloves on, weeding.

"Very subtle." She rolls her eyes at me. "So, what are you starting with?"

"I thought this one?" I hold up the one Lettie first gave me. The one with the girl and the horse.

"Ah." Lettie nods. "That was Lana's favorite."

"Was Lana your daughter?"

"Yes. She was."

"What happened to her?"

"She died."

Lettie's very still. Not looking at anything. Not moving to

make a cup of tea, or wiggling her toes, or scratching Splinter or any of the other things she does when we're sitting. I look down at the book in my hands and wonder if it's rude to ask how someone died. Or if maybe I should just start reading. I open to the first page.

"She was eleven, I told you that."

I nod and slip my finger in to mark the start, not sure if she's going to keep talking or if I should. She's still staring: her face hangs, mouth drooping from gravity rather than frowning. She's staring somewhere over my left shoulder. I turn and check. Just the door. I look back to the words on the page.

"It was flu. You wouldn't credit it, would you? Kids are supposed to be resilient by eleven. I thought she was improving, all her symptoms were improving. Then the fever came back with a worse cough. Rest, fluids, Panadol—everything they tell you to do. Nothing worked and by the time I called the ambulance it was too late. You're always made to feel like a bit of a ninny when you rush your kids to the hospital with a cold or flu, like you should just buck up and stop being so high maintenance. She seemed to be getting better. I thought, 'Oh, a little relapse—she was up and about too early is all.'" Her fingers pick at the checked wool of her pants, teasing out some fluff. "She was burning up, so hot she was delirious. So I called the doctor. They said he'd come around when he was done at the surgery. But then I called the ambulance anyway. I knew she wasn't okay. I should have called them earlier. They asked me that too. *Why didn't you call us earlier?* Doesn't matter what you do, it's wrong. First lesson." Her fingers leave the wool to pick at each other. "Last lesson too."

She looks at me. "She loved books." Her eye twitches, a little flicker over so fast I wonder if I imagined it. "I couldn't bring myself to get rid of them."

I twist around to look at the books on the porch behind me, getting more about Lettie in that second than I have the whole time I've known her.

"What about your son?"

She smiles. "Not so much. Chris was never much of a reader. He liked building things."

"No, I meant—"

"Oh." She nods. "You mean what about him in all the dying."

"Yeah, I guess."

"It wasn't a happy house after that. His dad left. I left too, really. I was here, but . . . not. I couldn't leave but I wasn't really there. I held on to him too tight and not tight enough. Held on because he was all I had left, not because of him, and he knew it. He studied hard, went to uni in Sydney and never came home again. Couldn't get out fast enough. Can't really blame him for that."

"But he gave you a car."

"Oh yes." She smiles and glances at it in the street, all white and shiny. "He gave me a car. And a hamper every birthday, flowers every Mother's Day, balloons and a bottle of bubbly for New Year's."

"He sends you balloons?"

"Yep. They're all in—" She gestures into the house, smiling; catches herself. "They *were* all in there." Her fingers pick at the back of her hand. She looks at me and smiles again, only not quite: her lips pull down at the corners rather than up. "Big outrageous things filled with glitter. He's got a sense of humor. Wish I'd known that." She picks at her fingernail. "Never mind."

"Do you see him?"

"Sometimes. On my birthday. On Lana's he always calls. Takes me out to lunch when he's in town. A sweet man. He just doesn't want to come here."

"Maybe he will now the house is all clean."

Lettie smiles that not-quite smile again. "I don't think that'll make a difference, kiddo. It wasn't that keeping him away." She's not looking at me. "The reason he doesn't come back is that from the moment Lana died everything changed. It all looked the same, had the same furniture, even smelled the same, mostly, but it wasn't. The home part of it died and all that was left was a house. I don't suppose that makes much sense."

I can't move. I want to tell her. I want to say that it does. I want to tell her our home ceased to exist with you. Instant desiccation. How it's a husk, with all the warm squashy bits that make it alive missing; a shell with brittle edges. How I feel it when I wake, the emptiness that's more than out of the room. And how it's worse that it's still here, that when I heard the rope creak and saw your feet the house should have disappeared in a mushroom cloud behind me. But instead I make believe, a husk in a husk with Splinter's warm body the only real thing.

I look at her. She's not looking at me. She's playing with the thread on her sleeve, her toes scrunching under Splinter. I can tell because his tail's making slow circles and his back foot's twitching in that way it does when you give his tummy a scratch.

I open my mouth but my voice has dried up. Even the breath coming out is shallow and hot. What would I say? *I understand*? Then what? Tell her where you are? She looks up and catches me staring. Splints sits up, his face hopeful. It's always about more pats with him. I shut my mouth and glance down at the pages, pretending to look for the start.

It doesn't feel right to start reading. But I can't say anything. I'm not sure I could read even if I wanted to. I think of the cushions I stole, the plants, the memories and words I collect and polish like shiny stones in my head. *Is this what happens?* But I don't ask that. I look down at the book, the wet lick of Splinter worrying at his groin the only sound between us.

Lettie slaps her thighs. "Right. Must be time for a warm drink. Have you got that page ready? I'll fill the kettle up and you can start reading."

"Lettie?"

"What?"

I hold my breath a second. Chicken out. "Can't you use an inside kettle now?"

She stops, kettle midair.

"Huh. I guess I can." She shrugs and continues over to the tap. "Old habits."

I nod, the words blurring in front of me. I get that too.

IT'S NOT A bad way to spend the day. Reading to someone. It reminds me of you reading to me when I was sick or scared of my new room with all the shadows and smells that weren't home. You read me books about horses too: those dancing horses that escaped from war over the mountains. I'd forgotten about that. You'd do all the voices and you'd read faster when it got exciting, then drop your voice and slow it down as it got to the scary parts. You'd always stop and wink at me as I squirmed and held on to your leg.

I don't do voices. Lettie sits in her chair and stares out to the street, listening. She smiles in a way that makes me think she's remembering too. She makes me so much hot chocolate that I have to keep stopping to pee. I go home for this. She offered her recently cleaned bathroom but I know what it was like before. I prefer ours.

Lettie just shrugs and waits. She breaks out those biscuits again. The ones from the fancy shop in Seddon, sweet and also cheesy ones this time. She has some fruit too, which we eat for lunch to *round out the biscuits*. She even bought some pigs' ears for Splinter. He lies pressed up against her legs and chews them into a slimy mess.

By late afternoon we've read most of the book. The story's getting quite good—I'm concentrating on reading and Lettie's staring off into space—so neither of us notices Lucy walk up until she's standing in front of us.

"Good book?"

I stop. Lettie gives her the side-eye.

"Sorry, didn't mean to interrupt, you two seem quite involved in the story." She laughs in that slightly too-loud way of adults being fake cheerful. What you'd call *jolly hockey sticks*. Which still baffles me.

"Can we help you?" Lettie tightens her lips into something kind of like a smile.

"I just want a quick word with Rae."

"Off you go, then." Lettie nods and sits back, hands in her lap, and stares at her.

Lucy's smile tightens but stays in place. She turns to me. "I'd still like to have a word with your mum, Rae. Is she home right now?"

The pages slip past my fingers. The good feeling from the reading and biscuits and hot chocolate vaporizes, leaving a burning cold in its place. She and Oscar have been in their front garden most of the day. She knows no one but me has been in and out of that house. She must.

I open my mouth. I speak the truth. "Yes."

"Oh, good." Lucy smiles and turns toward our place. The biscuits and hot chocolate threaten to re-emerge. I swallow them down, trying to think what I can say. *What can I say?*

"Don't you dare set foot on that front step." It's Lettie, in the voice that commands councilwomen.

Lucy stops. "I beg your pardon?"

"That poor woman is exhausted and is getting some much-needed rest."

"Is she sick?" Lucy tips her head to the side, eyebrows drawn together. She'll be at our front door with soup next. What's Lettie doing? She's making it worse.

"She's fit as an ox. But she *has* been up all week at ridiculous hours taking meetings with clients in the States. Ludicrous time to schedule them, if you ask me. But that's what happens when your company does business overseas. Globalization—not good for working parents, is it?" Lettie shakes her head.

"Oh. Poor thing, that must be exhausting." She flicks a glance at me again. "What does she do, exactly?"

Lettie laughs. "What do any of them do? This virtual digital stuff, it makes no sense to me!" I watch her, amazed. She pivots from businessperson to silly old woman so smoothly that it feels perfectly natural. Endearing almost.

"Oh. Righto, then. I won't disturb her." She gives me her full gaze now. "Rae, can you please let her know I'd still like to talk with her, when she has a minute?"

Lettie clears her throat and gives me a look. I shut my mouth.

"Oh, sure. I'll get her to call you? She's pretty flat out at work over the next week."

Lucy smiles. "That'd be great." She pulls a card out of her pocket. "My number."

I stand up. The book slips to the ground as I reach over for the card. "Thanks. I'll give it to her."

"Nice of you to read to Lettie here."

"Yes. She's a good kid. I love reading, but with my eyesight . . ." Lettie shrugs.

"You still drive, though?"

Lettie smiles. She's *enjoying* this. "Only during the day. And with visual aids." She pulls out her yellow glasses from her pocket and perches them on her nose. "Reading, though. It's the small type I struggle with, and those large-print books are just too damn heavy."

Lucy nods and walks off with a wave.

Lettie snatches the card off me. "You nearly dropped the ball there, kiddo." She whistles, looking at the card.

"What?"

She shows it to me: *Lucy Geddes, Department of Health and Human Services, Child Protection Operations Manager.*

I pick the book up and sit down. My hands are shaking. I find the right page. The looking calms me. Lettie tucks the card into her jacket pocket, settles back in her chair and gives me a wink.

I stare down at the book in my hands. The one her daughter had loved.

"Lettie?"

"Yep?"

"You were smiling before, when I told you I'd said you were blind as a bat . . ."

"What about it?"

"Was it because I reminded you of her, of Lana?"

She snorts. "No, you ninny. It was because you reminded me of me."

I find her answer oddly calming.

DAY 44

MONDAY

THE NOISE NEXT door starts up early. People banging around there from six thirty. I let Splints out for a wee and poo and put his dried-food bowl out with him. I'm going to leave him outside. They've seen him around now. And the garden looks cared for. I add some more blood and bone, a couple of piles near the fence. It seemed like a good idea but Splints is straight into it, snorting and sneezing, tail wagging like it might fly off. He'll either help spread it around or dig up all the plants trying. I watch him for a sec. All that hard work. I guess it'll look like the typical back garden of a family with a dog, all dug up. I shut the door on him. For once he doesn't notice.

I'm at school with time to spare. Lunch packed, homework done. I keep my head down, smile. The model student until the last bell.

* * *

I WALK PAST Oscar's place quickly: eyes ahead, no dawdling. I stop when I get to our gate, though. There's someone on Lettie's porch wearing one of those white suits, spraying down the front with a high-pressure hose. I wonder about their priorities. The porch was the only clean space she had. Lettie's nowhere to be seen; I can hear a sound like a humungous vacuum cleaner inside her house. I go into our house and straight through to the back, to find Splints a dirty stinking mess. He wiggles his bum off at the sight of me and tries to give me a lick. I push him away and lift myself up to peer over the fence.

What's left of Lettie's furniture is piled neatly in the backyard, covered in tarps. From the shapes I'm guessing the three bookshelves, the chair and coffee table from the front room and another couple of chairs, a few boxes and a bed. There are some of those plastic storage containers piled up outside the back door. Lettie's sitting on one of the porch chairs. I look around for more of those white-suit-wearing people but she seems to be on her own.

She waves at me.

"What are you doing?"

"What does it look like I'm doing? I'm sitting on a chair."

I roll my eyes. "But why are you out here?"

She looks around her. "Looks pretty good, doesn't it?"

I look at her backyard. It does. The jungle's been whipper-snipped to within an inch of its life; big wet clumps of grass lie in piles across the yard. There's even a birdbath the size of a small child in there. The smell of freshly massacred green is overwhelming. That and the fumes coming from her house. I'm glad of it as I hang propped by my forearms over the fence. Between that and the blood and bone, there's not much room for other smells.

"What's with the outdoor furniture?"

"The house is having plastic surgery. They've scrubbed it down, melted off the wallpaper, sealed it with one coat of paint and are about to add another. Latex paint! I've got rubber walls now. And they've even got a floor sander that vacuums as it sands. No dust. Painting and sanding at the same time." She shakes her head. "They reckon they'll have the first layer of sealant on the floor before they leave this evening."

"That's a lot."

"Yep. They've been at it all day. Using some pretty heavy-duty chemicals. Takes a while for the fumes to clear. So I could be out here all night."

"Oh." I'm interrupted by a white-suited mask-face peering out the back door. I drop back down and leave them to it.

Splints snuffles at my feet. He didn't get a walk yesterday. I sniff. I don't want to get that close to him. I also don't want to hang out the back of the house any longer than I have to. "I'm not bathing you again." He shoves his nose into my crotch. "Right. You asked for it."

I clip on his lead and head out the front, hook the lead over the side fence and turn on the hose. Anyone would think I'm trying to kill him. I give him a good spray. Some of the cleaners stop to watch, grinning with their masks hanging under their chins. I give them a tight smile and hurry up. Splints waits till I'm untying him from the fence to shake. There's a sympathetic laugh from next door. Now we're both wet. And a bit smelly. And the center of attention. I pull him out the front gate. We walk past Oscar and his mum pulling up in their car. I pretend not to notice and head to the dog park, the shadow-rat gnawing away gleefully at my insides.

* * *

THE DOG PARK'S pretty empty. I let Splints off for a run around and find a corner in the sun to sit and watch, trying to ignore the feeling of impending doom. I've got a week, maybe less, till a ton of stuff steamrolls over the top of me. I reckon I've got till Sunday before Lettie starts trying to call you herself. And that's not even thinking about Lucy nosing about, or school excursions, or bills or rent. I lean back into the fence. I'm tired. Tired like *if I close my eyes I might sink back through my head and melt into the fence* tired. I rub at my eyes and focus on staying awake. I wonder how conspicuous it'd be if I just let my eyes shut and napped here. Just for a little bit.

Splints skitters over, panting and stinky. He's dry now, at least. Cars are pulling up, loaded with kids and dogs for their after-school pre-dinner play. I heave myself to my feet, clip on Splints's lead and we head down to the river.

We sit, him and me, and watch the water. There's an old man fishing off the jetty with a bucket next to him. I wonder if it's empty; judging from his stillness there's not much biting. The noise of the container port washes over us, the low whine and reverse alarms of the straddle carriers: collecting containers, dumping them with a low boom. When we first moved here that sound in the middle of the night kept me awake. Every night I listened to the chaos of roadworks or building or something booming and beeping and crashing. It sounded like buildings collapsing. It frightened me. Every night I'd climb into your bed and try to snuggle under your arm, and you'd wake up and sigh. Until the night you lost it and shouted at me to go back to my own fucking bed and stop waking you up every night. I tried to explain but you threw my pillow out your door and screamed into my face and the streetlight from the gap in the curtains twisted you into something animal and furious. I could see the spit stretching from your front tooth to your tongue.

I went back to bed and lay with my head under the pillow, still scared of the noises but more scared of waking you. I was still awake hours later when you snuck into my bed. You asked me why I kept waking you up. I was too scared to tell you, but you figured it out. When you brought me down here in the predawn light in pajamas and sneakers, I was nearly as scared as when you screamed at me, but then you explained how it all worked. I saw it never stops here, twenty-four hours a day even on Christmas, like bees but harder working.

I slept after that. Now when I wake in the middle of the night to the boom and beep of the container yards and docks, I listen to it and imagine those straddle carriers lifting and lowering and whizzing around. So busy. Everyone's busy. The whole world is busy. If I keep my head down no one will look. Like now: me, Splinter and the old fisherman over there. We're invisible next to the bustle. We can just sit. Ghosts. With all the other ghosts.

I stare at the fisherman. I think of you, standing here, holding my hand. Of me here with you when I thought the worst that could happen was you screaming at me in the night or throwing something at the wall or staying in your bed for a week. Ghosts. Like the man fishing who was here last week and will be here tomorrow, fishing over ghosts of himself, fishing over the ghosts of others, of all the people who have stood here, real like us, drivers and fishers and workers and kids. Thousands of years of people, way back to when this was all wetlands, grasslands and rivers. People who stood here looking across the water being real and alive, not knowing what was coming. Just like I did, standing here in my pajama-clad legs, my hand in yours as you squeezed my fingers and said, *See? Nothing to be afraid of.*

The old man winds in his reel, checks his bait and casts out again. As we watch the river darkens, but it's the cool that lets us know about it first. That and the early dark: a dark that's not so much a fading day but a sucking-up of light. I look behind us. Clouds have gathered, building up a storm-head to the west so gray it's purple, a big ugly bruise of weather hanging on the horizon.

A gust of wind blows the old man's bucket into the river.

Time to go.

OSCAR'S SITTING ON our front step. I walk around him onto the porch. Splints gives him a lick. Oscar puts out his hand for a pat, catches a whiff and changes his mind. I hide my smile as I look at him. He looks back. He's holding my book in his hands.

I wait for him to say something. He waits back. We're not friends. Not not.

"Thanks for the book." He holds it out.

I stare at the familiar cover. "You can keep it. It was a gift." I hold the door key in my pocket and wonder how to make him leave.

"I liked it. It was funny." He smiles.

"Yeah. Probably because it was written this century."

The smile crumples into a kicked-puppy face. *Shit.* I glance toward his place. The lights from their front windows show through the branches in the gloom. I look back at Oscar. He's still sitting on the step, my book in his hands. He looks sad.

"Glad you liked it. Sorry about the whole hitting-you-in-the-face thing." I glance at my book. "So you read all of it?"

"Yep."

"Don't you sleep?"

"Not when I've got a good book."

I get that. He's holding it out to me again. "I said you could keep it."

"It's okay. I've read it now. I know what it's like to have a book that's special." His fingers flick to the title page and he holds it up. He doesn't need to—I know what it says. *Dear Rae, my bravest girl. Happy 10th birthday. Love, Mum.* The meaning's changed since you wrote it.

"It's not special."

"If you say so." He invites himself up off the step. Gestures a *do you mind?* at one of the chairs. Sits.

I let go of the key in my pocket. The wind's gusting; it bangs the gate shut, then disappears again, leaving the fence vibrating. The sensible strategy is to be friendly but not too friendly. Hopefully he won't be hanging around long anyway. I shrug and take the other seat. I wonder if I'm Lettie now. Should I offer him some hot chocolate?

He sniffs. "What's that smell?"

"Blood and bone."

"Oh. Right. I thought maybe it was coming from—" He glances across at Lettie's.

"I thought you were a gardener."

"We use chicken poo."

"You what?"

"On the veggies. Chicken poo. It's organic."

"You eat food you grow out of chicken shit but called the council on someone because her house is a bit smelly?"

He laughs. I wasn't expecting that. I was being mean.

"Your mum works a lot." The way he says it, it isn't a question.

"Yep."

"Do you get lonely?"

"No."

"I didn't mean . . . I, it's just that. Well, I do. A bit. Sometimes."

"With your mum and dad and school pickup and drop-off and gardening days?"

He shrugs and looks at his feet. "None of my friends from school live near me." He looks up. "I was wondering if, sometimes, we could hang out? Just at the park or whatever."

I did not expect this.

"We could walk your dog? Or kick a ball or . . . something?"

I think about what it'd be like to hang out with someone after school, someone my age to fill the time. He'd expect to come inside. He'd expect to see you.

"I just want to not be at home all the time, you know? Mum's great, but she usually has to work from home in the evening, and Dad's always late home during the week. I figured you'd understand what that's like, with your mum and all. Sometimes it's just nice to get out, right?"

I stare at him. Does he think we're the same?

"I could tell Mum we're friends, that your mum asked if it was okay for me to come over and play? Maybe then she'd stop trying to talk to your mum all the time."

He's not so stupid, then.

My face feels numb. "I need to check. With Mum."

He smiles, like my answer's already yes, and picks up one of the stolen cushions. "This is nice."

I shrug.

A banging from Lettie's makes us both look over. Two of the cleaners are carrying a big floor sander out the front door. A couple of others go in and out, carrying buckets and giant mop-looking things. They must be for sealing the floors.

Lettie comes out to the front porch. Her chairs and the chest are back where they should be.

She nods at me. "Kiddo."

"Old Goat-o."

She looks at Oscar, then turns to sit with her back to us. One of the white-suit people who carried out the floor sander sits next to her and pulls out a cigarette. It takes him a few goes to get it to light; the wind's picked up, and it keeps blowing out the lighter. Lettie makes him a cup of tea.

I've never seen her do that for anyone but me.

I turn to see Oscar watching me.

"How come you can call her an old goat and I can't call her anything?"

Because she's mine. I don't say that.

"It's respect, isn't it? She and I have a relationship. We joke with each other. It's affectionate. When you say things, it's just mean." The streetlights flicker on. "Shouldn't you be getting home?"

He stays where he is. "Mum knows where I am."

I bet she does.

"Right. That's it, Lettie. First coat's all done." Three more of the cleaners appear out the front door. The middle one's speaking to Lettie while the other two load up their van. "You can't walk on it for about six hours, though. We'll be back about seven thirty tomorrow to do the last coat on the walls, then finish the floor. Should be all done and dry in time to move your things back in by tomorrow evening, hopefully."

"What about—" Lettie's got her arguing voice on. She obviously doesn't like this one as much as the one she made tea for. I smirk.

"We've stacked all your stuff under tarps on the back porch." Lettie shuts her mouth. "We've got a new washer and some other things for you too."

"Rightio." She smiles and nods. I watch, openmouthed.

The smoking one tips his tea dregs off the edge of the porch, grinds out his cigarette on the sole of his shoe and stands to drop the butt into one of the bins. "You've got somewhere else to stay tonight, right?"

"Of course." She gives him the bird eye. "You think I'm going to sleep out here on the porch in winter?"

"Okay, good then. Weather looks like it might be a bit shit. See you in the morning." He joins the others getting into the van.

"Okay. See you then. And watch your language, there are kids around here." She gestures at me and Oscar without looking in our direction.

"Sorry!"

She dismisses them with a wave of her hand and gets back to her tea.

The wind sharpens into a pinching cold. It's not so much gusting now as just windy. Oscar stands. "I'd better get going."

"Bye, then." He looks like he wants to say something else, but I get up and turn away.

When he's gone I open the front door and flick on the porch light. He's left the book sitting on his chair. I look at Lettie, settled into her seat now with her gloves and coat on, blanket on her lap as she sips her tea.

I have to raise my voice over the wind. "You're staying there tonight, aren't you?"

She snorts. "Why wouldn't I? I've got a warm jacket."

I ask before I can think better of it. "Do you want to stay at my place? Just for tonight."

I'm filled with horror at what I've offered. But also not.

Lettie waves the idea away. I'm standing at the door, unsure if I should leave her and go in or offer again, when the bruised clouds open up with a gust of wind so mean the windows rattle. Sideways rain flies into the porch, blowing the cushions onto the ground and soaking my book. I grab it off the floorboards and drop it into my pocket.

I look at Lettie. The rain's hitting her in the face.

"Come on."

"Off you go." She gestures for me to go inside, ignoring the rain sliding down her cheek as she takes another sip.

"Lettie!"

"I'm fine." She has to shout to be heard.

"You're already soaked!"

"It's fine."

"It's not." I'm really yelling now.

She glances up the street. "All right. Don't be a pill about it."

And that's how the first ever grown-up who isn't you enters our house: wet, stubborn and bad-tempered. Seems our house has a type.

LETTIE'S SOAKED. I give her a towel and a face washer and an extra bottle of body wash from the cupboard. She looks like she might get offended, smells it and changes her mind. I push her into the bathroom, then shout instructions on where the shampoo is through the door.

"I can see it. I'm not actually blind, remember."

I hear the shower go on. When it's been running for a few minutes I sneak in and grab her clothes from the floor. I shove the lot into the wash with a bit more soap than I'd usually use. I find some track pants and a T-shirt and jumper from your stuff; a pair of cotton undies and some warm socks. I hold one of your bras, wondering how to work out if it will fit Lettie or not. I hold it up. Stretch the cups out. Thinking about Lettie's boobs feels weird. I get her a singlet instead.

I place them in a neat pile inside the bathroom door then go and top up all the vaporizers. Splints follows me around like an excited kid. The house hasn't been this busy and full since, well, you know. He still smells a bit. I find that dog deodorizer balm you bought last winter in the laundry and open it up. It smells better than he does. I read the instructions. It says to rub it in. I give it a go. I use the whole tub, finishing up with a good brush at the end. He's pretty shiny when I'm done. And pretty happy. He flops down on the kitchen floor with a contented huff while I sweep all the hair up.

The shower's still running. I dump the fistfuls of Splinter hair into the kitchen bin. It's dinnertime. What am I supposed to feed her? Two-minute noodles and a fried egg? I pull random things from the cupboard and fridge. Some eggs. Butter. A sad-looking tomato and a few wrinkly mushrooms. I feed Splinter. Turn on the lights and the heater. If you were coming home soon, would I really worry about the power bill? The little voice whispers, *Why worry? It's all skidding out of control anyway.*

I stand staring at the random food I've piled on the bench, unable to make a decision.

The shower goes off.

"Where are my clothes?" The voice is furious. Splints scrambles off the floor and runs barking to the bathroom. I follow him and yell back through the door.

"They're in the wash. I'll put them through the dryer when they're done." What's more power usage at this point?

"What am I supposed to wear?" She still sounds furious, but slightly less so.

"The clothes I put in there for you."

Silence. Followed by the sound of the hair dryer.

LETTIE STEPS INTO the kitchen, pink-cheeked, hair all fluffy.

Your track pants are a bit long on her. She's rolled them up at the ankles. And folded the sleeves of the jumper. They fit her differently to how they fit you. They barely look like the same clothes. I relax.

Lettie looks around, sniffs. "Why does it smell like orange and cinnamon in here?"

"Vaporizers. The house is a bit damp. It covers the smell."

"Huh." Lettie sniffs again and wanders toward the back door.

"Hungry?" I hold up a packet of noodles in one hand and the last frozen lasagna from the freezer in the other.

"No need to shout." She turns and peers at what I'm holding. "I hope that's not what you're planning on feeding me." This from a woman who until two days ago didn't have a functioning kitchen. "Oh, get that look off your face. If you're putting me up, then I'm cooking you dinner."

I think about arguing. For about two seconds.

Lettie moves around the kitchen confidently, opening drawers, finding things, testing out the oven and gas rings.

"Not much in the cupboards." She flicks on the light to the backyard, peers out through the rain. "You've got rainbow chard!"

She's out with a knife before I have time to stop her. I watch, frozen, from the back door.

"Phew, it's whiffy out there. A bit much blood and bone. Lucky it's raining, that stuff'll burn your grass to buggery."

She stands dripping under the back door overhang, a bunch of chard gripped in her fingers, looking out over the backyard. She sniffs again. "And I think there might be a possum or something dead in one of your sheds." She steps toward them. "Maybe more than one."

"Stop!" It's almost a scream.

Lettie stops, shocked.

I want her away from the shed. I want her back inside. "Don't walk all over everything! You'll ruin it all." I can hear the panic in my voice. Lettie just stares, the knife and chard still in her fingers. I can feel my breathing heading toward tears. I swallow and pull it back. "Anyway, I've smelled your place, so stop criticizing."

"Fair enough." She gives me a look but comes back inside.

She washes the chard in the sink. I sit on the kitchen stool, my hands squashed firmly under my bum until they stop shaking. Lettie looks at me while pretending she isn't. My breathing settles.

"Right." She gets to work and starts chopping and sautéing and generally treating me like a kitchen servant.

"Where's this?"

"Get that—"

"Do you have a—"

It's busy and chaotic; the room fills with steam and smells. Good smells. Lettie's hair curls at her ears, her cheeks turn pinker. She looks up to see me staring at her. "What are you grinning at?"

"I'm a bit surprised you know how to cook. I guess."

Lettie stares at me for a moment. "I genuinely don't know whether to laugh or hit you." She shakes her head. "Here, make yourself useful." She shoves a carton of eggs toward me. "Break four of those into a bowl." She gives me her bird eye. "No shells."

She sticks her head back into the fridge. "Got any ricotta? Sour cream?"

"Nope."

"What is this place? You live off two-minute noodles or something?"

I pretend to ignore her and crack the eggs into the bowl.

Lettie watches. "Got some skills, then. Hope for you yet."

LETTIE INSISTS WE sit at the table. She makes me set it, then tells me off for putting the water glasses above the forks. The woman who lived in a biohazard so bad she had to squat on her own porch is now lecturing me about dinner-party etiquette.

The food is good. Better than good. Sautéed chard and onion made into a frittata. I polish my plate and wonder why we didn't think to eat the food we planted.

I do the dishes, Lettie dries. Then we watch TV. Splinter on the couch between us.

"You let your dog sit on the couch?"

"Yes." I give her your *no arguments* voice.

"Does your mother know?"

I give her a bird eye of my own. "Do you see my mother?"

That gets a snort out of her. "Fair enough." She pats Splinter, then looks at her hand and sniffs it. "What the hell's on your dog?"

"Dog balm."

"Christ on a bike. They have balm for dogs now?"

"Yep."

She sniffs her hand again. "Not bad." She rubs it into her wrists.

We stare at the news. More dead people.

"Rae?"

"Mm?"

"Can we watch one of those cooking shows? The competition ones? I haven't had a working TV in so long, and I'd really like to watch one."

She doesn't have to ask me twice. We watch it to the end. Then find some other cooking shows on SBS.

Then it's nine. Lettie yawns. "I'm tired, Rae. I need to get some sleep. I can just sleep here, if you want to go on to bed."

"But I sleep—"

Lettie looks at the pillow, my duvet and yours folded neatly over the back.

"Ah," she says softly. "Seems like I'm not the only one who sleeps on chairs." We don't look at each other. "So, where do you want me to sleep, then?"

What would I do if you were really coming back next week? I'd offer your bed. I look at your duvet folded over the back of the couch. The last person to sleep in those sheets was you. They still smell like you. Or they did, before they started smelling a bit damp. "You can sleep in Mum's room." I stand up, pull your duvet off the couch and give it a shake. I don't think there's too much dog hair on it. "I'll put the electric blanket on for you." Lettie's probably been sleeping on a pile of rags for most of the time I've known her.

I try not to worry about the damp, unslept-in sheets and dog-hair duvet.

Lettie gets up and follows me in. “And you?”

I look back at the couch. “I’ll sleep in my bed.”

I PUT LETTIE’S things in the dryer before I go to bed. It rumbles, making the house breathe soft warm air.

I leave my bedroom door open. Splints pads in and lies on the floor. He’s asleep in minutes.

It feels odd to be lying flat; the sheets are cold and slightly damp against my calves. I close my eyes and listen to the house. The slow huff of Splinter’s breath mingles with the warm hum from the dryer and Lettie snoring like a bear, with the noise from the docks just audible underneath.

DAY 45

TUESDAY

WE BOTH SLEEP in until seven twenty-five.

Well, it's a sleep-in for me. I assume it is for Lettie too, based on the way she rushes around shouting about her clothes and her things and how people should *leave well enough alone*.

I get her things from the dryer. She snatches them off me but leaves your clothes on. I let her. Why not?

We eat breakfast in uncomfortable silence. There's only toast. I don't have enough milk left for more than two cups of tea. Lettie drinks hers, scowling, while I pull my uniform on. Should I offer her a toothbrush? She's already packing her clothes into a green bag she's found somewhere in the kitchen. Bugger her, then.

"Those people'll be over soon. I'd better get going."

"All right."

She stops at the door. "Sorry I'm a bit testy." She waves her hand in the direction of her house. "Thanks, Rae. It was nice to stay. You're good company."

"Okay."

"I'm just used to being on my own."

I nod.

"Okay. Bye."

"Bye."

The door clicks shut behind her: the house is ours again. Splints sniffs at the front door and whines.

I turn the heating off. I sit at the kitchen table and watch the clock tick to 8:00 a.m. I pull out my homework. I've got forty-five minutes till I need to leave. Just enough time to do a perfectly unremarkable job.

IT'S A BAG dump, oil burner top-up and a quick hustle out the door when I get home. I reckon I've got about a ten-minute window before Oscar comes around. Splints is okay with the hurry. I've got his lead on and I'm stepping backward out the door when I bump into something. Worse than Oscar, it's Lucy.

"Hi, Rae, is your mum home?"

"Oh, hi, Lucy." I give her my brightest smile and pretend like I didn't hear her question, pulling the front door firmly shut. Splinter bumps into her, forcing her back off the porch onto the front path. "We were just going for a walk."

"Is your mum home? I just wanted to have a quick word."

"Mum works late Tuesdays."

There's that frown again. "She leaves you alone?"

"I'm nearly eleven." I straighten up and look her in the eyes. "I'm old enough not to need after-school care now." Ha. Like I've ever been to that. "If I do all my homework before Mum gets home

I'm allowed to pick what I watch before bed." You always said it was the irrelevant details that convince people.

"And I keep an eye on things too." Lettie. She's leaning on the side fence. Nosy old goat. She gives Lucy a smile.

"Hm. Okay." Lucy gives her a tight smile and looks back to me. "Tell her I'd like to catch up for a chat. Okay, Rae?"

"Sure. I think we're free this weekend?" I can be out all weekend.

She goes. I don't like the look she gives me as she shuts the gate. We watch her walk back to her house.

"You're not going to dodge that one, no matter how friendly you get with her kid."

I shoot Lettie a look. Those cleaning people are still hanging around. They have a creepy habit of appearing out of nowhere.

Right on cue: "Okay, Lettie, that's all fine to walk on now." This one has the face mask off now. They all do. There are four of them peering out the front door, grinning. "All the furniture's in. And we've hooked up the washing machine in the laundry." They grin at her some more.

I can feel Lettie's bird eye radiating through the back of her head. They continue to grin, though it seems a little strained now.

"Come and see!" They look at me. "Your little friend should come see too." They turn their cheerful smiles my way. I lean away from the fence.

"She's not my little friend."

My cheeks heat up and I turn to go. Typical Lettie.

"She's my *friend*. Don't be so patronizing."

"Sorry, Lettie." Four grown-ups apologizing to her like kids who've been told off.

I smirk. She turns to me and winks. "Come and have a look, then."

I DON'T RECOGNIZE the place.

The walls are white, the floor polished and gleaming. There's neat uncluttered furniture, the comfortable basics only. A small couch and an armchair, the bookshelves and a side table. A bed and a dresser in the bedroom. A table and chairs in the kitchen. Empty shelves.

Everything's gone. After all the fighting and refusal to allow anything to be taken, *everything* is gone.

"Lettie."

She looks at my face. Her chin quivers slightly before her face sets into old goat. "Don't look so horrified. It's not all gone. I've still got the books." She gestures to the front room.

"Just the books?"

"And some other bits and pieces. The things that weren't broken or . . ."

"Where?" I look around at the rooms. There's nothing on any surfaces. Not a jar or a vase or even a coaster. I glare at the white suits. "What did you do with all her *stuff*?"

"Isn't it great?"

"No!"

They look shocked.

"What did you do with all her stuff? It was hers. You can't just *take* it." An image of Lettie's face when I tried to throw away the first pile of newspapers flashes through my mind. I glance at her. Her face is as blank as the inside of her house.

"What have you done?"

"Relax, kiddo. I told them to take it."

"What?"

"I couldn't watch. I just wanted to go out and have it all taken care of. I pointed out everything that had to stay. They called me about stuff that they weren't sure of. And I left. I've still got the books, and some other things in boxes." She walks over to the bed and lifts the hem of the quilt. Clear plastic containers are lined up underneath, each filled with things. One seems to be full of balls of wool. Another's a jumble of stacked papers. I spot some kids' toys, photo albums.

"Is this it?"

"No. The spare room has lots more boxes like this too."

"But why are they in there? Why not have them out? It's the same as taking them away. They may as well have—"

"Rae. They had to go in there."

"Why?" I glare at the white suits.

"It's okay, Rae."

"No! It's not. They've come in here and taken over your life, this is your house, your things. They were supposed to help, not . . . not *erase* it all."

"Rae."

"Lettie!" Her calmness is killing me. I want to stamp my foot. How can she be okay with this? I blink back tears.

"Rae, they *needed* to go in boxes." Lettie touches my arm. The white suits look awkward.

"No. It's not fair they've just come in here and—"

"Rae, they smelled. They even steam-cleaned what they could. Aired them out. But they're—"

"It never bothered you before!"

"Rae."

"Stop saying that! Stop it. Stop trying to pretend this is okay!" I wipe wet off my cheek. "That *you're* okay with this."

"I am okay with this."

"*No.* No, you're not!"

"It's not forever." One of the suits steps further into the room. "We've put odor-eating spray, bicarb and mothballs and things in with them—maybe in a while they might be okay again."

"Come on, kiddo." Lettie peers into my face and gives me a smile. I shrug her off. She hands me a tissue. I look at her feet. She's still wearing your socks. She sighs. "Okay. You wait here. I'll see everyone out."

I ignore their looks as they leave.

I can hear talking on the front porch. I catch snippets . . . *sweet she's so protective* . . . and Lettie's voice: *she's a good kid.*

I kick one of the boxes. It smashes into the wall behind the bed and the quilt slips down, covering them all up again.

The place is quiet when Lettie steps back in.

She hands me another tissue. "Come on. I'll show you something." She takes me to the spare room, opens the door. It's filled with large clear plastic containers. All full. All full of crap, floor to ceiling, with space left for the window and to squeeze in between, like tiny supermarket aisles.

She smiles. "See?"

"Is this everything?" I blow my nose.

"No."

"Did they throw everything else out?"

"Some of it."

I raise an eyebrow.

"A lot of it." Her smile fades a bit.

I sniff. “It’s pretty organized, I guess.” I glance up at the boxes near the top; they stretch up to the ceiling. “There’s a lot in here, still.”

Lettie smiles. “You should see the shed.”

“INSIDE KETTLE?” LETTIE waves a shiny new-looking electric kettle at me from the kitchen. “Shall we sit at the table?”

Her kitchen is nice now. Chairs; a table you can sit at. A gleaming clean floor. But it smells like chemicals and paint and whatever they put on the floorboards. And something else that I’m not sure is actually there or is just a nose memory. Something pungent, and animal. The scalpy overripe smell of its past.

I tell her I’d rather sit on the porch.

She nods and follows me out. Flicks on the old kettle on her tea chest.

“Aren’t you sad, Lettie?”

She watches the kettle boil. “I don’t know why I stay, really. It’s worse that it’s clean. It’s like going back to a place that you remember only to find it’s not there anymore.”

I sit very still.

“Memories are a bit like houses, don’t you think? They scaffold all this stuff. Curate it; give things a place so you feel safe and secure. And you step through the rooms and remember what was. But it’s not real, they’re just walls. And before you know it, most of your life is just memories, some of them not even that clear. And it’s just a house that reminds you what it felt like when you thought it was a home. You don’t realize how ephemeral it is. How temporary. That it’s just all going to be something you remember. And the memories that made you feel safe, made you feel like you, are just a flimsy reminder of what's gone to dust and that every second that passes is going to be the same, just something you remember."

She stares back at the house. "Past is past. The dead don't come back. Maybe it's best just to let them go." She gives me a bright smile, like she's just realized who she's talking to. "Anyway. Tea?"

I stare at her. The clink of the spoon comes from far away, a muffled underwater sound. The breath in my ears ripples into whispers in my head, all speaking at once, drowning out the sound in a rolling breaker through my brain. There are tiny little spots on the inside of my eyes, fogging up my sight, and no matter how I blink I can't clear them away. There's static in my head and my breath drags like a net. I'm drowning in breath. I'm losing you again. I hear the creak of the rope and the bang of the door and feel the air move against my skin.

Time stops. I hang in the dark between then and now. It's soft here. I can smell you. The you before. The you that smelled of citrus body cream and shampoo. I can feel your fingers on my hand. *We're all we've got.*

There's a weight in my lap and a wetness on my palm. My fingers curl around something soft and warm. Someone else is breathing, slow and wet. Then a sigh. Splinter. I open my eyes and watch him lick my fingers.

Lettie's talking to me, quietly. She's leaning across from her chair, peering into my face. "Just breathe, Rae. Nice and slow. There's no rush. Nowhere to be. Nice, slow breaths. We'll just sit here, okay? We'll just sit here quietly."

I look at Splinter's head in my lap. My fingers are tangled in the fur at his neck. After a few minutes Lettie leans back. I hear her opening a jar; that spoon tinkle.

"Here. Extra honey." She hands me a cup of tea that smells like grass. "Chamomile. Drink it."

I do. It tastes like grass. With honey.

"What happened there, Rae?"

I shrug.

"Want to talk about it?"

"Not really."

"Have you had anything to eat today?"

"Course I have. I'm fine."

Lettie makes a sound in her throat that tells me she's not happy about my response. "Want to know what I think just happened?"

I watch my fingers curling and uncurling in Splinter's fur. "Do I have a choice?"

"Not really." Her voice is gentle. "I think, Rae, that maybe you are not coping as well as you'd like everyone to think."

"I'm fine, Lettie. I'm just . . . tired." And I am. Stone body-tired. If she'd just be quiet I'd sleep in the chair.

"Maybe I should call your mum, just let her know it might be a good idea to come home a bit earlier. What do you think? Would that help?"

I close my eyes before they can betray me. "I'm fine."

"You're not." I've not heard this voice before. It's soft, the kind of voice that would be accompanied by a kiss good night and a big warm hug from above. The kind of voice that tucks you in at night.

I swallow the ocean and make myself look at her. "Just leave it, Lettie. Please."

She looks troubled.

I finish the tea and stand up. "I'm fine." I flash my teeth at her. Flick my fingers at Splinter.

She watches us until we go inside and close the door.

DAY 46

WEDNESDAY

OSCAR'S HANGING OVER his gate as I walk home from school. "Let me walk your dog with you?"

"Can't." I gesture at my bag and keep walking. "I've got lots of homework."

He calls after me. "Are you going to read to Lettie?"

"Why?" I stop, but don't turn around.

"Can I come?"

I'm too tired for nice. "No."

"Why not?"

"She doesn't like you." I start walking again.

"Mum asked me when I last saw your mum."

I stop. "What did you say?"

"Well, I thought I saw her out the window on Monday, walking toward the station. So I told her that."

I nod. "She leaves early."

"So, can I come over?"

I turn to look at him. "You liked my book?"

He blinks at the change of direction. "Yes? It was really different. I liked it."

"Don't you read stuff like that?"

"Not really."

"Maybe I could come and see what you've got? Maybe tomorrow or something? It's just I really can't today. I've got chores and homework stuff."

"Sure." He smiles happily. "See you then."

"Great." I walk off.

Seems I'm in demand. Lettie's waiting out the front of hers. For me, obviously: she's leaning on the fence.

"Good day?"

I shrug.

"Want a cuppa?"

"Nah. Thanks. I've got homework to do." I open the front door.

"I've got some more of those biscuits. And some pigs' ears for Dog-Balm."

Splints pushes past my legs and sprints over to the side fence, tail helicoptering madly. I give him a whistle. He ignores me and tries to scramble over to Lettie.

Lettie raises an eyebrow; she shakes the biscuit tin at me. I haven't been to the shops. My tummy growls.

"Fine." I dump my bag in the hall and close the door again.

"Oh, well. Don't let me twist your arm. I could just eat them all myself."

I ignore her sarcasm and open the gate for Splints. He doesn't need to be told; he's over to Lettie's so fast his paws slip on the footpath. I follow him and help myself to a biscuit as I sit down.

"I knew you couldn't say no to those." Lettie smirks and flicks on the kettle.

I speak around the delicious glug in my mouth. "I'm just saving you from yourself. You don't want to get diabetes."

"You're too kind."

I take another bite. "I know."

"Where'd a ten-year-old kid get such lip?"

"I learned from the best."

"Your mum?"

"No, you ninny, you."

Lettie laughs so hard she starts to cough and I have to make her a cup of tea.

WE'RE STILL SITTING on the front porch when the car pulls up. I should have known she'd be back. She steps onto the footpath, all business cardigan and sensible shoes. I can't get out of there without looking as if I'm running away. I have a go anyway.

"I'll give you some privacy, Lettie." I put my cup down.

"Sure." Lettie motions me to go.

The councilwoman stops me on the step. "Rae, isn't it?"

I nod.

"Yes. I spoke with your mum. Over here a lot, are you?"

"Not really. I just pop over. I read to Lettie."

She looks at Lettie. "Is there a problem with your eyesight?"

"No, no no no." She throws me a death stare. "She just likes to practice her reading."

"Is this every day?" She looks from Lettie to me.

"Most days." I give a toothy smile, willing my eyes to sparkle.

Lettie looks like she wants to kick me. The councilwoman looks at her. "Is this a formal arrangement?"

"No. No."

She turns back to me. "Your mum was aware of the state of—"

"We never went inside. I just visit for a bit sometimes."

"Hmm. And where's your mum now?"

I trot out the meeting line, a version of the ones I've given to Lucy. It doesn't sound as convincing in front of this woman, somehow. She eyes me like she's working out how much I weigh.

"Hmm. What school do you go to?"

Shit. I tell her. Big smile.

Lettie clears her throat. "Should you be getting home, Rae? I've got something to take care of here."

She doesn't have to ask me twice. I mutter something about homework and slink off.

I check the letter box on the way inside. There's a notice for you to collect something from the post office that requires *sighting photo ID.* I flip the card over. Anyone can collect it as long as the back's signed. I relax and look at the next letter. It's a fat envelope from the real estate agent. I open it and read the first page.

Rent is late.

I look up to see the councilwoman and Lettie watching me. I give them a smile and a wave.

Rent is *14 days in arrears.* I have *14 days to vacate.* I put the letter in my pocket and walk Splinter inside, slightly surprised that my legs still work.

I CAREFULLY PRINT my name on the back of the post office slip and then sign your name. There's a hollow buzzing in the pit of my stomach. Something hard and electric's sparking and spinning, twisting my guts into a knot, making the shadow-rat writhe and claw. The electric hiss fills my ears. I focus on finding my student ID, your phone and a beanie. I snap on Splinter's lead and walk out the front door with purpose, not looking to see if Lettie and Cardigan are watching. Not looking at anything at all.

It's raining. That nothing-drizzle that's close to invisible but soaks you through in minutes. I'm glad. The footpaths are empty. I tie Splinter to the pole outside the post office; he sits in the wet and looks pathetic. I wait in line behind an old lady with a shopping trolley, a man in a suit and someone carrying a pile of parcels so high they have to peer around it to see. There's only one cashier open, and it's taken up with a woman in a checked coat weighing tiny boxes and then passing them over the counter one by one.

Splinter barks outside. The woman weighs her last box. We all step forward. The trolley lady's buying stamps, all paid for with coins. Another person comes out from the back. They step out from behind the counter and shut the automatic door. Five o'clock. The old lady finishes with her coins. We step forward. She gets stuck at the door and has to be let out. Splinter whines at me through the glass. The suit man buys an Express Post envelope, the person with the pile of parcels stumbles forward and drops them on the counter. I look down at the slip and my photo ID.

"Next."

I look up. The other cashier's opened the second counter. It's a wonder that I can hear anything over the buzzing in my ears. I step up and hand over the slip and my ID.

She says something to me. I watch her lips to see if I can make sense of it. She says it again. "This has to be picked up by an adult."

"But that's my mum." I point at your name on the delivery slip.

"She'll have to come and collect it."

"She can't."

"Well, I can't give it to you."

"But she signed it. She put my name there. I've got my ID." I say it slowly, reasonably.

"I'm sorry, but I can't. You'll have to tell your mum to come and get it herself."

"But she told *me* to come and get it."

"It has to be signed for by an adult."

I point at your signature, the one I wrote. "She did sign for it. She can't come and get it, that's why I'm here."

"Can you get another adult to come and sign for it?"

I fight to keep my voice level. "No, we don't have anyone else."

The parcel person's gone. Both cashiers are staring at me now.

"My mum asked me to get it. She signed, see?" I point to the signature again. "I've got my ID." I pick it up off the counter and show them, keeping calm, keeping reasonable. Why can't they just help?

They look at each other. "We just—"

I want to scream at them.

"Oh. Sweetheart. Don't cry, just get your mum."

"But I can't! She's at work. She asked *me* to get it." I wipe at my face, making myself meet their gaze.

"Can you get someone else—"

"There is no one else!" To my horror it comes out in a sob, with a snot bubble. Then, so quiet I don't know if they can hear: "She signed it." I point to the signature again. My throat hurts. I try to breathe slowly, to swallow.

The cashier from the other counter gives the one in front of me a look. "I'm going out the back."

I watch her go. Is she calling someone? What was that look about? I glance back at the lady in front of me. She's holding the digital signing device.

She looks me in the eyes and speaks very slowly, like I might have trouble understanding her. "It has to be signed right here"—she points to the place on the screen—"with this." She holds up the stylus. "By an adult."

The other one comes back and slides an envelope onto the counter next to the stylus and leaves again. I stare at it. It's addressed to you. I look back up at the woman behind the counter. I think she winks at me; it's so quick I can't be sure. She pushes the stylus toward me. "*Must* be signed." She gives me a look and knocks the slip onto the floor. "Oh dear, I'd better pick that up."

Has she gone crazy? She disappears beneath the counter. I stand there. There's a movement in the door to the back. The other woman's head pokes out, she waves her hand at me frantically. Does she want me to leave? She makes a writing motion in the air, points at me.

"I just can't see where this went." The voice comes up from behind the counter. "For all I know an authorized adult could come in and *sign for that* and *take the envelope* and *go*."

I step forward, glancing at the head peering around the door again. She nods at me. I pick up the pen thing, waiting for her to tell me off. She smiles and disappears.

I swallow and sign, grab the envelope and get the hell out of there.

My fingers are shaking as I untie Splinter. I risk a glance as I pull him away. The two women are behind the counter again. They give me a wave.

I walk to the playground round the corner, my legs like planks.

I sit in the dry under the play equipment, grateful for the drizzle. There's no one else here. I open the envelope.

It's got the same stuff as the other letter. I read each page carefully. Not much of it makes sense but I get the message: fourteen days' *Notice to Vacate*, and there's a copy of the *application to the Tribunal for a Repossession Order.* Repossession of what? Does it mean they can take our things too? Is that what happens when rent is late?

The last thing is a notice of objection. I do object. But what can I possibly say? It says to fill it in and return it by *4:00 p.m. of the last day of the notice period.* I don't know what that means. Do they mean before the fourteen days are up? They say I can contact the Tenants' Union for advice. I look at the number. What would I tell them? It'd be the whole *you have to be an adult* all over again. I stare at the first page. *Notice to Vacate.* Where will I go?

Rent in arrears. How? It should have been paid.

I pull out your phone and log in to the bank account and . . . I don't get it. There's still money there. Last time it just took the rent out automatically.

I look again. It says the rent came out two weeks ago, but there's a note next to it. *Insufficient funds, transfer declined.* I don't understand. I checked weeks ago that there was enough money.

I look down the transaction history. Automatic deductions for internet, Netflix, power, phone; transactions at the gas station, the gas station, Coles, Coles, Chemist Warehouse, Coles, pizza . . . The list of transactions is long. I look at it all: it's food, essential oils, vaporizers, mosquito coils, gas bill, pizza.

I spent the money. It seemed like there was so much there.

This is my fault.

I don't know what to do. I look at the notices on my lap, trying to force back the hissing in my head. Trying to focus. What does this mean? Will someone come to the house and kick me out? Will they take all our stuff? Should I just take what I can and leave before they get there?

Then I think about you and the hissing gets louder. My tongue swells to twice its size in my mouth. What about you? I try to swallow, working hard to push the saliva down. Do I leave you behind? I vomit into the wood chips under the slide, long throat-wrenching heaves that leave me breathless; ribbons of drool hang from my lips.

I move away and put my head on the ground. The wood chips are cool and painful under my cheek. I just want to lie in a ball and rest my head here.

I'm so tired.

I wipe my mouth on my sleeve and watch as Splinter licks up my spew.

OSCAR MUST HAVE been watching out his window, waiting for us to walk by. We're only about five steps past his gate when he comes racing out his front door.

"Rae!"

"What." I turn to look at him, hoping the look on my face will be enough of a hint to go away.

"Wow. You look awful."

"Shut up."

He looks shocked, then gives me a half smile like I must be joking. "Do you want to come over?"

"Oh my god, no! Can't you take a hint? Just leave me alone." I don't wait for his reaction. I leave him standing in the drizzle. I dare the world to make this worse. Let it try. I don't even care anymore.

DAY 47

THURSDAY

WHAT AM I doing here?

I don't sleep. I'm back on the couch, with Splinter asleep on the floor beside me. I watch the night go black. Then, eventually, back to gray.

When the currawong's finished its morning shout-out I pull on your dressing gown and go sit in the damp grass next to you. I sit with my back to the door. The long grass I left near the door is up to my shoulders now. I lean my head back against the wood. I imagine you sitting on the other side so we're back-to-back, the door between us.

"What do I do?"

I imagine you breathing. Tracing your fingers across the ground, like you'd do on the kitchen table when you couldn't look at me. Like you'd do on my back when I couldn't sleep.

"I don't know what to do."

I hear a scratching. Splinter's at the back door. I can see his paws reaching up onto the glass, his claws tapping, his nose breathing onto the panes. He keeps at it for a while before I hear a loud snuff. He's settled with his nose pressed underneath. Smelling us, out here, without him.

I can feel my bum getting wet through your bathrobe. I pull the towel away from under the door. If I sniff under it like Splinter, will you hear? Will I smell you? I pull out some grass stems and poke them under one by one.

I picture you watching them come through, one stem at a time. Like the drawings I used to post under your bedroom door when I was little, trying to get you to come out.

I hold my breath and listen.

"Mum?"

I know you're not there. But the silence is like a held breath, the silence of listening, the silence of our life.

I stand up and press my hands against the wood. I feel you stand up and press your hands against mine.

"Mum?"

I open the door.

I DON'T GO to school.

I don't answer your phone.

I shut the curtains and leave the lights off.

I pretend no one's home and I'm the house: an empty shell house, all my people gone. Just walls and unused furniture. I lie on the floor and watch the ceiling. Tiny half shadows from the top and bottom of the curtains pass across it with the sun.

Lettie comes knocking.

"Rae? Rae. I know you're there."

I'm not. I speak it in my head because houses have no vocal cords.

"Let me in."

No. It sighs out my windows.

I feel her waiting at the front door. I blink at the shadows on the ceiling. They wave back.

"Come over. No pressure. I'm cooking. Come over."

I close my eyes.

DAY 48

FRIDAY

I'M WOKEN BY knocking at the door. My shoulders ache from the cold floor. Splinter lifts his head off my thighs; I feel his alertness in my bones.

There's more knocking.

"Rae?"

It's Lettie. Again.

"Rae? I know you're in there. Are you okay?"

I let the house speak for me. It chooses to say nothing.

"Are you sick? Rae?" I hear the door handle rattle.

It's too much for Splinter, he skittles long-legged and hungry to the front door. Gives her a yip.

I wonder if I'm covered in dust. Maybe I'm one of the floorboards now. I wiggle a toe experimentally and feel it move. Not floorboards yet, then.

"Rae, I'm worried." The whole door rattles now. Splinter barks.

The noise makes the house flinch. "I'm not going away, Rae. Not till you open the door."

"I'm fine." I wonder if I spoke out loud or just in my head.

The door rattles again. "Rae? Come on, I'm worried."

I'm tired. I want her to go away. I try again, forcing my vocal cords to work. "I'm fine." It comes out croaky. But the door stops rattling.

"Can I come in?"

"No. I'm just tired. I'm sleeping."

"Rae."

"I've got a headache." That's true, I have.

"I'm cooking lasagna. Come over, okay?"

I turn my head so I can see down the hall. There's a shadow across the bottom of the door. Splinter paces back and forth in front of it.

"Go away, Lettie."

It hovers for a bit. Then it goes.

SPLINTER'S PACING. I hear him pushing his water and food bowls around. I don't need to see them to know they're both empty. He pads over and sticks his tongue in my ear, then blows a snuff into the side of my neck. He nudges my cheek.

He's had nothing but salt water off my face since yesterday morning. Is that how long I've been here? I think it's possible I've always been here. He snuffs again and puts his paw on my arm. My bones ache.

There's no food left in the house. Splinter's hungry.

I LEAVE YOUR damp dressing gown on the floor, crumpled in my outline like an old shell that doesn't fit. I pull on socks, a jumper, your jacket, a beanie. I'm still cold.

Splints sticks like a shadow, his nose glued to my leg. He's so clingy I don't even bother with the lead. I just put my hand down and there he is. I sink my fingers into his coat. They're the only warm part of me.

There are lights on at Lettie's. I can see through gaps in her curtains. I can see floor. I knock. She opens the door and nods for me to come in.

The house smells less chemically. Smells like food, even. Lasagna. I wonder if she can hear my stomach growling. She sits me at the table. She's bought some mince for Splinter. He inhales it from a plate in the corner—it literally takes less than a second. I watch her move around the kitchen. She has to keep checking to see where things are. She opens the same drawer three times before she pulls out a large serving spoon. There's a pile of empty tomato cans, rinsed and stacked in a box next to the bin.

She's still wearing your tracksuit.

She serves me a plate full of steaming lasagna. It burns my mouth but I eat it anyway; it scalds my throat as I swallow, making my eyes water. But there's heat in me now. I feel it radiating out of my belly.

I take another mouthful. It's good. I shove another forkful in before I've finished the first.

Lettie picks up her fork. I ignore her.

"So, it's Friday today."

I keep eating. "It usually is after Thursday."

Lettie rubs at a spot between her brows. "What I mean is, it's nearly the end of the week." She looks at me like I should know what she's getting at.

"Yep." I speak around the lasagna.

"You told me your mum would be back."

"Yep."

"Yes. You told me on Sunday that she'd be back next week."

I shove another mouthful in. "Well, that's not till after the weekend then, is it?"

"You said next week on Sunday, Rae. I assumed you meant this week."

"Well I didn't."

Lettie puts her fork down. Rests her hands on the table either side of her plate. I concentrate on my lasagna, now it's just a gloopy mess in my mouth. I chew it, swallow, take another forkful.

"Rae."

"Lettie."

She lets out a hiss through her teeth. "By god, you can be exasperating."

I keep eating; I must have swallowed some molten cheese because my throat hurts and my eyes are stinging. I take another bite.

"Kiddo, I'm just concerned—"

My fork slips out of my fingers. *Concerned*. The magic word that makes my stomach hurt. *Concerned* pretends care but it's all about making you do things. Concerned means *I know best*; *I know better*. Concerned is when your life is *not good enough*. Your mum *is not good enough*. You are *not good enough*. Concerned is a load of shit. It's a clanging warning bell to get the hell out of there, the sign that the person saying it can't be trusted. It's a door-slam of a word that means a storm is coming that will upend my life and I will have to leave. Again.

This time without you.

I didn't expect it from Lettie.

"Don't look at me like that, kiddo. I just think it's time you let me give your mum a call, okay?"

"No. Not okay."

"Kiddo."

"Just leave it, Lettie."

"I can't, Rae. You understand that, don't you?" Her voice is kind. Her face is kind.

My chest hurts.

"You shouldn't have to look after yourself. You need your mum. She should be here."

I stand. Splinter yelps. I've pushed the chair back over his tail. My fork clatters to the floor. I can't hear properly. Lettie's gesturing for me to sit down. Her mouth's opening and closing like there are words coming out.

My ears ache. "Don't yell at me!" Splinter's barking. I can't breathe. "Stop shouting."

"Rae, I'm not."

"Stop it. You don't know what I need. You don't know anything."

"Rae, please—" She stands and reaches out, her hand stretching out from your tracksuit top.

"Leave me alone." I think I must have screamed it, because she steps back, shocked.

I run for the door, Splinter at my heels.

And we're gone.

We don't go home.

We just run.

IT'S COLD. NO-CLOUDS, pinprick-stars cold. I fog my breath in front of me; it points the way, we follow.

It's too cold to stop. Too cold to sit. My back's still stiff from the floor; it feels good to move. We walk in step, Splinter's head pressed against my hip. I curl my fingers into his scruff and every now and then he turns his head and licks my wrist. We do our streets. There are new pots and chairs to replace the ones we took. We keep moving.

Even Splints tires eventually. There's barely any traffic now, so it must be late, just the regular rumble of trains and their hoots as they speed through the station. We pass under the train bridge and stand on the bottom side of the hill to watch as they speed above us, rumbling snakes with glowing bellies full of empty seats.

We end up at Yarraville Gardens. They've replaced the plants I took. Splinter flops in the wood chips near the sandpit and I swing, my back to the road, watching the lights of the docks shimmy through the trees. The cold air passes through my shoes as I swing up—hang—and down. It pushes through my socks, making my toes tingle, desperate to stretch.

The swings squeak rhythmically, a daytime sound in the dark, punctuating the random bangs and beeps from the docks. My fingers hurt on the cold chains. I bite my lips, they're numb, and I skid the swing to a stop. It's time to go home.

Splinter pounces on a stick as we walk toward the main road. I pull it out of his mouth and throw it ahead. He bounces after it, his front legs wide like an unco puppy. He snorts it back to me, weaving in tight circles around my legs, turning his head so I have to tackle him to get it back. I throw it again and he's off like a mad thing and then he's racing back, snorting like a pig and prancing like a pony as he twists himself round my legs and ducks out of reach. I lunge at him and he skitters away, shaking his stick, making me laugh. I chase him, the movement warming me up.

We burst out of the park entrance and onto the footpath. The orange of the streetlights filters through the giant branches of the overhanging trees, throwing broken shadows across our faces. Splints shakes his stick at me, and I launch myself at him, hands outstretched. He skips out of reach, eyes on me as he bounces over the grass of the nature strip. I lunge again, laughing, but he sidesteps me neatly into the gutter.

"Off the road, Splints." I go to grab his collar, using my *game's over* voice, but he snorts and pulls the stick out of reach, jumping further away from me. Something massive looms, rushing shadows into a bang-splitting screech, blowing cold air on my face, pulling the darkness into a hissing metallic howl.

I blink.

I lock my gaze back to Splints. He's not there, but there's a soft gray shape bowling across the road into a crumple in the gutter.

The smell of hot rubber in my nose. I can feel every part of my body, my limbs dread-weighted. In the quiet after, I can hear an engine tick. The cooling sound of hot metal. And then a whimper from the gutter. I move, pulling my legs under me, trying to get to upright. The air's got thick; it's hard to push against. Then the whimper comes again and all the sounds rush back.

"NONONONONONONONONONONO—" SOMEONE'S YELLING. I scramble over the road, tearing the skin on my hands. There's a truck stopped with orange lights flashing but I've no time to wonder about it. I'm kneeling beside Splinter, knees in the gutter, my hands on his big jerky body. I roll his muzzle into my lap. His mouth's a mess of foamy bubbles. He's juddering on my knees. I push my hands into his coat to try to stop his shudders; his fur's sticky and warm. I pull my fingers back and hold them up to the light. They're dark, wet and slippery. There's a metallic smell.

"Splints, it's me. *Splinter*."

An eye focuses on me and he whimpers, it comes out quiet and unbroken like he's trying to whistle. He lifts his nose, his muzzle's wrong. His lip's torn and it folds back to show me his teeth, like he's trying to smile. He manages a half lick of my hand and then his head's back down and he's shaking like an Elmo doll, a mass of twitching, jerking fur and blood. I push my palms into him, trying to make it stop, and scream for the only person who can make this all right. The only person I need.

I hear you running. The thump of heavy footsteps on tarmac. I scream your name and you slide down beside me.

"Oh my god. Oh my god, I didn't see. Are you okay? I didn't see." But it's not you. It's a big man smelling of sweat and grease, boots bigger than my forearm. The look on his face makes me feel sick. "Was it just—are you okay? Did I hit you?"

"No. I don't know. No. We have to help him. You have to help me help him."

But he's not looking at Splinter; he's looking at me. His hand hovers, afraid to touch. "There's blood on you. And on your face. Are you okay? Did I hit you?"

"I'm fine!" I hold up my bloody hands. "But he's not." I push my palms back onto Splinter's jerky body. "He's not. You have to help my dog." He's still looking at me and not Splinter.

"Ah, Christ. Sit tight. I'm calling an ambulance, okay? And the police, they have to come to an accident too, right?"

I shake my head. "No. No police. No ambulance. Just a vet, okay? We need to get him to a vet."

He's got his phone out now, but he can't swipe it open. He wipes his shaking hand on his jeans and tries again. The phone slips out of his hands and lands next to Splinter's head. He picks it up again, hands still trembling. "What are you doing out here? It's two a.m. Christ, I didn't see you. I just didn't see you."

I spot the stick in the gutter, half under Splinter's head. It must have ripped through his lip when the truck hit him. "We were playing." I rest my hand on Splinter's ear, rubbing the tip between my fingers in that way he likes. He's still whimpering but there's an edge to it now, a sharpness I've never heard before. And I know all his sounds. This one rips my stomach, letting the cold in.

The driver's still struggling with his phone. "Come on!" He swears, apologizes, wipes his hands on his jeans again. I try to shift my lap further under Splinter's head; I place one hand gently under his neck and the other on the ground near his hips so I can lever myself under him. The ground's warm and sticky. I look at his hip. His leg's hanging at a funny angle, I can see inside it, like one of the lamb legs hanging in the butcher's. There's a lot of blood. I gently touch his leg, trying to lift it back into place, trying to stop the bleeding.

"Help me." I look at the driver. I don't understand why he's wasting time. "What are you doing? You have to help me!"

He's still swiping at his phone. "I am! I'm calling for help. I'm trying. I just didn't see you." He's crying now. "Oh shit. You're covered in blood."

I look down. "It's not mine."

"You're bleeding!"

It's even in the gutter. "It's not mine."

He's sobbing now. His whole giant-man body shaking. He must be in shock. I'm vibrating with it all, Splinter shuddering on my lap and this giant man quaking at my side. I can't hold Splinter's leg in place with this crying man rocking back and forward, swiping uselessly at his screen. I don't have time for shock. I lean back as far as I can with Splinter's head in my lap and, with one hand holding Splints's leg together, I slap the driver hard across the face.

He drops his phone and looks at me. I speak at him, clearly and slowly.

"Help. Me. Get. My. Dog. To. A. Vet."

He touches his cheek with his palm. "What?"

"My dog." I gesture at Splinter. "My dog needs the help. Not me. I'm fine." My voice cracks. "I think he's dying. Please." I make eye contact, willing him to understand. "Help me get him to a vet."

He nods and puts his big hand on the shoulder of your jacket, and relief floods through me, making my hands shake. I start to move, ready to gently slide Splinter over to him.

He squeezes my arm through the jacket. "Just relax. You're in shock. I'll call the ambulance. You'll be okay." He picks up his phone again.

"No!" I slap it to the ground. "Why can't you understand?" My face is wet. "Help me . . ." I shuffle to my knees, raise Splinter's shoulders and try to lift him up; I lose my grip on his leg and it hangs out like something out of a circus. Splinter screams, the sound of it tears through me. I'm losing him, he's slipping out of my hands and the man's tugging me back down. Splinter's head slips and hits the street, the sound of it as loud as the impact of the truck. He's so broken already. The man's pulling at my jacket, trying to keep me down.

"Stay still! You're hurt. You have to keep still."

I can't see if Splinter is breathing. I kick at the driver and scream. He stands and takes half a step back. I bend over Splinter. I can hear his breath, it's uneven but it's there. I lift the front half of his twitching body into my arms, trying not to look at his back leg, trying to keep him in one piece.

I look at the driver again. "Please, help me, he needs to get to the vet." Snot bubbles out of my nose. It pops across my cheek. I'm not letting go of Splinter again. "Please!" I plead.

But the driver's shaking his head. "I have to stay here. I can't leave the scene of an accident." He's picking up his phone, swiping at it again. I can see the cracked screen in the streetlight. "I have to get help." He looks up, sees headlights on the main road.

"Help *me*!" I scream it at him, but the words don't come out right, they're all strangled, and he's running away. He yells something over his shoulder as he runs, but I can't hear it over the sound of Splinter whimpering and the strange noises coming from my throat. I place my hands gently on the underside of Splinter's rib cage. *Breathe.* I have no one to help me. I push everything else away. The man. The truck. The pain. It's just me and Splints. It's always been just him and me. I brace my legs and heave the whole of him into my arms, barely keeping his head from hitting the gutter. His yelp pierces me. I hold his shuddering body tight and stumble onto the median strip. More whimpers.

Think. Think. Think. I shake my head, keep walking. There's a vet in Yarraville. It can't be more than five or six blocks away. My arms shake; I don't know if it's me shaking or Splints. I knot my fingers in his fur, clench my teeth, and keep walking.

My arms scream, my shoulders feel like they're pulling off my back. I keep walking. The streets pass in a fog. Two steps to breathe in, two steps to breathe out. My muscles scream to stop but I don't. One step, another. *It's okay, Splinter, not long now.* My arm's wet with his blood, my face just wet. I lower my head to wipe my cheek with his fur. His marionette-jerks and his weight turn me into a heavy-legged doll.

One step, another. Hours pass, or seconds; it's just pain and fear and me and Splints.

I carried him like this when he was a puppy, but he could fit inside the circle of my arms then, not like this with his head lolling and drooling off to the side and his legs twitching like demented feelers, one hanging at an angle it shouldn't. Two steps to breathe in, two steps to breathe out. Every step makes him whimper, every whimper makes me cry. One step, another. Time stops. We have been like this always, me carrying him. Him carrying me. Two steps to breathe in, two steps to breathe out. I stumble across the main road and nearly trip over the gutter on the other side. His yelp cuts me, then he's quiet, his body heavy. He's dying and all I can do is walk. One step, another. Forever and ever. Two steps to breathe in, two steps to breathe out.

And then I'm there. It's dark. It's the middle of the night. But I'm here. I'm standing on the corner with a giant silver dog and the words VET suspended over my head. I stare into the dark glass and see a blood-streaked kid staring back, a giant dog lying broken across her arms, its leg hanging off like a cut of meat. We're silver in the streetlight. It hurts to breathe; the cold air makes my lungs tight. The girl in the reflection stares back at me, helpless. She has blood on her cheeks.

I don't know what I thought I'd find. An emergency department? Someone waiting to rush out and help? The lights are off. It's closed. My front's warm and sticky. I turn away from the girl in the window. My legs are trembling. They won't take me any further. I slip. My bum hits the step hard. I keep hold of Splints. I cradle his body across my lap; my screaming arms keep his head off the footpath.

His eyes are closed. I pull your jacket down over my hand, ball my fingers to hold the material over my knuckles, I brace Splinter in place with one hand and twist at the hips to smash my fist through the glass. The alarm goes, shrieking. A blue light flashes over my head.

The pain in my hand's sharp and cold. I let it drop and cradle Splinter's head in the crook of my elbow. His legs sink toward the ground. There's nothing else I can do. I bring my face close to his, breathing his air. "Not long now, pup. Not long now." I hold his breath in my hands, willing him to keep going. The blue light above my head flashes with my heartbeat, with our breath, with my breath. I talk to Splinter. Tell him all the things we're going to do when he's better. The walks. The games. The whole roast chicken from the supermarket. He's quiet in my lap. Heavy. I think he's still shaking, and breathing. But that could be me. He's still and I'm cold. Then he's trying to get up, but it's not him, it's someone lifting him away from me. I look up into faces I don't know. There are more lights. Someone shines a light in my face. Someone's lifting me up. My legs don't work. There are voices, but I can't make out the words. I'm underwater and everyone's swimming away from me.

"Help him. Please."

TURNS OUT A girl sitting on the step of the vet's, bloodied dog in her lap, with a broken glass door behind her and the burglar alarm going off is—finally—enough to make someone call the vet.

And an ambulance.

And the police.

I don't care.

I just need him to be okay.

No one's telling me anything.

All I get is questions.

SOMEONE GLUES UP my hand. She seems nice enough. She keeps offering me something for the pain, but I don't feel anything.

LETTIE TRIES TO pick me up from the hospital. She's not meant to. She's not a relative. She lives next door.

Where's your mother?

I don't answer.

SHE WANTS TO take me home. They won't let her. They're arguing. Lettie keeps plucking at the skin on her hands and looking at me, and they're speaking to her like she's a criminal.

"Where's her mother?"

"Away overnight. On business." She's using her *do as I say* voice but it doesn't work on them.

"Are you looking after her?"

She hesitates. Looks at me again. "Yes."

"What was she doing out on her own at two in the morning?"

"Well, I—"

"It's not Lettie's fault."

They all stop. It's the only thing I've said since I gave them Lettie's address.

"It's not her fault. She didn't know."

"If she's looking after you, she should."

"She's not looking after me. She's been looking out for me. Because she's kind." I wipe at my eyes. I can't look at her. I look at the tissues in my good hand. I still have Splinter's blood under my fingernails. "But she wasn't looking after me because she didn't know. I haven't told anyone."

They all go very still at that.

"Haven't told anyone what?"

Lettie clears her throat. "Her mum sometimes leaves, overnight, I suspect. So I've been keeping an eye out—"

"She hasn't left."

Lettie looks sad. "Away for work, then."

"Not that either."

"Where is she, then?" They're trying to be kind. But they're tired, and fed up with this kid who won't talk except to ask about her dog.

"She's at home."

Lettie's voice's gentle. "Come on, Rae, you have to tell them the truth now."

"I am. She's at home. She never left."

"Rae."

"She is." I look at Lettie, really look at her. "She's in the shed."

"Rae, don't be ridiculous."

I don't take my eyes off Lettie as I speak. "I left her there. I didn't know what else to do. So I left her there."

I see Lettie get it.

"Oh. Rae."

I can't seem to stop swallowing. She steps toward me. "Oh, Rae. Kiddo."

And then she has her arms around me. And she's still in your tracksuit, and she smells like you. And her. And Splinter. And it's the first time anyone's touched me properly since you died.

I let my head sink into her. Into Splinter. Into you.

I let go of the breath I've been holding since I first saw you there. Since I knew it was up to me.

I let go.

THEY STILL DON'T let me leave with Lettie.

They send a car round to my house. Take my keys.

It's Lettie who thinks to call Oscar's mum: she still has the card in her jacket pocket.

They let me go with her, a woman I've spoken to maybe three times. Over Lettie.

I DON'T ASK about Splinter again. The *we'll see what we can find out* answer tells me what I need to know. The way they won't meet my eyes. I don't want to know any more.

LUCY TAKES ME home. Makes me up a bed in Oscar's room. He doesn't even wake. She gives me some pajamas with cars on them; they're too big round the waist. She brings me a glass of water.

"Try and get some sleep." She touches my cheek. "Things won't seem so bad in the daylight."

I roll over to face the wall.

What would she know.

DAY 49

SATURDAY

I MUST SLEEP, because when I open my eyes Oscar's standing at the foot of the bed looking at me.

"There are police at your house."

I stare at him.

"Mum said not to tell you." He glances at the door. "But I thought, you know, that you should know." He's dressed in jeans and a green woolly jumper. He's wearing bright red socks. They look warm. He scrunches his toes up on the floorboards. "About the police, I mean."

I nod. I know what he meant.

I'M STANDING OUTSIDE, on the footpath at our front fence. I don't remember getting up, or coming out. My toes are warm. I look down. I'm wearing green wool socks, not mine. I can see the fuzziness of them poking out between my shoes and the too-short blue cord pants on my legs. Also not mine. I don't remember putting any of them on, but here I am, dressed, so I guess I did. There's a hand on my shoulder. I look up to my left. Lucy.

"Don't look, Rae."

I wonder if we came out here together. And why she's here with me if she doesn't want me to look. I can feel the weight of her hand through my wool jumper: also not mine.

I turn to see what I shouldn't be looking at.

Our front door's open. A man is walking out backward. Pulling something. You. Of course. I knew that, I knew that's what it would be.

"You don't have to look, Rae." That hand again, gently pulling at my shoulder. I know why she doesn't want me to. She thinks that if I see you like this, it's who you will be to me: that this is how I will remember you. She doesn't know about the first time when the breeze made the rope creak and your sneakers hung a hand's width above the ground. Or the last.

I watch.

I watch as they come out, and the bag looks much bigger than you on the trolley. The smell comes out too. Lucy coughs behind me, but it's not so bad. I watch as they wheel you into the back of the vehicle, the little legs of the trolley folding up neatly beneath you. They are gentle. They slide you in carefully and shut the doors quietly, no banging like a delivery truck. I wonder how often they do this. This collecting of other people's people.

The man slides into the driver's side. The woman goes around to the passenger side. She looks at me. Our gazes meet. She doesn't smile. Neither do I. She gives me a nod and I nod back because I know what she's saying with it.

She's seen you. She helped you down from where you were

stuck. She walked you through our house with the tidy kitchen and the key bowl on the table. She wheeled you past your neatly made bed and the towels hanging in the bathroom. She eased you head-first out of our home. She knows a tiny piece of you. And a tiny piece of me. And she knows that's all it is.

She gets into the van.

Someone puts the tape back across the front door.

Lucy puts a hand on my other shoulder, weighting me gently from behind.

"It's not her in there, Rae."

The things people say.

"Yes, it is."

"Well, yes, it's her body. But the her you knew, she's not in there. She's in your heart, in your memories. The way she was."

I know she means well. But she doesn't know. I know it more than she does. I know you're not one thing. Knowing you is not one thing, it was never one thing. It's a million things. And now the place holding them together is me.

I watch the van drive away.

And I say it because I never got to say it before. I say it because I wish I had, almost as much as I wish I didn't have to.

"Bye, Mum."

DAY 51

MONDAY

LUCY PUTS ME in the car and drives me somewhere, not telling me where we're going. I sit in the car and let her drive. I don't care.

I wait in the car while she puts money in the meter. We're back near the hospital, so I assume she's taking me to a head doctor. That's what they'll do now, right?

She opens the door and motions me out. I follow her through a gate. It's not the hospital. I look up to see the word VET over the door. I stop.

Lucy keeps walking for a few steps.

"I can't."

She stops. "What?"

"I can't."

"You can't what?"

"I can't see him."

She comes back and takes my hand. "It's okay, Rae."

I pull away. Remembering the weight of him. Remembering all the blood. "No, it's not. I can't see him like that."

"Like what?"

"All broken and lifeless." My voice cracks.

She smiles at me. "It's okay, Rae. There's someone waiting to see you."

I see the pet adoption sign in the window. Is she really this clueless? "No. I don't want a new dog."

Lucy frowns. "What? I'm not—"

"I don't want a new dog. I can't."

I watch her face change. "Oh god. Nobody told you." She looks horrified. She kneels on the asphalt in front of me. Takes my hands. "Rae, he's okay. He's a bit beaten up, and he lost his leg. But he's okay."

"What?" I barely get it out.

She smiles at me, still holding my hands, her stockings getting grubby. "He's inside, Rae. He's going to be okay."

Lucy has to run to keep up with me.

He's a mess when they show me in. Three legs; patches of fur missing with drips going in everywhere and stitches in his lip. He's wearing a cone of shame, and I stick my head in it and kiss him. I squeeze him too hard and he yelps and he's licking my face so much I don't know what's slobber and what's tears.

HE CAN'T COME home straightaway. Lucy tells me he can come back to her place when he's ready, which seems to make Oscar happy.

Turns out Lucy's pretty good at finding things. It's Lucy who tracks down my grandma.

I have a grandma. But you already knew that, didn't you?

Three hours after I find out she exists, I speak to her on the phone. Or rather we breathe into the same phone line. What do you say to someone you've never met? I ask her that, in one of the silences.

Her reply surprises me. "Oh, I've met you, Rae. I was there the day you were born."

That's weird. Someone who's known me since my first breath, whose face I don't even know.

I listen to her breathing some more. Then: "Do you want to come and live with me?"

What sort of question is that? I don't know anything about her. Except that you didn't tell me about her, so I guess she did something bad. Or you did.

I shrug. I know she can't see it, but I'm guessing my silence will get the message across.

I hear her clear her throat. "I'd like you to come and live with me. I haven't seen you since you were three. I guess you don't remember."

This shocks me. "No."

"Your mum and I—" And then she's crying. This woman I don't know, who's your mum who you never spoke about, who I'm now going to live with, who's known me my whole life but doesn't know me at all. I hear her take a shuddery breath. "I'm sorry about your mum, Rae. I loved her very much."

"Me too."

Then I put the phone down.

DAY 53

WEDNESDAY

LUCY TELLS ME Splints will be coming home tomorrow. I haven't been back to school yet. Lucy works from home at the kitchen desk, taking a million phone calls an hour and typing away on her laptop. I read in Oscar's room, mainly.

I want to see Lettie. But I assume I'm not allowed.

TURNS OUT I'M wrong.

Lucy has a meeting. I expect to be dragged along. I've not been more than five meters from her since she picked me up from the hospital. But when we leave the front door she doesn't walk me to the car, she walks me to Lettie's. She's on her porch. Of course.

"I've asked Lettie to keep an eye on you for a couple of hours. Okay, Rae?" She's not-smiling in that way that tells me she's really pleased with herself.

I nod, not knowing where to look.

Lucy rubs my back. "I thought it might be."

I walk up onto the porch and take my seat. It's weird doing it without Splinter.

Lettie leans forward and takes my hand. "It's good to see you, Rae."

I nod and squeeze her fingers.

She flicks on the kettle.

WE DON'T TALK much. What's left to say? We drink our drinks and enjoy the sun.

Lettie puts her cup down and gives me a smile. "I have something for you. Wait here."

She disappears inside. I wonder if she sometimes still moves like she used to in there, sideways and keeping her arms in tight against the memories of looming junk skyscrapers towering toward the ceiling, an ant in a city that threatens to collapse at any moment.

I settle into the armchair. If she's looking for something she could be a while. I can hear her muttering to herself and the containers in the spare room banging. The sound of tumbling plastic. And swearing.

"You okay in there?"

"Fine, fine." The voice gets closer, then moves away again. "I won't be a tick."

"Just making sure you weren't buried alive."

"You cheeky little—you're lucky I like you, or I wouldn't be giving you this."

"Giving me what?"

She swings the door open; it looks like there's white confetti in her hair. Or maybe feathers? And she's holding something with wheels. "This!" She holds the wheeled thing out to me.

"What is it?"

"It's for Splinter, of course."

"He can't ride."

"No, stupid. You fasten it around his middle like so." She demonstrates across her own chest. "The padded bit sits in his hip and voila! He has a leg again."

I stare at it. "It's a wheel."

"Yes. A wheelie leg."

"For dogs?"

"Yes." She's frowning at me now. Obviously she was expecting a more enthusiastic response.

"How does it work?"

She sighs, frustrated. "God, you're so dense. Like this." She crouches down so the wheel touches the porch, and mimes being a dog with a missing leg.

I bite the inside of my cheek. "Is it wheelie a good idea, though?" My voice comes out a bit squeaky. "I mean, there are no brakes, he could get wheelie"—a snort of laughter escapes, but I power through it—"wheelie hurt."

"Oh, you little—" She swats at me. But I can see she's trying not to laugh. "Do you want it or not?"

I wipe at my eyes. "Thanks, Lettie. Splints'll love it."

"A lot more grateful than you, I'll bet," she growls. But she's smiling.

I FINISH THE last of her hot chocolate. And her biscuits. The sun's still out but it's losing its heat the way it does in the afternoon in late winter. Lucy will be back soon.

"Did they let you get all your things?" Lettie tips her chin to the side, toward our house. I look at it. There's still police tape on the front door. But no one's been in there today.

"Lucy went and got some of my stuff on Monday."

Lettie nods.

"I gave her a list."

"Well, that sounds sensible."

All the unimportant things I don't know about swirl around my brain. I'm so used to keeping things in my head I don't know how to let them out. I take a deep breath and let my mouth take over. "I don't know if I'm allowed in. Rent was late, so everything probably belongs to the landlord now."

Lettie gives me a full-on bird eye. "What are you talking about?"

"I got a letter. Last week. When the councilwoman was here. Rent's late and they're going to repossess all our things."

Lettie blinks quickly for a bit then buries her face in her teacup. "They can't take your things, Rae. They can only take the house back." Her voice is gruff. "Is that why you were so upset?"

"Yes. And no."

She pulls a tissue out of her pocket and blows her nose before stuffing it back where it came from. "They can't take your things, sweetheart."

"You sure?"

"I'm sure."

"Can I go inside?"

Lettie sighs. "I don't know about that. I'm sure Lucy will help you sort something out."

I nod. "She's not so bad."

"No. She's all right, that one. For all her nosiness." She lifts the kettle. "Another?"

I shake my head. "I'm going."

"Oh." Lettie puts the kettle down and looks round. "Is Lucy back?"

"No. *Going* going." My fingers itch for Splinter's soft ears. I shove them in my pockets. "I have a grandma."

Lettie nods, like she's not surprised. "It's good, Rae. You can't stay here, in an empty house."

"You do."

She smiles a little at that. "Mine's a different kind of empty."

"Is that why you keep filling it up?"

"Touché." She pulls her jacket around her shoulders. "I'm old. I'm allowed to pretend. You're young. You shouldn't know about empty. Not yet."

"But I do."

"I know, kiddo." Her toes twitch. I wonder if they're missing Splinter too.

"I don't want to go."

Lettie nods. "That's understandable."

"I don't even know her."

"I imagine she's just as nervous as you are."

I hadn't thought about that. "But she lives three hours away. I have to move."

"Whereabouts?"

"I don't know. Somewhere down the coast. In the *country*."

"Well, that sounds nice." Her voice is pleasant. She smiles like we're acquaintances chatting in the supermarket.

"Does it? Does it, Lettie? Moving away somewhere hours from here, away from everyone, sounds *nice*, does it?"

Lettie tips her head to the side, her gaze steady. "And who would they be, these *everyone* you're going to miss so much?"

I look at my feet. She's silent, waiting for my answer. "Just you, really."

"Well, that's not a problem, then, is it?"

I glare at her.

She hands me a clean tissue from her other pocket. "I've got a lovely shiny car. And now I've got somewhere to drive it." She beams. "And bonus, that big hairy hound will already be down there, so I won't have his farts stinking up the interior."

"You'll visit me?"

"Of course I bloody will. You idiot." We grin at each other. "Now wipe your eyes before Lucy turns up and I get banned from spending time with you again."

DAY 54

THURSDAY

I MEET HER the day before we leave. How is that fair?

She comes to Lucy's place before lunch.

I sit in the kitchen and wait for Lucy to let her in.

She looks like you.

You but not you. I didn't expect that. Her hair's gray and her face is fuller, with the lines in different places, but you're similar enough that if I'd seen her in the street it would've made me stop.

She stands in the doorway.

"You look like her." We say it at the same time.

Lucy laughs awkwardly and offers some tea. Old-you sits down across the table. We look at each other while Lucy boils the kettle and gets out milk and sugar. She makes me an herbal tea, apple and ginger. It smells much nicer than that chamomile stuff Lettie gave me.

"I'll leave you two to it." She smiles at us. "I'll just be in the next room if you need me." She slips out. I notice she leaves the door ajar.

Old-you clears her throat. "So."

I take a tiny sip of tea so I can unglue my mouth. "So."

She doesn't take her eyes off my face. "I've enrolled you at the local school. It's a nice place. Your mum went there." I imagine you at school. "You don't have to go straightaway, of course. If you'd like some time to settle in?"

"I don't mind."

She nods and swallows. "Right. We'll play it by ear and see how it goes."

We look at our tea.

"How's your hand?" She peers at my bandage.

I hold it up. "It's fine."

"I'm very sorry—" Her voice cracks and she stops. She lifts her cup and takes a sip, swallows. Her hands are trembling and the cup hits the table too hard when she puts it down.

There's a crash outside the door. Old-you jumps slightly and turns just as Splinter pushes his head through the crack.

"Oh. A dog."

I get up to open the door for him. He's stuck. He keeps banging into things and getting his cone snagged. "This is Splinter." Splints hops in, his back stump still wiggling like he's moving his invisible leg.

"What's that plastic thing around his neck?"

"It's a cone. To stop him from licking his wound." I sit down again, and Splints hops after me and lays his cone-head in my lap with a sigh. I reach in and scratch between his eyes.

"What happened to his leg?"

I creep my fingers across and massage his ears. "He got hit by a truck."

"Oh. This is the . . . Oh, I see."

Splints sighs and goes to sit, and crashes into the table leg. I grab him to save him from tumbling over.

"He's a bit clumsy, isn't he?" Old-you is mopping up her tea from the table with a tissue.

"He's just getting used to it. They said that will get better after the first few days. As good as a regular dog."

I scratch him under the chin. He wobbles a bit and I help him down onto his side. He lies down with a soft huff and is asleep almost immediately.

"Everything okay?" Lucy pops her head round the door. She takes in the spilled tea and Splinter sleeping on the floor and smiles. "I see you've met Splinter."

Old-you gives a tight smile. "Yes."

I scratch his side gently with my toes. "He's sleeping a lot at the moment. It's the pain medication." His side where his leg used to be twitches in his sleep. "And maybe the shock."

"Well, losing a limb would be an adjustment for any creature, I suppose." Old-you peers at Splints sleeping on the floor.

"He's still a bit wobbly with sitting." I think about him crashing into the door. "And standing." I consider the last day he's been back. "And lying down and getting up."

"Sounds like a lot of work—"

"He's a bit clumsy at the moment," Lucy agrees. "But the vets tell us he'll be as good as new when the pain settles down, a few days, apparently. They're remarkably resilient, dogs."

"He gets his stitches out in a week."

"Well, it's good of you to take such good care of him. You've been remarkable. Two children, work and a handicapped dog." Old-you puts out a hand to touch Lucy's arm.

"He's not handicapped."

"Pardon?"

"He's not handicapped. He's a tri-pawed."

Old-you laughs at that. "Tri-pawed. That's great." She smiles at sleeping Splinter. "A tri-pawed dog."

Lucy gives me a wink and leaves us to it. Old-you gets out of her chair and crouches beside Splints. She pats his head gently. He opens an eye and gives her a half lick, before going back to sleep again.

"I'm not really a dog person. I've never had one of my own." She watches him sleeping, strokes his ear. "He's very soft, isn't he? He doesn't look like he'd be soft." I watch her patting him. "So, I assume he's named after Master Splinter from the *Teenage Mutant Ninja Turtles*?"

I look at her in surprise. "Yes."

"Hmm." She runs her hand gently over Splinter's neck. "They're still around, are they?"

I shrug. "I think so."

She peers up at me. "Well, that's a strange answer. Either they are or they aren't. Don't you watch them?"

"Not really. I didn't name him. Mum did."

She smiles. "Your mum loved those turtles growing up."

I don't know what to say to that. I just nod.

She stands up again, her knees cracking loudly as she sits back in her chair. She gives Splints a pat with her foot. "A good name, though. He looks a bit like a mangy old rat, except with longer legs."

I don't disagree. "That's what Mum reckoned."

"What is he? A deerhound? A wolfhound?"

"Maybe. We got him from the Lost Dogs as a puppy. They weren't sure."

"I bet he was one funny-looking pup."

I smile.

She scratches Splints's shoulder with her shoe, and he opens his eye and tries to give her foot a lick.

"What do I call you?"

"What?" The change of subject seems to confuse her.

"What do I call you?"

"Oh. I thought you knew." A shadow scuttles across her face, deepening her brow wrinkles. "Of course you don't remember. You called me Nenee." She smiles at me.

The name catches me by surprise. "I did?"

"You did."

So you didn't delete her completely. "Should I call you that again?"

"If you like."

Splinter claw-scrabbles to sit up and drops his head in my lap with a sigh. I consider if I should tell her, so she knows you kept a part of her with us.

"I have a bunny, a toy, called Nenee."

She smiles. "That gray one? With the big ears? I gave you that." For the first time she speaks like she's not measuring each word, and her eyes crinkle at the edges. "I never could work out if I was named after the bunny or the bunny was named after me."

I stare at her. For a split second you were looking out at me. When she smiled.

I don't like it.

DAY 55

FRIDAY

ALL MY STUFF'S in boxes. Lucy and I packed it last night, all the things I wanted to keep with me. There wasn't much. It fills three cardboard cartons and a couple of small bags. My books, Bunny-Nenee, my clothes. I packed your duvet and dressing gown. Lucy didn't question it, she just went and found one of those big checked laundry bags to fold them in. I put your broken alarm cube in with a bag of my books. We don't have a lot of photos. I packed what I could find, along with your phone and laptop.

When we were done I stood and looked at everything that was left, our whole life in objects. Lucy says people will come and pack it, put it in boxes, all labeled so we'll know where everything is. I don't know how I feel about that. More strangers touching our things. Part of me doesn't want our life boxed up; part of me wants it to go into the boxes and stay there.

Lucy says they'll pack everything except food, which she's donating somewhere. I don't bother to tell her there won't be much of that. I wonder if they'll pack the half-used laundry liquid and the bag of rubber bands and random pipe cleaners in the bottom drawer of the kitchen. The truck's coming the day after tomorrow. Lucy arranged that too. It's all going into storage near Nenee's till we *figure out what to do with it.*

I HAVEN'T BEEN back to school since before the letter. Lucy asked if I wanted to go back, just for the morning, to say good-bye. I like the kids there. I like my teachers. But I don't want to say good-bye. I don't want the questions.

Anyway, there's only one person I really want to say good-bye to. She's on her porch, as always.

"Leaving today, then."

"Yep."

She gets to her feet and holds out an arm. I wonder if she's going to hug me. She opens the door. "Come inside. I've got something for you."

We follow her in. It's still a bit of a shock to step into a hall that's so light and airy. Splints gets his cone caught on the doorway, so I help him through. There's a box next to the door half-filled with junk mail and catalogs. We trip over it and follow her into the front room.

"Here." She shoves something into my hands.

I look at it. It's a book. It's *the* book. The one we were reading, back when the stitches were still holding, before everything tore itself apart. Her daughter's book. Lana.

"But this is—"

"No. I couldn't give you that."

I swallow. "Of course not."

"It was too smelly. I got this one new, from the internet." She looks pleased with herself.

"You have the internet?"

"Of course I have the internet. The whole suburb has the internet. Haven't you heard of the NBN?"

"But you don't have a computer."

"True enough. I might get one, though. Read the papers online like you suggested."

I stare at her in confusion. "So how did you order the book?"

"On the internet."

"But you don't have a computer."

"I used my phone, you ninny."

"Really? I didn't think you even knew how to use the browser."

"The what?"

"The web browser. Safari?"

"What?" She looks at me like I'm speaking in Parseltongue. "No, I called Chris and he ordered it on the internet for me. They delivered it straight to my door. Very handy. Nicely packaged too. Look at this."

She snatches the book off me and slides it in and out of the cardboard packaging. "See?"

"That's great, Lettie."

"Yes. I thought so." She hands me back the book. "I think I'll keep this, it might come in handy." She drops the box into a basket next to the chair. "I wrote a little something in the front for you. You don't have to read it now."

But I've already opened it.

A book about a brave, resourceful kid for the bravest, most resourceful kid I've had the pleasure to spend time with. Don't forget me, kiddo. I'll never forget you. Lettie.

"I've put my phone number there too, in case you lose it." Her voice is gruff.

The words blur in front of me.

"Thanks, Lettie." I blink, but not in time to stop a tear from splatting on her neat writing. I wipe at it, my finger smudging the first *brave*. I rub at my eyes, mad at them for ruining something so special.

Lettie gently pulls my wrists away from my face. "Come on." She puts her arm around my shoulder. "Let's go have a last cup of tea, hey? You'll be off soon. And I bought a new packet of those biscuits."

I'M FINISHING THE last one when the little purple car pulls up in between our house and Lucy's. Nenee gets out, and I watch as she steps first toward our place, then changes her mind and turns toward Lucy's.

"That your grandmother?"

"Nenee. Yes." I'm not sure if I should call out to her. It feels disloyal to Lettie somehow.

"Call her over, then." Lettie starts waving her arms.

"Nenee." I keep my voice quiet.

Lettie shoots me a look. "She won't hear that."

I try again. "Nenee!"

Nenee turns to see Lettie waving at her frantically. She gives a half smile and looks confused.

I wave. *"Nenee."*

She smiles properly when she sees me.

"Rae, there you are." She walks over. "I thought you'd be at Lucy's house."

Lettie stands up. "Lettie." She holds out her hand. "I live next door to your granddaughter."

"Oh, so you're the one who—"

Lettie winces. "Yes. I didn't realize the whole situation, if I had of course I would have . . ." Her words come out more quickly than usual, until they dry up.

"Yes. Well." Nenee looks back at her car.

Lettie stands up, her fingers worrying at each other. "She's such a smart kid, so grown-up for her age, I just didn't realize. She's so capable. I had no idea what was—"

"Yes." Nenee steps back. "Well, I expect she and I will get to know one another, so you don't need to explain her to me."

"No, I . . ." Lettie reaches out a hand toward Nenee, before shoving it in her pocket.

Nenee's still looking toward the car, the corner of her mouth twitching down, up and down again. "My daughter and I have been out of contact for a long time, if I'd known I would have—"

Lettie holds up a hand. "I know." She rests the hand on Nenee's arm, making her flinch. "I have kids," Lettie says in a voice I've not heard before. "One dead and one in another state. We love them. They're not ours."

Nenee blinks and looks at Lettie for the first time. She nods and straightens her jumper. Holds out her hand. "I'm sorry, I didn't introduce myself. Noni." They shake.

Nenee clears her throat. "Thank you for keeping an eye on Rae. I'm glad you were here to do it." And they stand, hands still clasped, bird-eyeing each other. I think they've forgotten about me.

I clear my throat too. "Would it be okay if Lettie came to visit sometimes?"

Nenee looks at me and then back to Lettie. "Of course. Of

course it would." She gives a tight smile. "You'd be very welcome, Lettie."

"Thank you." They tight-smile each other. I've become invisible again. Splinter leans on my leg and I give him a scratch. He sneezes, making them both look.

Lettie coughs. "Now off you go. You've got a long drive ahead and you've not even got that car packed." I stand up for a hug. She gives my back a pat and shoves me toward the gate.

I help Splinter down the step and walk to the car. *Stupid old goat.* I look back at her. She looks smaller than usual standing on the porch. I drop Splinter's lead, run back and throw myself at her, balling the back of her jacket in my fists.

She staggers back a step. "Ooof. I think you've winded me." But her arms are strong, and they wrap all the way around. She leans down and whispers in my ear. "Good luck, kiddo. You know where I am." Then she lets go and gives me another gentle push toward the gate.

NENEE PILES MY stuff into her little car. She insisted we bring some of my bedroom furniture, so it *felt more like home* at her place. So my lamp, my duvet and the small step stool I use as a bedside table are coming too. I can't see how everything and us will fit in her little car. I sit on the doorstep, my arm around Splints, and watch. Splinter chews at the strap of his wheel leg. I haven't put it on him. The vet said he won't need it—as soon as he settles into three legs he'll be as fast and steady as he was with four. He likes to chew it, though, and push it around with his nose.

Nenee swears as something falls into the street. She shoves it back in and slams the door shut. Her face is red and sweaty when she turns back to me. "There. Done."

I stand up, Splints at my side, and walk to the back of the car. Lucy and Oscar are standing on the footpath, looking solemn.

Nenee looks at Splinter. "You'd better take him back to the house now." She nods toward Lucy and Oscar's.

"What?" My stomach drops away, the sensation making me slightly dizzy.

"He's staying here, isn't he?"

I mustn't be hearing right. "What?"

"I thought the dog was staying here?" She glances at Lucy in confusion. Oscar's beaming from ear to ear, while trying not to. Lucy catches my look, turns him around and walks him back into the house.

I sit down on the curb.

"Come on, up you pop! We'd better get going. We want to be home before it gets dark."

Splinter sits next to me. Neither of us look at her.

"Rae? Come on, it's time to go."

"I'm not leaving without Splinter."

Lucy's back; she squats next to me and puts her hand on my knee. "Rae, he still needs his stitches out and some follow-up care. I thought we'd take him to the vet for you. You can come and get him when you're all settled."

I turn my head away and wrap my arm more tightly around Splinter's shoulders, his cone digging into my cheek.

"Rae, we're just trying to make this as easy as possible. For everyone."

"For *her*, you mean."

I glare at Nenee.

"Rae—" But Nenee waves Lucy away.

When she's moved back toward her house Nenee starts to

speak. "Rae, sweetheart." She uses that fake-reasonable voice adults use when they're pretending to negotiate. "Be sensible. My house isn't set up for a dog, certainly not for a dog with special needs."

"He doesn't have special needs. The vet said when he's adjusted to three legs he'll be fine. He just has to adjust."

"Exactly." She doubles down on the tone. "He needs some time to *adjust*. It's much better for him to do that *here*, with his vet nearby and in more familiar surroundings."

"You're *transparent*." I spit the word at her.

She steps back slightly. "What?"

"You're pretending to be reasonable to make me the difficult one, when the truth is you just don't want him."

I watch her feet step closer again. "No, I just want what's best—"

"For *you*. Yes. I get it."

"No." Her toes scrunch up in her shoes.

"Yes. What's *best* for him is to be with me. *I'm* his familiar surroundings. Not their house." I point to where Lucy's standing, pretending not to listen. "He barely knows their house. He needs to be with me."

I wrap my fingers around his collar. "Everything's changed for him. He lost Mum, he lost his house, he lost his leg. And now you want *me* to abandon him because it's more convenient for you."

"Rae, I can see you're very upset."

"Stop it!" I want to kick her.

"Stop what?"

"Stop pretending to be on my side. You're not on my side. He's my side. If he's not coming, then neither am I." I watch her feet twitch. "That's probably what you wanted all along anyway."

"Rae."

I knot my fingers into Splinter's fur.

"Rae, look at me."

You used to ask me to do that too.

"Oh, for god's sake." I watch as one foot lifts and hits the footpath. She's shouting now. I knew it. *I knew it.*

"Will you stop being so bloody unreasonable? This is hard for me too. I haven't seen you since you were three, and now you're half-grown-up and god knows what happened to you in the years in between. I did a terrible job with your mother, and now I'm expected to pick up the pieces she left when she went and—"

I can't even look at her feet now.

Her breathing's harsh and frayed around the edges. She breathes like you do when she's upset. I squeeze my eyes shut. I can hear her swallow. "I lost her too. Twice." Her voice cracks.

I squeeze my eyes tighter.

I feel her sit down in the gutter next to me. I shift over. Not to make room for her, but so we're not touching.

She's quiet. I can hear her rubbing at her face. Another familiar sound.

"You look so like her." Her voice's soft and rough. "I'm so angry at her." I crack open an eye and look. She's looking at her feet. "I'm so angry at me."

I say nothing.

We sit in the gutter not touching. Splints tries to lick the salt off my cheeks but gets the cone stuck on my neck.

She stands, holds out her hand. "Will you come?"

I sink my face into Splints's shoulder.

"Please. Will you come?"

I still won't look at her.

"He can come too, okay?"

I point at her tiny purple car, parked between our place and Lucy's. "How will he fit?"

"I'll make room."

I watch her pile my junk back onto the footpath, then shove-stack it into spaces in the boot, the footwell and under the front seat, clearing a space in the back. I watch as she stands in the street, struggling to close the door, one hand trying to hold everything in. Your alarm cube tumbles from the pile and slips out the door into the street, along with the bag of my favorite books. She swears and scoops them back up and rests them on top of the box in the back seat. Holding everything on top of the box in place with one arm, she uses her hip to keep the box from falling out of the car as she winds down the window.

Even Splinter's watching with interest now, my salty cheeks forgotten. Stepping away from the pile on the seat, she slams the door shut with her knee, hand shoved through the window to keep what's on top from falling into the street. Only now she can't shut the window. Pushing the bag of books and your alarm cube back in, she leans in and winds it up as far as she can without getting her arm stuck.

"There." Her hair's in her eyes.

Your alarm cube slips and rolls across the seat and falls out the other door into the gutter, cracking the screen more.

"Oh." She looks like she might cry.

I stand up. "It can stay." I look at the space in the back. Splinter's pillow and bowl are in the footwell. "I've got all I need."

HER CAR'S NOT as neat as Lettie's, even accounting for all my stuff in it. Which seems more funny than it should be.

Oscar stands on the footpath, next to the car door. I wind down the back window so Splints can poke his head out.

"Bye, Rae. I'm glad you're okay."

I nod, not sure what to say.

"Will you write?"

I shrug. "You can if you want."

He looks hurt. "I don't know where you live now."

I step around him and slip into the front seat. I leave the window down. Oscar follows and stands there with his hands in his pockets.

I pull on my seat belt. "It's okay. I know your address."

He looks stupidly happy, and I pretend to be busy adjusting the seat belt buckle so he won't see me smile.

"Okay. Great." He stands there grinning like an idiot.

"Bye, then."

He gets the hint. "Bye, Rae."

Nenee starts the car.

Oscar steps back and waves. As we start to pull away I stick my head out the window and look out the back. Lettie's standing on her porch, watching. She waves. I wave back.

I watch her from the side mirror, watching us as we drive away. When we pull to a stop at the intersection she walks quickly to the footpath and picks something up out of the gutter. Your alarm cube.

As we turn the corner she's walking back to her porch. Then we're driving away, off toward the West Gate, and I imagine her sitting in her seat, kettle boiling, with your broken alarm cube on her lap.

ACKNOWLEDGMENTS

This book is the result of many hours at a desk, staring at the wall behind my screen. Those valuable hours would not have been possible without the support of my partner, Kevyn. Thank you for the winter weekends you spent at various parks in the rain with our kids (and the autumn, summer and spring ones too). A big thank-you also to my kids. When you're old enough to read this book you might find this at the back: thanks for teaching me that time is precious and that how I weight it matters.

A massive thank-you to my dear friend Jessica Brennan, the only person to read this before I sent it off to be judged. The first person (other than me) to cry over it. Thank you for your support and encouragement and for reading ten versions of an author bio with less than three words' difference between each one.

Dr. Tania Cammarano, my rock, thank you for the hours of writing (and nonwriting) conversations at parks and playcenters. Our friendship has kept me safely sane—well, sane-adjacent at least. *Please* consider doing a second PhD so I have someone to commiserate and whinge with in the writing trenches.

A huge thanks also to the amazing Stephanie Davis. Our early-morning fishbowl conversations about writing, creativity and everything helped motivate me when I was flagging. Thanks for always being curious; you're awesome.

An enormous thank-you to the ever-wonderful, talented and generous Toni Jordan, who volunteered her time to a virtual stranger as a project-management mentor. I agreed to timelines I never thought I'd hit and hit them all (because you made them sound so *reasonable*). Your suggestions of entering the Text Prize (for the ancestor of this book) and the Victorian Premier's Literary Awards were game changers. You have been so generous with your time and support, and I will be forever grateful. Thank you.

To the team at the Wheeler Centre, who do so much for writing and books, thank you for running the Victorian Premier's Literary Awards, for which the unpublished manuscript of this book was short-listed. A special thanks to Hiroki Kobayashi, Veronika Sullivan and Michael Williams for their time and advice. Thanks also to judges Ellen Cregan, Luke Horton and Natalie Kon-yu for reading so many manuscripts and liking mine.

Heartfelt thanks also to Kylie Scott (née McInnes), Belinda Monypenny and Carly Slater (and Jessica, of course) for reading, enjoying and responding to *Black Dog Small Bird*, the distant ancestor to this book. *BDSB* will never see the light of day, but this book grew out of it, and I will always be grateful for your time, thoughts and enthusiasm.

This would not be a proper acknowledgment without saying a big thank-you to my mum, Gillian. Thank you for your belief, love and support, always. x

To my dad, Gareth, thanks for keeping it real and for ensuring I know you're always there if I need. x

And last but certainly not least, a massive thank-you to the book-loving teams at Text and Berkley PRH. I've never met so many people so delighted that I'd made them cry (and laugh). Michael Heyward, thanks for loving my characters nearly as much as I do. Jen Monroe, your care and enthusiasm turned me into an excited dancing kid on more than one occasion. To David Forrer at Inkwell, thank you for your kindness and for your championing of this book. Mandy Brett, editor extraordinaire, thanks for taking the time to buy a Text Prize shortlistee a coffee and ask some direct questions. My answer? This. This book is what I would write if I ignored all the advice and ideas about what it *should* be.

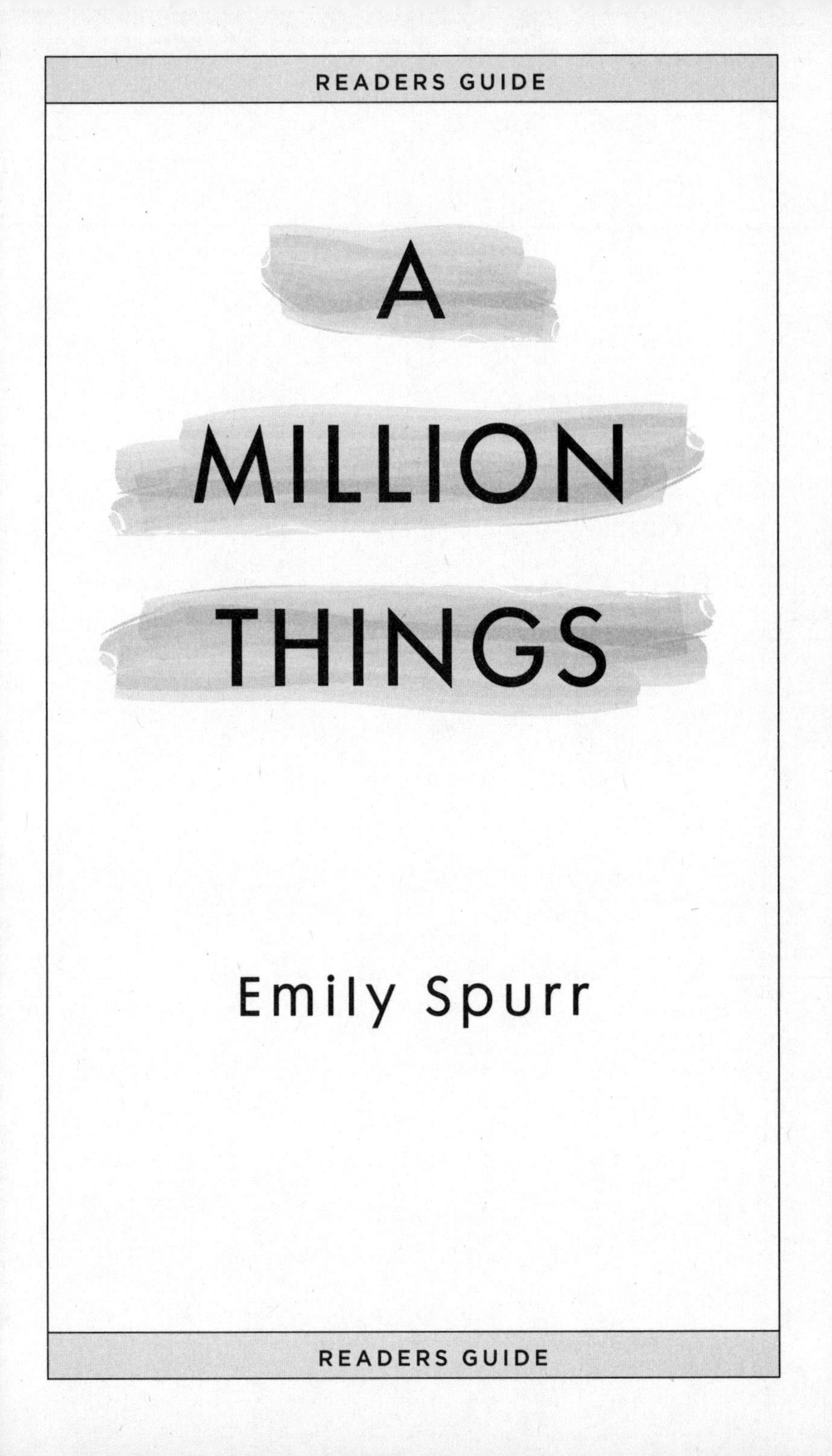
READERS GUIDE
A
MILLION
THINGS
Emily Spurr
READERS GUIDE

DISCUSSION QUESTIONS

1. How do you see the relationship between Splinter and Rae? Is he her protector? An extension of her? Her dependent (someone who needs her and keeps her going)? Or something else?

2. The character of Rae's mother, though central to the book, is never seen directly by the reader; we see her only through Rae's memories and thoughts. What sort of picture of Rae's mother do you, as the reader, form from this perspective?

3. Why do you think the author might have chosen to show you Rae's mother in this way?

4. The theme of home is strong in this novel. How do each of the characters Rae, Lettie and Oscar differ or coincide in their experiences of, and relationship to, home?

5. Consider what is unsaid in Rae's narration. Do you think there are insights to be gained into Rae's character and thoughts by

what she does not say or address? If so, what do you think the reader can learn from the things Rae leaves unsaid?

6. Rae has a strong reaction to Lettie's relationship with her son, Chris. What parallels do you think Rae might be drawing between Lettie's relationship boundaries with Chris and Rae's relationship with her own mother?

7. What do you think about Rae's reaction when she first sees Lettie's cleaned house? What do you think is behind Rae's response?

8. Briar Rose/Sleeping Beauty and the overgrown garden are reoccurring motifs in the novel. How do you feel these ideas tie in with Rae's situation and the extended in-between, or transitional, space in which she finds herself?

9. *A Million Things* deals with deep loss, grief and mental illness. Do you believe these topics are presented in a realistic way? How did you react to these themes?

10. What was your interpretation of the overall tone of the book? Was it sad? Hopeful? Or something else?

11. What are your thoughts about Lettie's future? Do you feel the implication at the end of the novel is that things will be better for her? Or is it that her life will go back to the way it was? Which one of these outcomes do you think is more likely, based on your reading of the book?

BEHIND THE BOOK

The idea for this novel grew from a what-if, as most stories do. It is a personal what-if, and I have wrestled with how much of it to share. That said, I believe openness and transparency are wonderful things, and I can't be truly open and transparent about the genesis of this story without revealing something of my own past. So, a little about me: in my teens and for a large part of my twenties I suffered with mental illness and the associated dark depression and anxiety. I'm well now and have been for many years, but I still occasionally have nightmares about being back in that headspace.

For those lucky enough to not have suffered from it, it can be hard to grasp the loneliness and trauma of mental illness. It isolates and shames. You're well aware of the effect your illness has on those you love, and the guilt of that is another rod the illness uses to beat you. You don't like yourself very much, and it's hard to accept that anyone else might genuinely like you. You're careless with yourself. In your own mind, you don't matter.

Parenthood can be isolating and lonely too (it is, of course, also many other things: beautiful, wonderful, funny, loving and deeply connecting). Standing in the shower one morning, washing away the horrible dream of the night before, I considered what might happen when the isolation and pain of mental illness collided with the isolation and guilt of parenthood—what would that do to a mother? How would she cope? How would she reconcile those experiences? The intense love to and from a child, the primal *need* to look after them, with an emotional life that is sometimes stretched to the limit just coping with existence. And that's where this story came from: what would this do to her child? What sort of person might they have to be to survive? What does that do to the feeling of *home*? A tough, frightened child stepped into my head.

This novel took a circuitous route to get to where it is now. When I started it, despite my best efforts to stay true to my idea, a lot of *should*s and *can't*s influenced what I was doing. It was suggested that I couldn't write an adult fiction novel told from the perspective of a child. I resisted, lost conviction, aged her up. Then, it was the idea that if the main character was a teenager it must be a young adult novel; I resisted, lost conviction, turned it into a YA novel. And there was the voice in my head asking: *Who would read this? This is so dark and depressing*. I gave it a plot that incited more action and excitement. I finished it. I entered it in the Text Prize, an unpublished manuscript competition for young adult novels with $10,000 and a publishing deal for the winner, and was shortlisted. I didn't win. What did happen, though, was that one of the senior editors at Text asked me out for a coffee to discuss my work.

I love a straight-talking editor, and you don't get much straighter talking than Mandy Brett. She looked at me over her coffee and asked me in her up-front way why I'd chosen to write a YA novel. I explained. We had a good chat about writing. Then came *the* question: *So, what would you write if you ignored all the ideas about what it should be, and wrote it as you wanted—what would that look like?* So I told her. I held my breath, expecting . . . I don't know what, fearful that she'd think it was terrible or that I was insane. She leant forward, and, using her finger to tap the table for emphasis, said: *Now that, I would read.*

So I stopped worrying about who would read this. And Rae was born, and Splinter and Oscar; then Lettie kicked her way in and took me on a road trip. In sixteen months I was done. I entered the finished novel in the Victorian Premier's Literary Awards, was short-listed, and found a publisher.

There are many ideas behind *A Million Things*, but for me, at its core, it is two things: it is a love letter to Rae and all the kids who cope with shadowy things outside their control, and it is a love letter to her mother, who did the best she could and loved her child fiercely, but, despite all the love, in the end it just wasn't enough.

READING LIST

A small selection of adult fiction with child protagonists from the author's bookshelf.

Say You're One of Them—Uwem Akpan

The Elegance of the Hedgehog—Muriel Barbery

Room—Emma Donoghue

Extremely Loud and Incredibly Close—Jonathan Safran Foer

Golden Boys—Sonya Hartnett

Of a Boy—Sonya Hartnett

Dog Boy—Eva Hornung

The Kite Runner—Khaled Hosseini

Let the Right One In—John Ajvide Lindqvist

Shadow of the Wind—Carlos Ruiz Zafón

Sour Heart—Jenny Zhang

The Book Thief—Markus Zusak

Author photo by Kevyn Lee

Born in Tasmania, EMILY SPURR lives in Melbourne, Australia, with her partner, their twins, and a deaf, geriatric cat. Short-listed for the prestigious Victorian Premier's Unpublished Manuscript Award, *A Million Things* is her first novel.

CONNECT ONLINE

EmilySpurr.com

SpurrEmily

Spurr.Emily